From the Ashes of Atlanta

A NOVEL BY

JEANNE HARDT

tending the vines that crept up the sides, mingled with blue morning glories.

Mama ...

Air puffed from his nostrils.

They could have let her be, but no. Hate spared no one. Not women, and not even ... *children.*

His legs shook as he forced himself to stand and trudge through the ruins of his home. He looked down at himself and grunted. Gray tattered trousers as dismal as the sight before him.

He stopped and turned to the stone steps that remained. Standing in the place that had once been their kitchen, he let out a long breath. The steps led the way from the root cellar. They would have hidden there. His gut twisted at the vision of his mama and Anna beneath the floor boards, praying they'd suffocated before they'd felt the heat of the flames.

He set his foot on the stone, then bent down and brushed away debris from a lower step.

What's this?

Rolling the tiny object in his palm, he gasped. Then his legs buckled beneath him and he dropped. All hope they'd made it out alive vanished. The tiny porcelain hand in his grasp told him all he needed to know. The hand of Anna's doll. She never went anywhere without it.

Frantically, he sifted through the grit, looking for the other hand, perhaps even the face. The rest of the doll was made from cloth and gone forever like the bones of his sister. Tears blurred his vision and he wiped them away with the back of a grimy hand.

Chapter 1

Nothing but ash. No longer warm from dying embers, but as cold as the hearts that ignited the flames.

Jeb Carter dropped to his knees and dipped his hand into the chalky remains. It fell through his fingers and drifted. Some cascaded down to the ground, as other particles were caught on the Atlanta winds and floated away. Just like everything else in his life.

He gripped another fistful. Tighter and tighter, as fury heated the dust between his fingers.

Why?

What sense was there in burnin' it to the ground?

His chest constricted.

"Yanks," he grumbled. "I hate every one of 'em." He wanted to scream, but there was no sense in yelling. There was no one left to hear his cries.

He closed his eyes and tried to remember his childhood home; three stories, white wood, six ornate pillars adorning the front. His mama had taken extra care in

Sitting down hard, he put his head against his knees and drew them toward his chest, still clutching the miniature hand in his own. He erupted into sobs that had been pushed down and not allowed until now. He would cry for Anna, but then he would never cry again.

Why'd I live?

It would have been much easier to die, than to face this.

Maybe it wasn't too late.

The cold metal pressed against his skin. Another reminder of the war and the lives he'd taken. His daddy had given it to him, but he never would have imagined he'd have to use it the way he did. It might have kept him alive in more ways than one. Knowing that the Yanks would pry it from his dead fingers, he wasn't about to give them the satisfaction. Aside from his blood, the Colt revolver was all that was left from his daddy.

This gift could take away all the pain. His daddy helped bring him into the world, and now he would help him leave.

Tucking the porcelain hand into his pocket, his chest heaved as he grasped the pistol in his palm. After checking to see that the bullet was still in place, he positioned the revolver. A simple squeeze of the trigger and it would all go away. The memories, the pain, the wretched life that was left for him. They'd taken away all he loved and he had no reason to remain.

With a quivering hand he placed the barrel in his mouth. It was the only way to be certain he wouldn't miss. After all the men he'd shot, this shouldn't be difficult. He bit down hard and his breath hissed out his nostrils.

Do it!

He scrunched his eyes tight and his mama's face shot into his brain faster than any bullet. Her blue eyes glistened with unshed tears. And then, all the years of *thou shalt nots* at the Baptist church rang out like bells hammering against the drums of his ears.

But it's too hard! What have I got worth livin' for?

Besides, what good did *thou shalt not kill* do for all those men who'd died at *his* hand? What difference did it make? Killing was killing. Why not take his own life?

Inhaling deeply, he sat upright, tasting the metal in his mouth.

Jeb, you're gonna grow up to be a fine man one day ... His mama's words stung more than those of any preacher. If she was looking down on him now ...

"No!" He flung the pistol into the rubble and it disappeared from view. His hands flew to his face and he bent over, crumpling to the ground; defeated. It would have been the easy way out of his misery. But what made him think that life was ever meant to be easy?

As he rose to a seated position, his shoulders slumped, then he jumped to his feet. He couldn't do anything right. After hording the revolver for years, he threw it away. What was he thinking?

He followed the path of the Colt, crunching over remnants of God-only-knows what. And then, finally coming to his senses, turned around. It wasn't worth it. He might as well leave it behind with everything else.

He couldn't stay here. If he was destined to live, then he would live, whether he liked it or not. But not in Atlanta. He wasn't about to wake up every morning to the reminders of what once was. He'd go west. Somewhere no one knew the difference between north and south. And if he had to fight, he'd be fighting Indians, not other white men. At least then it would be easy to know the enemy.

With no money to his name, the only way to get there would be train hopping, but he'd done it before.

Pausing one last time to look and remember, he tightened his jaw and headed down the dirt road.

* * *

At least Sherman's army had spared the church. Maybe there was something resembling a heart in the man's chest. Somewhere.

Jeb assumed the parishioners saw him as a poor beggar, not a boy who'd grown up, worshipped, and was baptized there. Looking at his reflection in the unbroken pane of glass in the church window, he understood why. He didn't recognize himself. The beard and filth were one thing—the fact that he'd lost at least a fourth of his body weight was another. He'd always had a muscular physique, but now his muscles had dwindled into skinny arms. Lack of food could diminish any man into a shadow of himself.

He was handed the clothes without a second thought. Charity. Years ago, his pride wouldn't have allowed it, but all that had changed when the south was lost.

"You'll need this soon enough," Mrs. Chambers said, with a nervous laugh as she handed him a flannel shirt. Her fear of him was apparent. Did he look that bad?

Even she doesn't know me and she was Mama's friend.

"Thank you." He tried to smile, but it wouldn't come. Maybe it was good that she didn't recognize him. If she had, she'd have told him how sorry she was about his mama. He didn't want to hear it. Didn't want anyone's pity. Charity was bad enough.

"You can change over yonder." She motioned toward a small room at the back. "There's a wash basin with water and soap." Her lips twitched and her nose wrinkled.

He nodded and walked away, clutching his new clothes. *Water and soap.* His body would welcome them, and though he'd grown accustomed to his own smell, he was certain it offended Mrs. Chambers.

Shedding the ragged uniform, he tossed it aside. The water was cool against his flesh, removing weeks of soil and sweat. With one finger, he pulled the wash cloth taut and scrubbed his teeth, then rinsed and spit. Not enough water to clean his hair, but no matter. He'd take a dip in the pond up the road before he hopped the train. For now, this brief washing should appease Mrs. Chambers.

New socks—probably knitted by her hands—molded to his feet, then he slipped into his old boots. They still had some life left. The tan trousers were too big, but he had the braces from his uniform to hold them up. The light-weight cotton shirt was just right for the August heat. Hopefully, by the time the weather turned, he'd be somewhere like Kansas. Maybe the winter would be mild. By then, he hoped to be employed and able to afford a coat. If things went well, he'd be a railroad man just like his daddy.

Sighing, he stopped to thank her again, but instead, he asked, "Why'd ya stay here? There's nothin' left."

She smiled a genuine smile and cast her eyes around the building. "The church is here. 'Sides, this is my home. Atlanta will grow again. Mark my word." She eyed him up and down. "Glad we could help ya."

He dipped his head. "Thank you."

"Come back tonight and we'll have soup. You look a might hungry."

She didn't know the half of it. "I will." A final meal before his departure. He'd have just enough time to go by the rail yard and figure out which train to hop. Then he'd take a swim in the pond before returning to eat. Everything was falling into place, except his smile. That was gone for good.

* * *

Dusk fell and the half-moon gave little light peeking through the clouds overhead. Jeb followed his feet and returned to the rail yard. Darkness would hide him from the view of the workers, but stumbling over the rubble didn't help. He slowed his pace, not wanting to twist an ankle or worse. Odd how he worried over harming his body when only hours ago he'd wanted to destroy it.

My mind ain't right.

At least his belly was full from three helpings of vegetable soup. It would have to last. Another meal could be far off.

Placing his hand against the crumbled brick that was once Union Station, he flashed another memory. Ten years old and his daddy had taken him and his brothers to see the fantastic brick dome. The center of the rail line and his daddy's pride.

Thank God, he can't see it now ...

No resemblance of the building it once was. Just like the rest of Atlanta.

Carefully stepping over the ruined rails and going around piles of debris from burned cars, he located the box car that he determined was heading north. Loaded down with cartons of unlabeled goods, he could easily hide between them.

If the train was going its normal route, it would take him to Chattanooga, Tennessee, then on north and west. In no time at all, Atlanta would be behind him. Though it might take years, he would make himself forget.

Chapter 2

Music filtered into Gwen's room and her heart danced along with the waltz being played.

"Hurry now, Gwen." Her mother's sweet face popped into the doorframe, her blue eyes lit with joy.

"Yes, Mother. I'm almost ready." She couldn't control the broad smile that covered her own face, making her cheeks hurt.

"You look lovely." Her mother's voice softened as she spoke. "I'll see you in the ballroom." She smiled and turned, her long, royal blue gown swished as she floated away. Her mother, Grace, was often mistaken as her sister. She'd aged well and Gwen hoped she'd do the same.

Gwen sat at her vanity and gazed into the mirror. She pinched her cheeks for color and primped her long, blond ringlets. Her gown was also blue—but light in color to match her eyes—and sat just off her shoulders, highlighting her long, graceful neck. Rising to her feet, she looked in the mirror one final time, then left her room and descended the grand staircase.

With every step, her heart increased its pace. Her palms began to sweat in anticipation of the affair. Dancing, food, but most importantly, she'd see David after his two year absence.

"Gwen!"

She nearly jumped out of her skin, startled by her little sister.

"Katherine, you almost made me lose my step." She was adorable in her pink, puffy dress.

"May I go in with you? Mother says I can dance one time with David, then I have to go to my room."

"You're only nine. When you're older, you'll be able to stay up late."

Katherine's mouth twisted. "I want to be older now."

"All things in time." Gwen touched her finger to the tip of her sister's nose, then took her by the hand. "And yes, you can go in with me. I'll even let you dance with David before I do."

Hand-in-hand they entered the ballroom. It had always been Gwen's favorite in the eighteen-room house. Designed with a smooth wood floor, high ceiling, and walls that enhanced the quality of the music being played by the eight-piece orchestra, the ballroom welcomed every guest. The space glimmered with candlelight from six candelabrum suspended from the ceiling and the glowing lanterns attached to the walls. But the greatest light of all was in the eyes of their guests. Joy filled the room.

"David!" Katherine jerked her hand free and ran across the floor, drawing the eyes of everyone. They chuckled over her enthusiasm.

Gwen covered her mouth and laughed as any proper woman should, watching her sister weave through the hoopskirts and suits, making her way to their brother. David couldn't have been more dashing. His uniform was crisp and his medals glistened.

"You've grown!" David exclaimed, hoisting Katherine into his arms.

She hugged his neck, then kissed his cheek before he set her back down again.

Gwen gracefully made her way through the crowd and stood facing her brother. "Welcome home, David." He extended his arms and she gladly went into his embrace.

Though she would never bring it up in conversation, she was relieved that the rumors of his capture had been false. Thank God the war was over and he was home.

"Winnie," David said. "You look more beautiful than ever." Katherine tugged at his shirt sleeve. "And so do you, Katie."

Katherine grinned, satisfied.

"Thank you, David," Gwen said. "And I've never seen an officer more handsome. Blue suits you."

"I'm just glad to be home—at least for a while." His attention moved to the far side of the room and Gwen turned to follow his gaze. Of course, Martha Clayton caught his eye. She was more interesting than his sisters.

"Go to her, David. We can dance later." Gwen gave him a gentle push.

"What about *my* dance?" Katherine asked.

Gwen smoothed Katherine's long golden hair. "Let him dance with Martha first. Besides, that means you can stay a little longer."

Katherine's face brightened, then she tugged Gwen toward the food table, as David bowed and hurried off to Martha.

Servants bustled about, bringing fresh drinks, clearing plates, and setting food on the table. David's homecoming had been planned for months and their father had spent a great deal of money making certain that it would be an event worth remembering.

Her younger brother, Henry, had arrived home a month ago with little fanfare. But Henry wasn't an officer, nor was he in line for a position in Washington. This party was more than a homecoming; it was a way to show off David to all the important people of Boston.

"Doesn't he look brilliant?" Her mother tucked her arm into Gwen's.

Gwen cocked her head. "Brilliant? An interesting term for handsome." She laughed aloud. "I always thought *I* was your brilliant child."

"You are, but as much as I hate to say it, being a man gives your brother an advantage. I'm sorry, dear, but even with all the education the world has to offer, women will always be best suited in the home."

"Then why is Father spending so much on my education?"

"Because you asked for it." She placed a gentle hand on Gwen's cheek. "He'd do anything for you."

Katherine tugged on Gwen's sleeve. "I don't want schooling. Mother says all I need to do is marry well and I'll be taken care of."

Gwen sighed. Her nine-year-old sister was already talking about marriage. It couldn't be further from *her* mind. Being born female shouldn't have set the mold for her life. She should be able to choose a profession, just like her brothers. But she'd had this discussion with her mother more than once and she was tired of it. Tonight was meant to be a celebration and nothing would squelch her good mood.

"You marry well, Katherine," Gwen said. "And when I'm an old maid, you and your wealthy husband can take care of me."

Katherine giggled, but her mother cast a look of disapproval. "Albert Finch is here," she said. "Have you seen him?"

Not Albert Finch ...

"No. But I wasn't looking for him. There are a lot of people here."

"*Important* people." Her mother's brows rose. "Sadly, Mr. Longfellow declined your father's invitation. The poor man is still suffering from the loss of his wife."

Henry Wadsworth Longfellow, the pride of Massachusetts. Or at least, one of them. Literary masters seemed to emerge from every corner of Boston.

"That's a shame," Gwen said. "I would have liked to hear one of his newest poems."

Her mother excused herself to tend to guests. The room was quickly growing warm to the point of stifling.

August was almost too warm for a ball, but David was important and this was for him.

He approached them with Martha attached to his arm, beaming like an exploding star. "Martha has agreed to give me up for a dance. Are you ready, Katie?"

Katherine nearly skipped onto the dance floor, leaving Martha with Gwen.

Gwen smiled graciously at her brother's *intended*. The marriage had been arranged while the two were babies. Fortunately, Martha had grown into a woman they all cared for. Things could have turned out much worse.

Martha stood rigid. Shoulders back, breasts full up.

"How can you tolerate that corset?" Gwen whispered in her ear.

Martha's eyes widened as she pushed a strand of her auburn hair from her face. "It's the style. Mother says that beauty is supposed to be painful."

Though corsets were fashionable, Gwen refused to wear one. Why go through all the discomfort, only to enhance one's figure? She had no intention of impressing any man. Comfort made more sense. Besides, she wanted to enjoy the evening and the food. Corsets bound the stomach.

"Nothing is worth that much pain." Gwen shook her head. "How do you eat?"

"I don't." Martha batted her eyes and stood even taller.

They watched David and Katherine parade around the dance floor. What they were doing wasn't a typical dance, but their smiles were all that mattered. When the song ended, David swung her around with erupting giggles, then returned her to Gwen's side.

"Your turn." He took Gwen by the hand.

Cheers resounded through the room as the band began a polka.

"Polka?" Gwen giggled. "You requested it, didn't you?"

"I know it's your favorite."

"But it's so warm. I may faint."

"Then I'll catch you." David gave her hand a little jerk, then whisked her away.

They'd mastered the dance long ago, after many bruised toes. As the room whirled in circles, Gwen's face grew tired from laughter. People stepped aside, allowing them to take the full floor. And though Gwen didn't care to be the center of attention, she loved the dance.

She caught Albert Finch's eye during a spin. Sooner or later, she'd have to speak to him.

When the music stopped and the applause thundered through the room, she nearly swooned. But true to his word, David held her upright.

"I need some air," she huffed, and he led her out of the room, then out the back door. The patio was lit with torches and several guests were enjoying the night air. They nodded as they passed and Gwen took a seat on a wrought-iron bench.

She fanned herself with her hand. "Thank you, David. I've not had so much fun dancing since you left."

"It was my pleasure." He sat beside her, then rose again as Albert Finch approached.

"Fine dancing." Albert nodded his head to each of them in turn. "When you've caught your breath, Miss Abbott, I'd very much like to waltz with you."

Before she could respond, David rested his hand on her shoulder. "I'll leave the two of you. Martha expects my return."

She smiled at her brother, who bowed slightly and walked away, then forced a smile at Albert. "Would you like to sit, Mr. Finch?"

His brows rose. "Yes, thank you."

Because he sat a bit closer than she was comfortable with, Gwen scooted away from him, then turned her body to face him. "You're looking well." Truth be told, Albert Finch always looked well. Until he opened his mouth for more than a brief *hello*. Appearances weren't just about stylish ash-brown hair, deep brown eyes, and a pronounced chin. Yes, he had a remarkable stature and was a well-structured man—tall and lean—but his good looks stopped there.

"You're looking well ... as well." He took her hand and gave it a brief kiss. He then promptly wiped his mouth with the back of his hand. "My ... you did perspire, didn't you?"

She covered her mouth to stop a giggle. Served him right for taking liberties. "Do you still wish to waltz?"

"Of course. In time."

Yes. Enough time for her to dry out. She fidgeted with her skirt, wishing he would leave.

"Are you still attending that woman's medical school?" He crossed one leg over the other and leaned toward her.

"Yes."

"But, why? A woman with a face like yours needs only to capture the heart of a man. Why fill your head with unnecessary things?"

If only he'd remained silent. "Unnecessary? What I'm learning will help others."

"You have other talents which would benefit those closer to you. Of that, I'm certain." He raised his hand to touch her cheek, but she backed away. His implications churned her stomach.

"Oh, there you are." Her mother bustled to them, looking happier than both of them combined. "We're about to serve the cake."

"Wonderful!" Gwen stood. The timing couldn't have been better.

Her mother pulled her to the side. "Mind what you eat," she whispered in Gwen's ear. "Limit your amount of cake and stay away from the cucumber sandwiches. Though I know they're your favorite, we can't have you belching in front of our guests."

"Mother, I promise I won't embarrass you."

"Good. Now see to Mr. Finch." She floated away, then turned and waved for them to follow.

Albert extended his arm and Gwen dutifully tucked her hand through it. He smiled a wry smile and escorted her to the ballroom.

Servants weaved in and out of the guests, distributing slices of cake. Gwen searched the crowd for Katherine, but their mother must have already sent her to her room. She hoped she'd been given a piece of cake before she was told to leave.

Gwen eyed the cucumber sandwiches. She'd been chided many times for belching. Another unladylike problem that her mother was trying to correct. It seemed pointless. Why should women be denied the elimination of gas? The double standards for men and women were so unfair.

On the far side of the room, she spotted Henry. Unlike David, he wasn't in uniform, but looked just as handsome in a three-piece black suit. Two years separated them, but there was no denying they were brothers. Same nose, same chin, and the same sandy-colored hair.

He caught her eye and must have noticed she was standing beside the stacks of triangular sandwiches. He covered his mouth, pretending to belch.

Very amusing.

Nothing like a good family secret.

Once all the cake was distributed, her father gave a brief speech thanking everyone for attending, then the music started again.

Albert appeared to be a permanent fixture by her side. The moment a waltz played, he extended his hand and without saying a word, escorted her to the floor.

He wasn't as capable on the dance floor as her brother, but he wasn't horrible and didn't cause her to stumble. When they began, he positioned her with a proper amount of space between them. But as the song progressed, he drew her closer.

"You're by far the most beautiful woman in this room," he said with a cool, suave air. His lips pursed and his hand at her waist moved inappropriately.

What could she say? She certainly didn't want to encourage him. "Thank you." She looked downward, not about to look him in the face. Truthfully, she was tempted to slap it.

"Do you find me handsome?"

Perhaps she was supposed to return the compliment. "Yes."

His brows jiggled. "Then we make the perfect pair, don't we?"

No. This time, she wasn't about to respond. Rude or not. He didn't seem to mind. His head rose higher than ever and his grip grew tighter and tighter. She breathed a relieved sigh when the music stopped.

"If you'll excuse me." She stepped away. "I need to tend to personal matters."

"Of course." He dipped his head. "I'll be waiting here for you." He started to take her hand, presumably for another kiss, but pulled it back to himself.

She walked away, shaking her head.

* * *

Once her head hit the pillow, Gwen fell immediately to sleep. Cradled in a soft bed, with a light-weight blanket pulled to her chin, she drifted off with sore feet, but a happy heart. She'd managed to avoid Albert for a good portion of the evening, snuck a cucumber sandwich, then hid when she got a case of the hiccoughs. Not as offensive as belching, but still socially unacceptable.

Knowing that something sweet would sooth her disorder, she ate two cinnamon buns, then got a bout of indigestion. All in all, she had a wonderful night and wouldn't have changed a thing. Except, perhaps, sitting with Albert Finch on the patio. How dare he say that her education was unnecessary? And such arrogance ...

Now, after a restful sleep and a belly full from a good breakfast, her father wanted to see her. Alone. Everyone knew it wasn't wise to keep William Abbott waiting.

She stood facing the heavy oak door, which led to his smoking room. Even with the door closed, the aroma of pipe smoke filled her nose.

Her stomach fluttered as she rapped softly, then slowly pushed the door open. Although she'd always been close to her father, something about this particular summons didn't feel right.

"You wanted to see me, Father?" She approached him as though nothing was wrong. He was seated comfortably in a brown leather chair; legs crossed and pipe in hand. Her brothers were the exact image of him. Even his graying sideburns didn't diminish his good looks and he was fortunate to have retained all of his hair.

"Yes, Gwendolyn. Please, sit down."

Gwendolyn? This *was* serious. Her throat became dry. Was he going to remove her from school?

She gracefully took a seat next to him, then crossed her feet at the ankles. Her yellow day dress was more comfortable than the dress she'd worn last night, but the discomfort hanging in the air made breathing almost impossible.

After taking a puff from his pipe, he smiled. She let out a large breath.

At least he's smiling.

"I have some very good news, my dear."

"Yes, Father?" She sat a little more upright.

"You'll be happy to know that Albert Finch has asked to court you. As the eldest son in the Finch family, he's in line to take over his father's mill. That being said, he'll have the means to support you and eventually a family. So, I agreed to his proposal."

Her shoulders slumped and her heart stopped. She couldn't have heard him correctly.

She swallowed the lump in her throat. "You agreed to his proposal?"

"Yes. Aren't you pleased?"

"Pleased? Father—why didn't you ask me first?"

He drew back. "I assumed you would be grateful. You're not getting any younger, Gwendolyn. You'll soon be twenty and few men care for women declining in age."

"But ... I don't-"

"Your mother told me that Mr. Finch is what most women consider pleasing to the eye. Because of that, his eventual affections shouldn't cause you offense. With that and his wealth, you should have no objections."

"Father, I don't love him. I find him ... *offensive*."

"Offensive?" He chuckled, then waved his hand. "As for love, my dear ..." He patted her head, just as he'd done when she was a child. "Love comes in time. Your brother and Miss Clayton are a prime example. When they were younger, they cared little for one another, but now, he can scarcely take his eyes from her."

Probably has something to do with her corset.

"But ..." How could she make him understand? She didn't want or need a husband. She wanted to finish her education.

"There's nothing more to be said. Mr. Finch will be calling on you Saturday and you *will* receive him. This is a courtship, not an engagement. Give the man a chance. He may be your last."

She folded her hands in her lap and stared at them, thinking of the way Albert wiped away his kiss. She didn't want his affections or any part of him. "May I continue going to school?"

"For now."

"Thank you, Father." She stood and kissed his cheek, relieved that everything wasn't being taken away.

"Your mother and I feel this is for the best. And if all goes well, you and he shall have handsome children."

She curtsied, then left the room. Her life was no longer her own.

Chapter 3

Gwen looked upward at the three-story hospital, wondering what was in store for her today. Anything was better than being at home. She did her best to keep the anger toward her father at bay, but how could she not be furious? He was orchestrating her future without her consideration.

Saying *for now,* in regard to her schooling, didn't help matters. How long would *for now* be? Until Albert Finch proposed? She shuddered.

Though she wasn't a nurse, Massachusetts General Hospital required her to dress as they did; floor–length, blue cotton dress, topped with a white bibbed apron, which covered most of her dress. Her hair was pulled into a tight bun and covered by a white cap.

Some of the nurses stuck up their noses as she passed by. She couldn't help that she was given privileges most women were not. After all, she deserved her place here, studying with Doctor Young. Her grades at the women's medical school earned her the position, not her father's money.

"Miss Abbott." Dr. Young peered over the top of his wire-framed glasses. "You're just in time."

She smiled, remembering the first time Katherine met the doctor. She'd giggled over the fact that Doctor Young was quite old. With silver hair and a slight hunch in his back, he may be old, but had more knowledge than all the other doctors put together.

"In time?" She followed him down the hall until he stopped just short of entering the room at the far end.

"Yes. I know you're interested in the psychological well-being of our patients and I thought this one might pique your interest."

It was already piqued. "What's wrong with the patient?"

Doctor Young inhaled deeply and sighed. "Many things, but mostly his disposition." He motioned to a bench and they sat.

"Go on ..."

"He was brought in last night. He's dehydrated—nearly starved. And he has a broken femur."

"Oh, my. That's terrible."

"That's only the beginning. When we tried to administer ether, to reduce his pain while setting the bone, he fought us. Even with his poor physical condition, we couldn't calm him and had to use restraints. Now, he's refusing laudanum."

"Refusing? But, why? Does he give a reason?"

Once again, the doctor took a very deep breath and shook his head. "He doesn't speak."

"A mute?" Gwen leaned in toward the doctor. This was more intriguing than she could have imagined.

"It would seem so. But he has no difficulty hearing— or throwing things."

"Throwing things?"

"It was his way of refusing the laudanum."

Intriguing though he may be, was he safe? Gwen sat perfectly upright, shaking off the thought. She never shied from a challenge. "Where did he come from?"

"He was found in a box car on a train. They thought he was dead. A stowaway. The broken femur was a result from a shifting carton that fell on him. I imagine it rendered him unconscious. The pain must have been excruciating."

"I'd like to see him." She had so many questions.

"There's a station for you in his room. Paper and pen are available. He should prove to be your finest study."

"So, I'm only to study him? Won't you need someone to help with his recovery?"

A brief chuckle came from deep within the doctor. "If you're able to get close enough to help him, so be it. But I doubt he'll let you near. The poor man is troubled and not simply from the pain of a broken limb."

"Very well, then." Now it was her turn to take a large breath. In her time at the hospital, she'd seen numerous injuries. Blood didn't bother her, as long as it wasn't her own. She'd have to be careful.

As they entered the room, she stayed behind the doctor, expecting to see a beast of a man. But he was no beast. His small frame looked scarcely able to lift a feather. His brown hair was mussed and he was unshaven, but appeared calm. Perhaps because he was sleeping.

"So, we don't know his name," she whispered, and the man's eyes popped open wide. Her heart jumped.

He scowled in her direction, then turned his head. What could make a man so hateful?

"This is Miss Abbott." Dr. Young addressed the man. "She's here to assist you. I expect you to treat her with kindness. She'll be logging your progress in a journal."

Did he grunt?

"Yes, I'll be sitting there." She pointed to the desk, but realized it was senseless. He wouldn't even look at her.

Doctor Young placed his hand on her arm. "If he gets out of hand, seek an orderly. You're not required to tolerate poor behavior." He smiled and walked out of the room.

Gwen pulled out the chair at the desk, tucked her skirt under her bottom, and sat. After smoothing the paper with her hand, she dipped the pen into the inkwell and began her journal.

MGH – August 29, 1865

Patient name: unknown

Patient is a male, approximate age ...

She glanced over her shoulder, then whipped her head around and stared at the paper. His eyes were on her. Returning the pen into the ink, her hand shook. It was as if his mean spirit had covered her with an invisible mist.

perhaps twenty-two. Or so.

Per Doctor Young, patient was found in a box car as a stowaway. Hungry, thirsty, and with a broken femur. Bone has been set. Patient is most likely in pain, but will not speak.

Will not, or *cannot* speak? Slowly, she swiveled her head. "C-Can you hear me?" *Why did I stutter?*

His lip curled into a snarl and he folded his arms over his chest.

Yes, he can hear me.

Once more, she dipped her pen.

"*Irritable.*" She wrote and spoke the words simultaneously. "*Uncivilized.*" She lifted her head and sniffed the air. "*In need of a good bath.*"

Again, he grunted. She covered her mouth to muffle a giggle. At least she was reaching him. Whether or not that was a good thing remained to be seen.

Her head jerked toward the desk as a pillow struck it from behind.

What?

Picking the pillow up from the floor, she stood facing the intolerable man. "Is that the best you can do? A pillow?"

His eyes widened and air hissed from his nostrils.

"Next time, why don't you try throwing your drinking glass? Or perhaps that Bible on your bed stand? It's much heavier and could cause me some pain. But then again, you'd do better to open it and read it!" It was doubtful he *could* read.

She was tempted to toss the pillow back at him, but instead, lifted his head and put the pillow beneath it. He made no attempt to stop her.

Then, returning to her desk, she picked up the pen.
Patient threw a pillow at me. No damage was done.

* * *

Jeb stared at the woman. This nurse was different from the others, but it didn't matter. He hated every one of them. How could he have made such a mistake? The train he'd hopped was bound for Chattanooga, so how did he end up in Boston, Massachusetts?

He closed his eyes, tired of looking at the back of her blond head. The last thing he remembered was falling asleep on the train, then he'd woken up on a table having his leg stretched and nearly pulled from his body. The moment he'd heard them speak, he knew they were Yankees. Their uptight accents gave them away. When they'd told him where he was, he'd made up his mind. He wouldn't speak. It would give him away.

They'd try to poison him, if they knew. And maybe they already suspected it. He'd never trust them.

Why don't she leave?

She obviously thought she was better than him. Calling him irritable and uncivilized? What did she know about him? She'd just walked in the room.

Reckon I shouldn't a thrown the pillow.

Maybe he *would* try something heavier the next time. She'd dared him to.

He opened his eyes and looked at her more closely. She didn't look old enough to be a nurse. Not even as old as him. She sat upright with good posture. His mama sat the same way when she wrote letters.

A dull ache tugged at his heart. And then a sharp pain shot up his leg.

"Ugh ..." The sound came out of him before he could stop it.

She jumped from her chair and came to his side. "You're hurting, aren't you?"

He turned his head. *Don't speak ...*

"Why won't you let us help you?"

I don't want nothin' from you.

If he didn't look at her, he wouldn't be tempted to open his mouth. All his life he'd been courteous, spoke when spoken to, and kind. But not now.

"Fine. If you don't want help, then ... lay there and feel sorry for yourself." Her skirt brushed the edge of the bed as she returned to her desk.

Sorry for myself?

He didn't feel sorry for himself. He simply wasn't about to give her the satisfaction of caring for him. He didn't want her help. And as soon as he could walk, he'd be gone.

She was mumbling, but he couldn't make out what she was saying.

She's writin' again.

Ignoring the pain, he lifted himself up in the bed, craned his neck, and watched her. He hated to admit that of all the nurses he'd seen, she was by far the prettiest. But she had the temperament of a mean possum.

"Miss Abbott?" Another nurse stood in the doorway holding a tray. "I've brought some soup for the patient. Do you believe you can get him to eat it?"

"Bring it to me. He'll either eat it or wear it."

He met Miss Abbott's gaze and she had the nerve to smile at him.

If anyone wears it, it'll be you.

The pleasant aroma of chicken soup drifted into his nose and his stomach grumbled. He didn't know how many days had passed since the vegetable soup from Mrs. Chambers. If he was going to get his strength back, he had to eat.

It was just the two of them again and Miss Abbott looked at him with pity as if he was a helpless baby. She pulled her chair up beside him.

If she tries to spoon feed me, I'll throw it at 'er.

"You need to eat. I promise you, it's good." She dipped a spoon into the bowl and took a bite, then handed him a spoon. She grinned. "I should have had her bring two bowls."

She started to hand him the bowl, then pulled it back. "You aren't going to throw this at me, are you?"

He shook his head. He was too hungry to be hateful.

"Good." Her fingers trembled as she placed the bowl in his hands. Maybe he shouldn't have been so hard on her. Looking at her face now, he could tell she was young. Her eyes were blue. Lighter than his, but … *kind.*

Quickly, he shifted his attention back to the bowl, but not fast enough. Their eyes had momentarily locked.

She scooted her chair back. "Eat as much as you can. I can get more if you want it." Before he'd even taken one bite, she was back at her desk.

It was for the best. There was something about her that made him uneasy.

He took a bite. Better than the vegetable soup. Even so, as hungry as he was, anything would taste good. It didn't take him long to finish the entire bowl. He tipped it up and drank the last drop.

"More?" Miss Abbott looked over her shoulder and grinned.

He frowned, but nodded, hating giving her any kind of satisfaction.

She stood, took the bowl from his hand, and left the room.

Why did he suddenly feel more alone than ever?

He lay back against his pillow and closed his eyes. Not only was his leg sore, but his entire body ached. He'd never liked being idle. How long would he have to be here? Staying quiet and still was almost as bad as being dead.

Turning his head, he glanced at the Bible perched on the bed stand. Maybe she was right. He needed to read it. God kept him alive for some reason, but why bring him here?

"Ready for more?"

Miss Abbott's cheerful voice tugged at his heart. It was hard being hateful to her.

He scooted up in the bed.

"Here, let me help you." She set the bowl of soup on the bed stand, then adjusted the pillow behind his back. "Better?"

He nodded. His heart wanted to thank her, but his mind told him *no*.

After finishing a second bowl, he needed to sleep. It seemed to be the only way to forget the pain.

"You did well." She smiled at him again. Not such a mean possum after all. Of course, now he was behaving himself. Maybe that made the difference.

She took the bowl and left the room, but this time, she didn't come back.

Chapter 4

Doctor Young stared at Gwen, holding his chin with one hand. "He actually ate for you?"

"Yes, sir. Two bowls of chicken soup."

They sat in his office, and as they talked, Doctor Young took notes. She left her journal in the man's room, knowing no one would disturb it. There would be many more entries. A broken femur would take at least three months to heal. Thank goodness the hospital was charitable.

The doctor stopped writing. "I wish he could speak. I'd like to know why this was in his pocket." He opened a desk drawer and held up a tiny white object, then passed it to her.

"A hand?" She turned the porcelain piece in her palm and studied it. "From a doll?"

He nodded. "An odd thing for a man to possess."

"Does he know you have it?"

"No. It was almost thrown away with his blood-soaked clothing, but I decided to keep it."

She rubbed her finger over the tiny thing. "May I have it? I'd like to see how he reacts to it."

"Studying him as any good medical student should." Dr. Young smiled. "Yes, you may keep it. I'll wait for your report."

It was time to go home, so she excused herself.

"You're the first person he's allowed to get close," Dr. Young said, as she walked away.

She stopped and faced him. "Perhaps he was afraid I might throw something at *him*." She left with the doctor's chuckles following her.

The walk home was welcome. It gave her time to gather her thoughts. The weather was pleasant, but when the cold set in, she would need to be brought by carriage. That is, if her father allowed her to continue at the hospital through the winter. She'd have to persuade him. At least for the three months that her new patient was healing.

New patient …

It would be so much easier if she knew his name. She didn't want to keep referring to him as the mute or the irritable man in room 107. She laughed aloud, remembering the look on his face when she'd hovered over him with the pillow. He was expecting her to hit him with it. He seemed to find it just as painful when she hit him upside the head with kindness.

Maybe he fought in the war.

She quickened her pace. Talking to her brothers might give her the answers she needed.

Once home, she rushed to her room, changed out of her uniform, then went down the stairs to the main floor. The house was unusually quiet. Being that it was only an hour until dinner, she continued down the hallway to the kitchen.

The enormous room was the envy of many of their neighbors. Having hired help, her mother rarely set foot in it, but she insisted that they have all the finest accessories and latest gadgets.

Violet, their cook, was at the stove, cutting potatoes into a pot. She'd been with their family since Gwen was a child, and though she was now fully gray-haired, she'd kept her health, and her petite frame was still capable of maintaining a well-run kitchen.

"Miss Abbott," Violet said, acknowledging her.

"Roast chicken?" Gwen sniffed the air.

"Yes'm. Your brother is bringing Miss Clayton to dinner."

So, David was with Martha. Not a good time to talk to him. "Is Henry here?"

"Yes'm. I believe he's in the library."

Perfect. "Thank you, Violet."

She hurried down the hallway to the double doors which led to the library. She'd spent many hours here reading all her favorites more than once. And when the weather turned, she intended to take her place in the most comfortable chair by the fireplace. There was nothing quite so wonderful as a warm fire and a good book on a cold day.

Henry was at the desk in the corner by the window, reading. He looked up when she shut the doors behind her.

"Home from the hospital?"

"Yes. May I speak with you?"

He set the book aside. "You sound serious."

She sat on the sofa across from him. "I have a new patient."

"Now you sound like a doctor." He folded his hands on the desk and stared at her. "Remember, you're a medical *student*."

"Yes, I know. But, he *is* my patient. For *study* purposes."

She proceeded to tell him about her irritable mute. And even though Henry was often times more playful than David, he listened intently.

"So." She took a deep breath. "Do you believe he may have been in the war? That his demeanor and difficulties might have been because of something he was exposed to? Something horrible?"

"Other things than the war can cause a man to have difficulties."

"But he seems to be the right age. And from all you and David went through ... I thought-"

Henry held up his hand. "There are some things I don't want to talk about."

"But-"

"Gwen. You can't push anyone to tell you things they don't want to discuss. As for your patient—being that he's mute—you may never get your answers. But at least he's eating. Heal his body and don't worry yourself so much about his mind."

She sighed and stood. It wasn't what she wanted to hear.

Henry picked up his book and she walked away. Although dinner would be ready soon, her appetite was gone.

* * *

Throwing the bed pan wasn't the smartest thing he'd ever done, but how else would Jeb make the nurse realize he didn't want her helping him? *There are some things that a man has to do privately.*

And why hadn't Miss Abbott been back to see him? The other nurses were nowhere near as pleasant.

"Throwing things again?" Doctor Young crossed his arms over his chest. "We're trying to help you."

Jeb pointed to the bed pan and looked intently at the doctor. He then pointed downward and followed it with a tap to his chest.

Doctor Young nodded. "You want to do it yourself, hmmm?"

Jeb nodded. *Thank God he understood.*

"I'll empty it for you when you're done."

Again, Jeb nodded. Even this was humiliating, but at least Doctor Young was a man.

The doctor handed him the pan and left the room. Even though Jeb's broken limb made everything difficult and painful, he didn't care. When the doctor returned, he'd finished.

"You need to be bathed. Shall I assume you want to do that yourself?"

Of course I do. He didn't have to nod this time. His eyes must have been speaking loud and clear.

"Fine. I'll have the nurse bring in some warm water, soap, and a wash cloth. Please take care not to dampen your dressings. But I must say that we'll all benefit from your bath." He tilted his head and peered at him over his glasses.

Why is my smell everyone's concern?

When the nurse—whom he was told was Nurse Phillips—brought in the bathing supplies, she was accompanied by two orderlies, who lifted him from the bed and placed him in a chair. With his leg casted and splinted, trying to sit was nearly impossible, and the pain unbearable. Unable to help himself, he moaned.

"I'm changing your bedding," she grunted. She was the most unpleasant woman he'd ever met, with looks to match her demeanor. Maybe it was her behavior that made her appear so haggard. As large and manly as the orderlies, if she wasn't wearing a dress, Nurse Phillips could easily be mistaken for a man.

Fortunately, she was quick and soon he was reclined back in bed. She left the bathing supplies and a clean gown, then went out of the room without another remark.

Hateful ...

As he scrubbed his body, he chided himself. Of course she was hateful. He'd almost hit her with the bed pan. He couldn't expect to be treated well if he was cruel. Is this what the war had left him? No family and a heart filled with hate? He couldn't live like this. He didn't *want* to live like this.

* * *

MGH – August 31, 1865

Gwen looked over her shoulder. He was sound asleep and impossible to evaluate. But she didn't want to wake him.

Patient asleep when I arrived. Appears to be resting peacefully and without pain. Not making any sound, except for a slight snore.

Some medical journal. Sleeping and snoring?

She arose from the desk and moved to his side, quietly pulling a chair up beside the bed, and smiled as she inhaled the air around them. Fresh, clean-smelling air. He'd been bathed.

Tilting her head, she studied his features. With a good shave, he might be a handsome man. Well, *that* and a better disposition.

What made you so angry at the world?

She reached into her apron pocket and fingered the tiny porcelain hand. Soon, she would have something worth writing in her journal. Would he be even angrier? What did this mean to him?

He stirred and she held her breath as his blue eyes opened and took her in. For a moment, it seemed that a smile might form on his face, but then it vanished and his brows furrowed.

"Good afternoon," she said as cheerfully as she could.

His lips screwed together.

"You're looking well. Are you in pain?"

He sighed.

How could she reach him?

Her hand slipped into her pocket. Whether or not this was the right time didn't matter. She had to know.

"When you were brought into the hospital, your clothes were discarded, but Doctor Young found this in your pocket. Is it something you'd like to keep?" She held up the piece and as quick as the strike of a snake, his hands gripped hers. He wrenched it from her fingers with fire-filled eyes, and his unclipped nails scratched her skin.

"Fine! Take it." She examined her hand. No blood. "I'd have given it to you if you'd asked. You didn't have to pry it away."

Silly thing to say. How could he have asked?

He clutched the little hand to his chest, breathing heavily. Then his face softened and he nodded toward her hand, questioning with his eyes.

"You scratched me, but it didn't hurt ... much." She stood and paced the floor. "If only you could talk to me."

She took a seat at the desk and dipped her pen.

Doctor Young gave me a tiny porcelain hand found in patient's pocket. Showed it to patient. It means something to him. He grabbed it out of my hand. Received mild scratch. Believe he felt badly for hurting me.

A loud rumble from the man's throat turned her head. He pointed toward her.

"What?"

He pointed again.

She glanced at her hand and then showed it to him. "It's fine. You didn't hurt me."

He shook his head and pointed again, then acted as though he was writing in midair.

"Oh. You want the pen, is that it?"

He nodded rapidly and scooted himself up in bed.

This was promising. If he could write, then maybe they'd actually get somewhere.

As she crossed the room to him, she looked cautiously at the pen. It was pointed and could be used as a weapon if that was his intent. There was only one way to find out.

Lifting the Bible from the bed stand, she placed it on his lap. She laid a sheet of paper on the book, dipped the pen, and handed it to him. It was doubtful he would try to do something mean while holding the Good Book.

Sitting down, she waited.

He stared at her for a moment and then wrote, *WHERE HAVE YOU BEEN?*

She read it three times. Why did he care?

"I go to school most days. I study with Doctor Young two afternoons a week."

He frowned—but there was nothing unusual about that—and wrote again.

THOUGHT YOU WAS A NURSE

Poor grammar, but she wouldn't hold that against him. At least he could write. "No. Not yet." And what she truly wanted to be was a doctor, but no man would understand that.

He nodded toward the ink well, so she held it in her hand close to him. She had so many questions and didn't know where to start.

"What's your name?"

He hesitated, then wrote, *CARTER.*

What a relief. Finally a reference.

"It's good to meet you, Mr. Carter."

His eyes lowered.

"Can you tell me about the hand?" Even though he was no longer holding it in his fist, it lay atop the blanket.

He shook his head, then turned away. The pain in his face made her heart ache. Maybe in time he'd be able to tell her, but for now, she'd let it lie.

"How about where you're from?"

He handed her the paper and grasped the porcelain. It seemed they were done for today.

"Why don't you get some sleep, Mr. Carter? I'll wake you when they bring your dinner."

She lifted the Bible from his lap and returned it to the bed stand, then watched him inch down under the covers.

Returning to her journal, she added to her entry.

Patient's name is Carter. A deeply troubled man.

Chapter 5

Jeb stared at the white walls, feeling as empty and plain as the drab color surrounding him. Maybe he felt sorry for himself, just as Miss Abbott said. He'd never spent this much time in bed. If only he could run, however, running away was what got him into this mess.

Miss Abbott's journal lay on the desk, far from his reach. Aside from the comments she'd made the first day, he didn't know what she'd written. Did she genuinely care about his well-being or was he simply a case study?

Did it matter?

Yes, for some reason it did.

Since she said she only came to the hospital two afternoons a week, he doubted he would see her again until next week. That alone made his day drearier. The other employees who entered his room were cold and unfeeling. Although, Doctor Young seemed all right. For a Yankee.

Maybe he shouldn't have shown that he could write, but he hated not communicating at all. He feared that when the time came to use his voice, he'd forget how. And when would that be? No one had told him how long he'd be here.

He rubbed the porcelain between his fingers. He hadn't meant to hurt her.

She must think I'm insane. Maybe I am.

* * *

Gwen lay in her bed, unable to sleep. Tomorrow, Albert Finch would be calling on her.

God help her ...

She tossed about in her store-bought bedding, feeling guilty. She'd never wanted for anything—never gone hungry. Her mind was plagued with thoughts of Mr. Carter. But she'd much rather think about him and his perplexing life than think about Albert Finch.

To make matters worse, having David and Martha announce their engagement at dinner last night had her parents thinking about weddings.

She clutched her pillow to her face.

Why can't I be like all the other women I know?

It was every girl's dream to marry. Every girl, but her. Her dreams were much larger. From the time she'd helped the baby bird that fell from its nest, her heart had moved her to heal. It was a love that went much deeper than feelings she could ever have for a man.

Maybe that was why she was drawn to the animals on the estate. She used to spend hours on end with the horses. Somehow, just looking into their eyes told her whether or not they were hurting. Their gentle manner soothed her, and she even found grooming them enjoyable. They were never disagreeable.

"Another family secret," she mumbled into the pillow. "Gwen talks to horses."

They didn't talk back with words. They didn't have to. Maybe it made dealing with Mr. Carter easier. She was used to working with mute patients.

Furry mute patients.

She giggled. Mr. Carter was slightly furry, and definitely unable to speak. But it was the sadness behind his eyes that tugged at her heart.

How could she heal him? He was no horse or baby bird, but he'd certainly fallen from somewhere.

She fluffed the pillow and placed it under her head.

"If I have to face Albert Finch tomorrow, I've got to fall asleep." She needed a fresh mind to deal with him.

With slow breaths in and out and thoughts of Mr. Carter's big blue eyes, she finally drifted off.

* * *

"Gwen, Mr. Finch is here!" Katherine popped into Gwen's room, grinning from ear-to-ear. "He brought flowers!"

Gwen closed her eyes and sighed. Flowers. She should be elated.

"Please tell him I'll be right down."

Katherine giggled and hurried off.

Looking down at her green gown, she hoped it was appropriate for whatever he'd planned. Being told he would call on her didn't tell her much. Did he plan to simply sit with her and talk, or take her on a carriage ride? Certainly not unaccompanied.

She took her time descending the stairs and there he was, waiting at the bottom in a fine gray suit, holding a bouquet.

He pulled his shoulders back and extended the flowers. "For you."

"Dahlias." She smiled and took the bright purple and pink bundle. "They're lovely."

"Not as lovely as you are." He reached for her hand and gingerly kissed it.

Her parents entered the hallway, smiling as though it was Christmas morning.

"Mr. Finch asked my permission to escort you to his home for dinner," her father said.

"Oh." Gwen's lips pushed themselves upward with great effort. "And you gave it?"

"Of course I gave it." He patted Albert on the back.

Her mother took the flowers from her hand. "I'll put these in a vase and let Katherine take them to your room."

"Thank you, Mother."

Albert extended his arm. "Shall we go, then?"

It wasn't what she'd expected, but what choice did she have?

She placed her hand into the crook of his arm and followed him out the door. Then they walked down the curving pathway to the waiting carriage. The driver tipped his hat as Albert helped her inside. It was a fine carriage, with red velvet seats, nicely padded for long journeys.

She'd never been alone with a man in a carriage. *Why did Father agree to this arrangement?*

After adjusting her skirt and smoothing it over her knees, she made herself comfortable, assuming he would take the seat across from her. To her dismay, he sat beside her. So close, it pulled on her dress.

"Mr. Finch." She swallowed hard. "You're on my skirt."

"Oh. Forgive me." He lifted his body and she jerked the fabric from beneath his rump.

Sweat beaded on her brow as well as her palms. Silence hovered around them as thick as mud. She attuned her ears to the sound of the horse's hooves on the dirt road and the rumbling of the carriage wheels. Yet she still could not ignore the hiss of air that came from Albert's nostrils every time he exhaled.

She couldn't think of a single thing to say.

Tentatively, she turned her head to look at him. Perhaps it would spark a thought for conversation. But rather than sparking conversation, it ignited anger. His eyes were on her bosom. It appeared that a corset was unnecessary for drawing the attention of a man.

She cleared her throat, lifting his gaze. A slight amount of color filled his cheeks.

"Your dress is ... *lovely.*" His lips pursed, then formed a sly smile.

Lovely.

"It's kind of you to notice. Most men aren't interested in women's fashions." Did he feel the ice coming from her words?

"Oh, *I* noticed. And tell me. What fabric is this?" His hand brushed over her leg.

"Mr. Finch!" She slapped it away. "I doubt my father gave you permission to fondle me in your carriage. We may be courting, but that doesn't give you the right to take liberties."

He placed his hand to his chest. "Fondle? Miss Abbott, you mistook my action. I was merely feeling the fabric."

"I'm not ignorant, Mr. Finch." She crossed her arms, shielding him from further advances. This could not be what her father intended. He'd mentioned eventual affections, but he had to have meant *after* a proper wedding.

They remained silent for the remainder of the ride.

In *her* mind, the evening didn't get any better. But for some reason, Albert continued to grin as though he'd just acquired a prize bull. And his parents lit up just as hers had, brighter than any candelabrum. Everyone seemed pleased with this arrangement. If only she felt the same.

The food was good, and the custard for dessert was better than Violet made. It was the one thing that made her smile. But conversation was forced and she heard more about the weather than she cared to know. Her attempt at discussing the use of anesthesia dropped like a hot potato and Mrs. Finch looked at her as though she'd just crawled from beneath a rock. Why was it improper for a woman to speak intelligently?

And now ... rain?

They bustled quickly to the carriage. Thank goodness she'd be home soon.

She took her seat—this time in the middle of the cushion—and fanned her skirt to take up space. Albert cocked his head, staring at her, then sat on the opposite bench.

"I assured your father that I would return you before dark." He crossed one leg over the other and leaned back in the seat.

"Thank you." The last place she wanted to be was with Albert Finch in a dark carriage.

"Miss Abbott? Since we're courting now, I believe it would be appropriate to address one another by our given names. May I call you Gwendolyn?"

Coming from him, she would prefer it over *Gwen*. "You may."

He slapped his hands against his thighs. "Good! And you may call me Albert."

"Very well."

Silence.

He cleared his throat. "The rain seems to be coming down harder."

"Yes, it does." More weather.

If he goes into detail about just how wet the rain is, I may retch.

"I'm afraid you may get your dress dampened when you leave the carriage. I neglected to bring an umbrella."

"It's a warm rain. I don't mind being *dampened.*"

She peered out the window. Almost home.

He grasped her hand, startling her. Her eyes popped wide, glaring at him.

"Gwendolyn, I should very much like to hold your hand."

"I can see that. Shouldn't you have asked first?"

He chuckled. "May I hold your hand?"

His thumb brushed over her skin. As long as he limited his affections to hand-holding, she wouldn't raise objections. "Since you already are, I shall allow you to continue doing so."

"You have very soft skin."

His eyes penetrated hers, so she quickly looked down. Perhaps he didn't see her cheeks flush.

The carriage abruptly stopped, jolting her. She pulled her hand from his and steadied herself on the seat. Her heart raced, though it wasn't from the sudden stop.

Albert stood and opened the door, then stepped down and extended his hand. Since he was willing to get out in the rain to assist her, her opinion of him improved *somewhat*.

Ducking her head, she placed her foot on the carriage step. Rain pelted through her hair and trickled down her cheeks. "It seems you're also being dampened ... *Albert*."

"It was worth every raindrop to hear you use my name."

Why couldn't *he* be mute?

He steadied her as her foot came to rest on the wet ground. She tucked her hand into his arm and he escorted her to the door.

"I sincerely apologize for our misunderstanding during the onset of our carriage ride." He kissed her wet knuckles. "I shall plan something more entertaining for next Saturday." He jiggled his brows.

More entertaining? Was she supposed to be giddy with anticipation of what was to come? She smiled, but didn't reply.

"Shall we sit together at services tomorrow?"

"I usually sit with my family."

Her remark prompted him to take her hand. "I'm quite certain your father would raise no objections."

"Then ... I shall sit beside you."

Again, he kissed her hand. Rain water didn't appear to offend him.

"Goodnight, Gwendolyn."

"Goodnight." She curtsied, then waited while he opened the door. At least he didn't pose that courting included a real kiss goodnight. She wouldn't allow that form of entertainment.

Chapter 6

Tuesday. Jeb thoroughly scrubbed his body and cleaned his teeth. Feeling stronger and very alert, he adjusted the pillow behind his back and waited. It was well past noon.

Where is she?

A bit of ice melted from his cold heart the moment he heard her laughter.

"Hush, Joanna," she said, calming. "We don't want to disturb Mr. Carter."

He strained to hear her.

Who's Joanna? Immediately, he thought of his sister and his heart sank. He would never forget who took her life.

Two big brown eyes peered around the corner of the doorway, then disappeared.

"Come now, Joanna. You need to return to your room."

Miss Abbott's voice drifted away down the hall. Thankfully, it wasn't long before footsteps approached. He sat up taller in bed.

She walked in with the smile he'd been waiting for.

"Good afternoon, Mr. Carter."

He nodded. Still, no smile would come.

"You have more color. Doctor Young said you've been eating well. I'm certain you found food to be more beneficial in your belly than thrown in someone's face."

She knew how to speak her mind. So much like his mama ...

"Oh, good!" She clasped her hands together. Two orderlies entered the room. One pushed a wheelchair.

"It's time to get you out of this room."

What?

Where would they take him? Though he was tired of staring at the empty walls, he wasn't ready to leave.

"Don't look so frightened." She leaned toward him. "I'm taking you for a stroll outside." She nodded to the orderlies, who lifted him into the chair.

The chair had a long extension to accommodate his leg. Miss Abbott tucked a blanket around him, making him feel like a baby in a carriage.

"Here, this will help your leg." With a gentler hand than that of the doctor, she raised his leg enough to place a pillow beneath it. "Good?"

He nodded, then she stepped behind him and gripped the chair.

After being in the same room for more than a week, even the plain hallway was interesting. They passed by a room and he met the same dark eyes that had peered at him earlier. Her face was framed by long, dark locks.

"That's Joanna," Miss Abbott whispered. "A very sweet eight-year-old. She'll be going home soon. She had the fever, but will have no lasting effects."

The little girl waved and they continued on.

"It's a beautiful day. We may as well enjoy it before the cold sets in."

Cold. Something he wasn't used to. It was rare in Atlanta.

They passed by one of the nurses. Why did she scowl at both of them?

"Don't mind her. Some of the nurses here don't care for me. I'm sorry if they're taking it out on you."

Why? Where was the pen and paper when he needed it?

They reached the front door and a tall man opened it for them. He smiled broadly at Miss Abbott, then gave him a sympathetic frown.

Reckon he'd shoot me, if he knew where I came from.

Squinting in the bright sunshine, Jeb shielded his eyes with his hand. Sparkling water glistened before him.

A river? He knew little about Boston—just that it was on the Atlantic.

"I love this time of year. The leaves will be turning soon."

She pushed him further along a concrete walkway. When he turned and looked behind him, he gasped. Tilting his head back, he scanned the three story building. Tall white pillars adorned the front of the white brick structure. Brick. Everything reminded him of his home, except that. Brick wouldn't burn like wood.

"Are you in pain, Mr. Carter?"

No ache that she could heal. He slowly shook his head.

"Here. This is the perfect spot." She positioned the wheelchair beside a wooden bench and sat. "I sometimes come here when I want to think."

They were shaded by four large trees; three maples and one oak. He spotted a squirrel scurrying up the trunk of the oak.

"Getting ready for winter." She nodded toward the squirrel. "Do you like snow?"

He shrugged. He'd seen a few flurries, but nothing that stayed long on the ground.

"I like to watch it fall. My sister is fascinated with the different shapes of the crystals. She's nine."

Mine was five ...

No, he wouldn't allow tears to form. He rubbed his eyes with his palms.

"Does the sun bother your eyes?"

He nodded, though he didn't like to lie to her. Then again, his entire existence here was a lie.

"We'll go in soon, but I believe fresh air is good for recovery."

Aside from the fact that around every corner something reminded him of his losses, he liked being out here. Truthfully, he liked being with *her*.

"I should have brought pen and paper. There's so much I want to know about you. When we return to your room, will you answer my questions?"

Depends on the questions.

He shrugged. She giggled. She must have understood his meaning.

* * *

Talking to Mr. Carter was effortless for Gwen. Unlike talking to Albert. What made the two men so different? Aside from the fact that one *couldn't* talk and the other *shouldn't*.

Mr. Carter seemed to be enjoying the outdoors, so why didn't he smile? Was he still in too much pain? Doctor Young told her that as long as he didn't put a lot of weight on the leg, his pain should be minimal. In time, they would help him walk with crutches.

Everything in time.

She wheeled him back inside, with a promise of another outing on Thursday. Weather permitting.

As they passed Joanna's room, Mr. Carter waved.

Hmmm ...

After the orderlies put him into bed, she sat at her desk and started her entry, allowing him time to get comfortable.

MGH – September 5, 1865

Took patient outside. Appeared to enjoy fresh air and sunshine, yet something still troubles him.

Observed that Mr. Carter is fond of children.

He cleared his throat. Very promising. Hopefully he was ready to do some writing himself.

After placing the Bible on his lap, she handed him the pen and paper and took her place beside him. Before she could ask him a question, he began writing.

WHEN CAN I LEAVE HERE?

"Oh. Hasn't Doctor Young told you?"

He shook his head.

"Well ... we need to get you on your feet. As long as you're eating well, and have your strength, then we'll get you up on crutches. But you'll be in the cast for at least three months. You should be grateful that the fracture wasn't severe."

His eyes widened and his hand flew over the page.

WILL I HAVE TO STAY HERE?

"For now. I thought you would have to stay for the full three months, but after talking to Doctor Young, he said that in time you'll be able to leave, as long as you can get around by yourself. Even in the cast."

His body seemed to deflate. She thought it would be good news.

"Do you have family near here who can help you?"

She didn't think he could deflate further, but she was wrong. He closed his eyes and his shoulders drew in. He almost dropped the pen. Then with slow deliberation, he opened his eyes, and his hand moved.

NO FAMILY

"Anywhere?"

He shook his head.

Her throat tightened and she had to turn her head to keep him from seeing the tears pooling in her eyes. "I'm so sorry." Though compelled to touch him, she held back. It wasn't her place.

"Do you live in Boston?"

NO

"Where do you live?"

HERE

He rolled his eyes and looked around the room.

She persisted. "But, where are you from?"

He handed her the paper and she scolded herself for asking the question he didn't want to answer. Twice asked. Twice avoided.

"Very well, then. Get some rest and I'll see you on Thursday."

She stood and was about to return the writing materials to her desk, when she changed her mind. Instead, she left them on the bed stand within his reach. Thursday, she would add to her journal, but for now, she hoped he might feel inclined to do a bit more writing himself.

* * *

Gwen hastened down the hall, anxious to see what Mr. Carter had written on the paper since their last visit. She'd drifted through her studies yesterday with little concentration. All she could think about was the mysterious man at Mass General.

She froze. He wasn't alone.

Joanna?

Gwen leaned against the wall and listened.

"I'm going home today, Mr. Carter." Joanna's sweet voice warmed the air around her. "I'll take this with me and treasure it forever."

What did he give her?

With a thumping heart, Gwen cautiously peered into the room. She jerked back, praying she wasn't seen. Tears filled her eyes and she had to control her breathing. Touched beyond words, she wiped her damp cheeks. With arms encircling the little girl, Mr. Carter smiled.

She counted to thirty, making certain enough time passed, then walked into the room as though nothing had happened.

"Well ... Good afternoon Mr. Carter *and* Joanna." She smoothed her hand over the little girl's head.

"Look, Miss Abbott!" Joanna exclaimed. "Mr. Carter made this for me!"

An intricately folded paper rose was placed in Gwen's hand. Beautifully formed with stem and petals. She'd never seen anything quite so *lovely*.

"Mr. Carter. This is fantastic." She smiled at him, hoping for one in return, but his face remained solemn. Although she'd hoped to find written words, this flower said more.

"Maybe he'll make one for you, too," Joanna said, taking the rose.

Mr. Carter lowered his eyes.

"I believe you're special, Joanna."

The girl beamed. "I need to go, now. Mommy and Daddy are coming for me." She hugged Mr. Carter, then wrapped her arms around Gwen. "Thank you for being so nice, Miss Abbott." She tugged on Gwen's arm and pulled her to the other side of the room.

"Miss Abbott," she lowered her voice. "Mr. Carter isn't as mean as everyone says." She pulled her down and cupped her hand over Gwen's ear. "He smiled at me."

Gwen knelt down in front of her, then gave her a kiss on the cheek. "Thank you."

"What for?"

"For helping me."

The little girl tilted her head and wrinkled her nose. Maybe she didn't understand, but no matter. She'd made today very special.

Joanna giggled, skipped out of the room, and waved as she left. Gwen's heart felt as light as the child's laughter.

She stood and moved toward Mr. Carter. "You surprised me, Mr. Carter."

He looked toward the ceiling.

"You did a very nice thing. Do you have a soft spot for little girls?"

His head dipped in a slow nod.

She had to try. She handed him the pen and paper, then put the Bible in its place on his lap. "Who?"

His hand trembled, hovering over the paper. Finally, the pen rested against the sheet.

HAD A SISTER

Progress. "What was her name?"

His chest heaved.

ANNA

So close to the name Joanna. No wonder she touched his heart. "How old was she ... when she died?"

He gulped. Tears glistened in his eyes. Maybe she was pushing too hard. Her heart ached as his hand rested on the paper.

5

He shoved the paper away and it floated to the floor. Then he placed the Bible and pen on the bed stand. They were done for today, but at least now she knew something. His leg was not the source of his pain; this poor man had a broken heart.

Chapter 7

At least it wasn't for a meal. Wearing a corset was the last thing Gwen wanted to do, but her mother and Martha insisted on it. Told that she would be an embarrassment to society without one, Gwen had to succumb. After all, they were attending Boston Theatre; Albert Finch's promise of something more entertaining.

The good thing was that they weren't going alone. Martha and David were invited, so the couples would share the carriage. That meant she would have to sit beside Albert, but would have the protective eye of her brother at all times. Unless, of course, his eyes were affixed on Martha.

Gwen sighed. It was the last time she'd be able to breathe before her mother came in to cinch up the torture chamber.

"Don't look so sad, dear," her mother said, entering her room. "You'll be pleased with the results."

Pleased? It had to have been a man that invented this horrid undergarment. Every bit of it was for his benefit, not that of the woman wearing it.

Standing in her chemise and bloomers, Gwen closed her eyes as her mother lifted the device over her head and positioned it into place.

"Reach under your chemise and lift your bosoms," her mother said with as much calm as she would if she were instructing her how to lace her shoes. "You won't want them pinched."

No, they wouldn't be pinched; they would be lifted for the entire world to see. Much to the delight of Albert Finch.

She dutifully did as she was told, then gripped her bed post and braced herself for what was to come.

Dear Lord!

"Hold your breath, Gwen." Her mother yanked and pulled.

"I'm forever bruised," Gwen muttered. "Mother, I'll be sitting like a tree stump for more than two hours. How will I endure this ... *thing?*"

"There!" She patted her back. "Now, we'll place your dress and you'll see how it looks."

Gwen turned to face her mother, stiff as a board. "I'll be walking like a penguin."

"No, you'll walk like the refined lady you are."

After placing her crinolines, her mother lowered the lavender dress. The neckline scooped just enough to re-veal the outcome of the corset; fully rounded breasts. The view looking down terrified her.

"Mother, I'm exposed." Gwen pulled the lace bordering the neckline upward, trying her best to cover herself.

Her mother immediately grabbed her hands. "Gwen, dear. You look like a woman. What you're showing is socially acceptable."

"I don't want to be this social."

"Come here." She led her to the full length mirror. "Look at yourself. This color is splendid with your hair, and once I place your hat, you'll be stunning."

Gwen scanned her image. Her long blond hair was pulled up in the back, dropping into ringlets. Her bare neck appeared exceptionally long and she fingered it uncomfortably.

"Don't move," her mother instructed and left her standing there.

I can't move.

When her mother returned, she fastened a string of pearls around Gwen's neck.

"Oh, Mother." She gulped. "Are you certain you want me to wear these?"

"Yes." She smiled and kissed her cheek.

Gwen had a good reason to return the smile. The pearls were exquisite. White, like the satin bows adorning her lavender skirt. Once the matching cap hat was positioned, Gwen was ready to face the city of Boston and the eyes of the social elite.

"We must show your father." Her mother took her by the hand and led her down the stairs.

With each step, the bone ribbing of the corset dug into her flesh. The only time it didn't hurt was when she held her breath. An impossible way to go through the afternoon.

Her father came out of the library puffing on his pipe. When he saw her, he stopped and stared, shaking his head. "Grace, I believe our daughter has finally become a woman."

Gwen stood tall, sucking in her breath. "One that shall faint from lack of air."

Her father chuckled. "Now, now. You've always been my dramatic child."

She couldn't have been more serious.

Katherine bounded down the stairs. "Gwen! You're beautiful!" Her enthusiasm was appreciated, but Gwen stopped short of hugging her.

"You don't want to muss her gown," her mother said to Katherine.

"I wish I could go." Katherine's large eyes blinked slowly.

"In time, my dear."

"Yes," her father said, "for now, be my little Katie."

Footsteps turned their attention. David and Martha were coming down the hallway, arm in arm. Martha wore navy blue and David was in a deep gray suit.

Gwen wished she had Martha's grace. Martha had more practice wearing fashionable undergarments and floated over the floor, not seeming to be in any discomfort.

Gwen shifted her eyes between Martha and herself.

Hmmm ... matching bosoms.

She tittered, then covered her mouth when her mother admonished her with her eyes. Although she didn't speak her thoughts, perhaps it wasn't appropriate to find humor in them.

Martha pulled her to the side. "It's not so horrid, is it Gwen?"

"Yes."

Martha laughed aloud, then returned to David's arm.

"Albert should be arriving soon," David said. "The matinee is at one o'clock." He drew a chain from his front pocket and flipped open his gold watch. "Noon."

A knock on the door made him smile. "He's punctual."

"Wait until he sees you," Martha said, grinning at Gwen.

Gwen looked down. The mounds of her breasts seemed to be glowing. She wanted to hide—to run away. Anything, but have Albert Finch see her like this.

"Mr. Finch!" Her mother exclaimed and pulled him inside. "So good to see you again."

Albert took her mother's hand and kissed it, then nodded at her father. "Mr. Abbott, Mrs. Abbott, it's my pleasure."

His gaze traveled to her and landed right where Gwen feared. His eyes popped wide, then he caught himself, breathed, and raised them to meet hers.

Stepping toward her, he took her hand. "Gwendolyn, you look ..." he paused.

Lovely?

"Glorious."

Oh. "Thank you, Albert." He looked a bit *glorious* himself. Dashing in black.

He kissed her hand, then kept hold of it as he escorted her out the door. "Your carriage awaits."

She caught a faint giggle coming from Martha, who followed behind them with David.

No wrap was needed. The sky was clear and bright and the temperature comfortable. A horizon without clouds promised no rain. All-in-all, the perfect day for a carriage ride.

Boston Theatre was a twenty minute jaunt across town and with Martha and David in the carriage, conversation was light and easy.

Albert's warm body butted against Gwen's, and his fingers remained entwined with hers. Looking across at her brother and Martha, Gwen sensed a great deal of difference between the pairs. They appeared to be very much in love. They frequently locked eyes and their bodies tipped toward one another. Gwen did all she could to tip *away* from Albert.

At one point, Albert rubbed his thumb over the back of her hand, then jiggled his brows at her. All it accomplished was a flip of her stomach—and not in a good way. Would her feelings ever change?

"So ..." Albert sat straight up and pushed his shoulders against the back of the seat. "Shall I tell you about the production we're about to see?"

He looked from person to person ... waiting.

"Oh, please do," Gwen finally said.

He repositioned himself and puffed out his chest. "It is entitled, *The Streets of New York.* Their newly acquired actor, Frank Mayo, will be playing the part of Badger."

"Badger?" Martha's brows dipped. "Is the play about animals?"

Albert rolled his eyes. "Not *a* badger. Badger is his character name. He plays a clerk."

"A clerk named Badger? Seems rather silly to me." Martha folded her hands in her lap.

Gwen could tell David was suppressing a laugh. It wouldn't be wise to laugh at one's host.

"Martha," Gwen said. "I'm certain it's a very good play. Tell us more, Albert."

Albert squeezed her hand and smiled. "Very well. All I can say is that you'll certainly laugh and perhaps cry. And ... the audience is encouraged to boo and hiss at the villain."

"A shame that Katie couldn't come," David said. "She loves to boo and hiss."

Albert's shoulders drooped. "I assure you. You'll enjoy yourselves."

"I know we shall," Gwen said with a smile. Albert went to a lot of trouble arranging their tickets and she didn't want him to feel discouraged. Whether or not she genuinely cared for him.

The carriage stopped and the door opened. The men helped Gwen and Martha step down. Everywhere Gwen looked, people dressed in fineries walked toward the theatre entrance. She was grateful she'd listened to her mother. Her dress was in fashion all the way down to the corset. She touched the pearls at her neck, making certain they were still there.

"Lovely," Albert whispered in her ear.

With shoulders back and the grace of a *female* penguin, Gwen strutted beside Albert. Her eyes widened, taking in the enormous auditorium. There were four tiers encircling a large stage and a high domed ceiling painted with posed ladies entwined with flowers. Each tier had intricately carved wood railings and padded seats which were filling to capacity.

Excitement surrounded them and Albert beamed as he showed them to their prime seats, only three rows from the stage. "It's far enough back so that you don't strain your neck. Or for that matter, get spit upon by the actors." He chuckled. "Yes, they sometimes spit."

"Even the women?" Gwen asked.

He looked sideways at her. "Women don't spit."

Or release gas. Enough said.

Gwen was glad to take her seat, until the ribbing rode up and rubbed her the wrong way. She adjusted herself by twisting, turning, and holding her breath. It would be a very long afternoon.

As Albert promised, they all hissed and booed, and although it caused her pain, Gwen even laughed. But she was haunted by a line from the play that repeated itself over and over again in her mind: "'Tis my happiness that renders me silent."

Although it had nothing to do with Mr. Carter's situation, once the line was said, she couldn't get him out of her head. What kept him silent? It couldn't be happiness. Perhaps lack thereof.

On the ride home, *she* was silent. In tune to her thoughts alone.

"Gwen?" Martha patted her leg.

"Yes?"

"You didn't answer my question."

Gwen stared at her. "I'm sorry. What did you ask?"

"I asked if you would stand up with me at our wedding."

"Oh. Well ... of course I will. I'd be honored."

"Good!" Martha cuddled her shoulder into David. "And since Albert agreed to stand for David, we'll be perfectly matched."

Albert turned his head and gazed downward at Gwen. His eyes lit up and he squeezed her hand. By the end of their outing, her hand would be kneaded as well as any lump of bread dough.

Once home, Martha and David exited the carriage first. Albert pulled the door closed behind them.

"Why did you do that?" Gwen asked, pointing to the door.

"Privacy."

"But it's highly improper."

"Gwendolyn, we're courting, and we're both adults. Five minutes alone in a carriage will not create scandal."

He took both of her hands in his, then drew them to his lips, kissing each knuckle one-by-one. He paused and peered into her eyes. "You take my breath, Gwendolyn."

Oh, dear Lord. He intends to kiss me.

"Albert—we must exit at once."

He placed his cheek against hers. "Please ... just one kiss?" His lips were in her ear.

She shuddered. "No."

"No?"

"No."

"Oh ..." He hissed air through his nostrils, then pulled back. "You wound me, Gwendolyn."

Perhaps I should.

"Everything in time, Albert. And now is not the time for affection." She stood her ground, swallowing hard.

Reluctantly, he opened the carriage door, then stepped down and extended his hand. When she stooped to exit the carriage, his face was mere inches from her bosom. Not what she intended.

"As I said ..." He held his hand against his chest. "You wound me. Deeper than you realize."

She planted her feet firmly on the ground, then he once again took her hands.

"Gwendolyn," he breathed hard. "I shall have to marry you soon."

Soon?

Deciding to make light of his words, she giggled. "Dear, Albert. You're overcome from the production. We've only just begun courting."

"It doesn't matter. Your beauty moves me beyond words."

She felt nauseous. The only thing moving him was the view of her bare skin. No matter how socially acceptable it might be, she would never dress this way again. "I'm sorry for your torment, but I beg you not to rush me."

He cupped her cheek with his hand. "I'll wait for you, but please don't make me wait forever."

She swallowed hard, feeling heat in her cheeks. Thank goodness, her mother was coming toward them.

"Gwen, you did invite Mr. Finch to dinner, didn't you?"

It had slipped her mind.

"Will you have dinner with us, Albert?" Gwen asked, appeasing her mother.

"The more time I can spend with you, the better my life shall be."

He can't be serious.

Her mother's face lit up and they all walked inside. But before dinner was served, nothing would stop Gwen from going to her room to change into something more comfortable—with a high neckline.

Chapter 8

The time it took to get from Thursday to Tuesday, seemed like forever. Jeb wrote for no one but Miss Abbott, and even though one of the other nurses tried to get him to, he wouldn't do it. It had always been hard for him to trust folks and being in the north made trust almost impossible.

Nurse Phillips was the assigned weekend nurse and she fussed at him, telling him how lucky he was to have a room by himself. And then she sneered and said it was because he was hateful and they feared for the safety of the other patients.

Hateful? He wasn't hateful, he was trying to survive. But why? What did he have to live for?

"Good afternoon, Mr. Carter." Miss Abbott's voice warmed him. Was she his reason?

He nodded. He wanted to speak.

She crossed to the desk and immediately began writing. Then she stopped, rubbed her hand along her side, and groaned. Was she in pain?

He cleared his throat, causing her to look over her shoulder. Tipping his head, he questioned her, pointing to her mid-section.

She rolled her eyes upward. "You don't want to know."

He nodded, encouraging her.

After looking from side-to-side, she arose and pulled up a chair beside him. "You're certain you want me to tell you?"

Of course he was. He wanted to know everything about her.

"Very well, I'll tell you. Besides, you won't tell anyone else." She grinned, but then softened to an apologetic smile.

He waved his hand. She didn't have to apologize. If she discovered his farce, he'd be the one apologizing.

"Though the subject matter is of a delicate nature, I doubt I'll offend you."

He raised his brows. This could be interesting.

"Are you familiar with women's corsets?" Her voice was barely a whisper and she continued looking toward the door as though she was afraid they'd be interrupted.

Though his cheeks heated at the mention of a woman's undergarment, he managed to nod.

"I was forced to wear one and am paying the price. My skin is bruised, but that's not the worse part."

Should he allow her to continue?

"Wearing the garment sparked my beau's affections. Of course I refused his advances. I shouldn't have succumbed to wearing something that would arouse his interest. It was highly unfair to him."

Jeb's chest tightened and his palms became damp. A mixture of emotions stirred and he was literally at a loss for words. Her beau? Of course she had a beau. A woman as beautiful as Miss Abbott would likely have more than one suitor. But hearing her say the words was painful.

He looked away.

"I've embarrassed you, haven't I?" She touched his arm, causing him to jump. "Forgive me. Sometimes I speak without thinking."

One of us has to.

He mimed writing, so she handed him the pen, paper, and Bible.

ARE YOU MARRYING HIM?

"We're courting. My parents are pushing the relationship." She shifted her eyes to the floor. "It wasn't my choice."

WHY DO IT?

"My parents believe that every woman needs to be married. And—Albert comes from a well-to-do family. He'll be able to provide for me."

Albert? Yes, he sounded rich.

DO YOU LOVE HIM?

She looked him in the eye and struggled to speak. "I—I don't. Not yet."

Not yet? Did she expect it to happen suddenly, or grow from years of waiting on him hand and foot and rearing his children?

DOES HE MIND THAT YOU WORK?

She shrunk at least two inches, shook her head, then rose to her feet.

"Enough about me. It's time we get you on your feet."

He'd forgotten that today was the day for walking. He hesitated.

I'M SCARED

She touched her hand to his face, making his admission worthwhile. "I won't let you fall." After slowly pulling her hand back, she walked out of the room, then returned with an orderly who held crutches.

Jeb's cheek tingled, recalling the feel of her soft skin. And now, she would have her arm around him to steady him. How could he think clearly being so close to her? He had to stifle his feelings or he was bound to be hurt. Chiding himself, he focused on the task at hand.

She set aside his writing tools, then smiled and touched the porcelain hand which he now kept beside the Bible. He wanted it within view as a constant reminder. She must have come to the conclusion that it belonged to his sister.

"Are you ready?"

He sighed, but nodded. Was he ready for anything?

She pulled back his blanket and the orderly helped swing his body to the side of the bed. Then the large man reached under his arm and hoisted him up. He stood on his left side, which was the side of his broken limb. His good right foot rested on the floor. "Here." The orderly secured a crutch under his armpit. "Put your weight on the crutch and no weight on the left leg."

Miss Abbott placed her arm at Jeb's waist, stood on his right side, and positioned the other crutch. "I'll help you until you're steady. You've been in bed a long time."

He considered never being steady again.

Even though he felt vulnerable wearing only a simple hospital gown, he stood tall, towering over her. Being so close, he caught a whiff of her clean hair. When it wasn't in a tight bun, did it fall all the way to her waist?

Her head tilted upward and her blue eyes blinked slowly.

What's she thinkin'?

"You're taller than I thought," she said, while turning to face forward.

And you're too pretty.

He put weight on his left foot and received a jolt of pain, snapping him out of his ridiculous thoughts. She had a beau. A *rich* beau.

I'm her patient. Nothin' more.

"I told you not to do that," the orderly said.

"Yes," Miss Abbott added. "Please be careful. Doctor Young entrusted me to help you. I don't want to let him down."

What would Doctor Young think if she had to write that he'd further damaged his leg? He decided to comply to keep her in good standing with the doctor.

They walked into the hall. The orderly was the first to release him, and after about five steps, Miss Abbott also let go, hovering close. The crutches were uncomfortable, but after a few more steps, he got used to them and made his way with little difficulty. Maybe this wasn't wise.

Where would he go when they released him from the hospital?

"I don't want you to overdo," she said. "Let's get you turned around and back to your room."

She placed her hand against his back as he swiveled and faced the other direction. It was surprising how tired he was after so little exertion.

They helped him back into bed and the orderly left them alone.

He grabbed the writing tools.

DID IT HURT YOU?

"Hurt *me*?"

He pointed to her waist.

"Oh—no. I didn't even think about it. I was too worried about you."

GOOD. DIDN'T WANT TO HURT YOU.

"Mr. Carter ..." She folded her hands in her lap. "You're a very kind man. And though I'm sorry you were injured, I—I'm glad you came here."

What could he say? I'm glad to be here, too?

"Have you always been mute?"

NO

"How ..." She stopped and he was glad she did. She must know him well enough now to know that there were some questions he still wouldn't answer.

She started to speak again, but stopped as if her mind reeled in different directions. She'd never been at a loss for words with him before.

WHAT?

She looked away, so he tapped her shoulder, then pointed to the page.

"When I come on Thursday, would you mind if I brought my sister? I'd like you to meet her."

Though he didn't understand *why* she wanted him to meet her, he nodded his agreement.

"Her name is Katherine."

9, RIGHT?

"Yes. You remembered." Her face lit up with a bright smile. "You rest now. If you feel like walking again, be sure to have an orderly help you—or one of the nurses. Katherine and I will help you on Thursday. And, if the weather is pleasant, perhaps we'll go outside again."

Something to look forward to.

"Goodbye, Mr. Carter. And—thank you for listening to me earlier. I find it easy to talk to you."

He waved his hand, then without thinking ... *smiled*.

* * *

Gwen's heart raced. Prior to leaving, she grabbed her journal, then darted away before he realized what he'd done. His smile warmed the room and every corner of her heart. She'd known it was there somewhere. Joanna had brought it out in him, and now, so had she.

She couldn't wait to tell Doctor Young, but first, she'd write about it.

MGH – September 12th, 1865

Excellent progress with Mr. Carter.

Today he not only walked with crutches, he also smiled.

Not sure which was the greater accomplishment.

Intend to bring Katherine for Thursday's visit.

Want to see how he interacts with her.

After reporting to Doctor Young—who was pleased with her progress—she floated home. Lighter than air. The joy of her accomplishment kindled her spirit. Maybe this was how the doctor felt when he'd repaired Mr. Carter's limb.

She wouldn't give up her education or her time with Doctor Young. It was where she belonged. But maybe it was more than that. Maybe it had to do with Mr. Carter specifically. She shook her head.

No, it can't be. He's my patient, nothing more.

So why did his smile reach all the way to her soul? And why did he matter so much?

Slowing to a snail's pace, she considered every moment she'd spent with him since he came to the hospital, then muffled a laugh, remembering how he threw a pillow at her the first day. He'd come a long way. *They'd* come a long way.

"Why did I tell him about Albert?" She mumbled the words aloud, then looked around to make certain no one heard her. "And my corset ..." Her cheeks warmed. If her mother knew she'd discussed her undergarments with a patient, she'd be ashamed of her.

What was I thinking?

At least she'd have Katherine with her on the next visit. She would keep her in line. And even though Mr. Carter was easy to talk to, from here on out she'd make a point of keeping her personal matters behind closed lips.

* * *

Gwen clutched Katherine's hand as they walked down the long hallway. She'd explained to Doctor Young her reasons for bringing her sister to the hospital and he found them fascinating. He wanted her to continue her journal and be as specific as she could in regard to Mr. Carter's recovery.

"Now remember, Katherine. Mr. Carter can't speak, but he can write. Just be yourself and I know he'll like you."

"Does he like *you*?"

The question brought warmth to Gwen's face. "Yes, I believe he does."

"And you like him, too. I can tell."

Perhaps bringing Katherine wasn't such a wise idea. Would she embarrass her?

Gwen received the usual looks of disapproval from the nurses she passed. She'd thought that by now they would have accepted her role at the hospital and be happy she was there. After all, she wasn't receiving pay for all her hard work and she was doing things they would have to do in her absence. They should be grateful.

"Why don't they smile?" Katherine asked, after receiving a scowl from Nurse Phillips. "The nurses here look like they drank sour milk."

"Shh ... We'll speak about it later."

"Do you think Mr. Carter will smile today?"

Gwen probably shouldn't have told her sister about him smiling at her. She had to remind herself again why she chose to bring her in the first place. *Research.*

Gwen stopped her sister just outside Mr. Carter's room. "You look very pretty today, Katherine." Her yellow, ruffled dress was adorable, accented with a matching yellow ribbon in her hair.

"So do you," Katherine said. "Even in that ugly uniform."

Sisters were obviously created to speak their minds. Especially *little* sisters. Granted, the uniform might be unattractive, but it was something she was required to wear. There was no choice in the matter.

Katherine could have at least been more grateful that they'd come by carriage and she hadn't made her walk the entire way. But even then, Katherine had teased her about talking to the horses prior to entering the hospital. What had been so unusual about giving the mare a pat on the nose and telling her that they wouldn't be long? It seemed that today her sister was determined to point out her every flaw.

Gwen took a deep breath and sighed, then escorted her into the room.

Mr. Carter sat fully upright in bed and met her gaze the moment she walked in. For a brief instant, she thought the corners of his mouth were rising, but then his face lost all expression.

"Good afternoon, Mr. Carter. This is my sister, Katherine."

Katherine crossed the room and stood beside his bed. "My brother, David, calls me Katie. You can, too, if you'd like."

His head tipped and he looked at Gwen with the usual questions lurking behind his eyes. When she went to hand him the writing tools, she noticed that he'd been busy. A paper rose, similar to the one he'd given Joanna, was atop the Bible.

Now it was her turn to question *him*. "For Katherine?"

He nodded.

Gwen handed her sister the rose. "Be very careful with it."

"It's beautiful. No one has ever given me flowers of any kind. Thank you, Mr. Carter." Katherine leaned over and kissed his cheek.

The surprise in his eyes softened into joy and a slight upturn of his mouth lasted a few moments.

"Mr. Finch gave Gwen flowers. But they've already died. My flower will never die."

He pointed to the paper, and when Gwen gave it to him, he wrote:

GWEN?

Of course. He didn't know her first name. There was no need. But now ... "Well, then. Since you know my given name, I believe it would be appropriate for me to know yours. I've assumed all along that Carter is your surname."

He nodded.

"So, will you tell us your given name?"

J

After writing the single letter, he stopped and stared at the page.

Katherine giggled. "It's a game. He wants us to guess."

"Oh?" Gwen looked at his face, but didn't see a trace of playfulness.

"Let me try." Katherine rolled her eyes upward, thinking. "Jacob?"

He shook his head.

Katherine moved closer and peered into his face. "Julia?" She laughed aloud, then covered her mouth.

He hesitated for a moment and shook his head again.

Did he chuckle?

Gwen decided to play along. "Jeffrey?"

Another shake of the head.

She studied his features. What would his mother have named him? Something strong.

"I know what it is." Gwen lifted her chin, confident in her guess. "It's John."

This time, she received a satisfying nod.

"Not fair," Katherine pouted. "I wanted to guess it."

John reached out and patted Katherine's hand, then wrote on his paper.

YOU HAVE A ROSE. GWEN DON'T

"So it seems," Gwen said. "And it also appears that you want to be on a first name basis. Is that correct?"

YES

What could it hurt? Perhaps it wasn't appropriate, but since she wasn't a nurse and didn't have to adhere to all their rules, maybe this was what she needed to break further into the shell he'd built around himself.

"Very well, John." It was odd saying the name. "I'm going to leave you and Katherine for a moment to get the wheelchair. I believe we all need some fresh air."

She shook her finger at Katherine. "Don't give away any more family secrets."

"What secrets?" Katherine asked, wrinkling her nose.

Gwen shook her head, then rushed out of the room. She didn't dare stay away long.

Chapter 9

John Carter.

The lie was bigger than ever. But he couldn't tell her his real name. The name *Jeb* screamed *southern born*. So, he would learn to answer to the name John and keep his mouth shut tighter than ever.

The weekend brought even more problems. Doctor Young proclaimed him *healthy* and wanted to release him from the hospital. Though his entire stay had been written off as charity, it seemed their goodwill only carried so far. And now that he was strong, eating well, and walking proficiently with the crutches, they wanted him gone.

"But don't go far," Dr. Young said. "I want you to come and see me every week so that I can monitor your leg. Eventually, we'll remove the cast."

Jeb stared at him. And then, he did what he swore he wouldn't. He picked up the pen and paper to write a message for Doctor Young.

HAVE NOWHERE TO GO

Doctor Young took the paper from him, read it, then peered at him over the top of his glasses. "You may. Miss Abbott has been working on that."

What?

"Don't look so surprised. She cares about you—medically speaking."

Of course he would add those words. How else would she care about him? After all, he was a poor mute, with no prospects.

"She's coming by this afternoon when she gets out of class. Hopefully, she'll have good news for you."

Coming by on a Monday? Unexpected, but good.

"Mr. Carter." Doctor Young moved in closer. "Whatever happens from here on out, I want you to know that I doubt your recovery would have been so successful without the help of Miss Abbott. So please, always be kind to her. She's a special young woman."

He nodded, then the doctor left him alone. He didn't have to be told that Gwen was special. It took only five minutes alone with her to make him realize that. And after he'd allowed his stone heart to soften, she'd managed to work her way into it.

What did she have planned for him? In his condition, manual labor was impossible. He wasn't good for much of anything. Except making paper roses ...

* * *

It seemed strange walking into the hospital in a regular day dress. When Gwen realized John had never seen her out of uniform, she froze.

Looking down at her long, green dress, she smoothed the fabric with her hand. What would he think of the plaid print and the ribbon in her hair? Hair worn down over her shoulders rather than high upon her head?

You're being silly, Gwen.

John Carter was a patient. A patient whom she'd helped to recover, and would hopefully continue to work with, if he was agreeable to her proposal. And thank goodness her father had agreed to it. Apparently, she still had the ability to have him do her bidding, except where Albert Finch was concerned.

Throwing her shoulders back, she pressed on. Her heart thumped the closer she came to his room.

Silly, silly girl.

She held Henry's contribution under one arm as she walked through John's door. Depending on how he coped with outright charity, she might have something thrown at her again.

"Good afternoon ... John."

His head moved slower than ice on a frozen river as he scanned her from head to toe. Then his Adam's apple bobbled and he swallowed hard. His blue eyes finally locked with hers and she knew her cheeks must be glowing brilliant red.

"Goodness, John," she choked out the words. "You look at me as though you've never seen me before."

He whipped the paper from the bed stand.

BEAUTIFUL

She couldn't breathe. This was far worse than the discomfort from the corset. As many times as Albert had told her she was *lovely*, it had never affected her this way.

Needing to sit, she dropped into the chair closest to the bed, then sat as upright as possible. "Thank you."

After nervously toying with her skirt, she extended the bundle of clothes to him. "I believe you're about the same size as my brother, Henry. I knew you'd need clothing to leave here. Please don't take offense. He gave them willingly."

John held up the black wool trousers and white cotton shirt, then nodded.

THANK YOU

"The weather's getting colder. The wool should keep you warm, even though I had to split the left leg to accommodate your cast. And—I can get you other shirts. Maybe some flannel?"

He looked down with eyes sadder than ever.

"John?" Taking a deep breath, she prayed that he'd agree. "I know you have nowhere to go."

Once again, he met her gaze, warming her to the tips of her toes.

"My father is a charitable man. As a matter of fact, he donates funds to this hospital." She shook her head. She didn't want to sound like a braggart.

"What I'm getting at is—we have a guesthouse. It's currently unoccupied. I asked Father if you could stay there until your cast is removed."

His brow crinkled.

"Of course, there would be something expected from you in return. This isn't charity."

He sat up a little taller.

"If you haven't already discerned this, my father is William Abbott. Abbott's Department Store?"

He shrugged.

"You truly aren't from Boston, are you?"

She stood, then scooted the chair closer and sat again. "Abbott's is quite successful and Father's good sense of business has brought our family the means to ..." *Bragging again.* Would she ever say the right things?

He placed his hand on her arm, then motioned for her to continue.

"What I mean to say is that Father would like to employ you."

HOW? CAN'T WALK

"No, but you write wonderfully. And you can get around with crutches. You can count, can't you? Do simple addition?"

YES

"Then you're perfect for the job. With Christmas coming, Father is taking inventory. As large as the store is, it takes some time. He's aware of your impairments and is actually fond of the idea that you can't speak. One of his former employees had a tendency to run off at the mouth."

The frown on John's face was not what she'd expected. She assumed he'd be overjoyed at the prospect of a job.

"What is it, John?"

TOO KIND

"No. I'm doing what's right. I've always believed that God meant for us to help one another. You've had some bad fortune, and need a leg up—so to speak. Father needs the help." She grinned, hoping to brighten his mood.

His single chuckle was all she needed to hear.

"So, is that a *yes?*"

YES

"Very well. Once you're working, Father will give you a discount on some new clothes. Ones you can choose for yourself." Again, she smiled, thankful he wasn't offended by the used clothing. "I'll return tomorrow morning with a carriage. My brother, Henry, will likely come to assist. It wouldn't be wise for me to ride alone with you—since I'm being courted by *Albert Finch.*" She had to push the man's name from her lips, and force herself not to cringe.

I UNDERSTAND

She stood and walked toward the door, but stopped and looked at him one last time. "I hope you'll like my home."

As she passed through the doorway, she felt his eyes on her, covering her like a warm blanket.

* * *

Jeb's heart raced, following Gwen out the door. Until he came to Boston, he'd never met an angel. This one had golden hair, just like the ones pictured in his mind when his mama read the Bible to him as a child. And now, not only had he agreed to work for her daddy, he'd be living at her home. Regardless of the fact that he'd be in the guesthouse, he'd more than likely see her every day. The thought both terrified and elated him.

Reckon I'll meet Albert Finch, too.

Not such a pleasant thought. And when he realized just how jealous he was of *Albert,* he knew he was putting himself in a horrible position. He'd have done better to stay in Atlanta. At least there, he could be himself

Knowing that he was completely alone, he made sounds in his throat, even attempted humming. He feared that his voice might never come back, so he tested it from time to time. But he had an even bigger fear of being discovered, which kept him silent.

He glanced again at the clothing she'd brought. From her brother, Henry? And she had another brother, David. Did she know how lucky she was to have living, breathing kin?

He would enjoy being around Katherine, but didn't know what to expect of the brothers. Yet, he had no choice. Gwen gave him an opportunity to make a living while he finished his recovery. When he had the cast off, he'd hop another train. Boston was not for him. Then again, it wouldn't be easy leaving an angel behind.

Chapter 10

With the help of Doctor Young, Jeb dressed in the clothes Gwen had brought. Though he could have done it by himself, the doctor said he wanted to be there when he left, ensuring he didn't fall and reinjure his leg.

The clothes fit, but he hated that she'd had to cut the trousers. The fabric felt expensive. Before, he would have thought nothing of it, but now that all his wealth was burned to nothing, every penny counted. His old boots would have to do.

"I nearly forgot," Dr. Young muttered, then left the room.

Jeb sat on the edge of his bed and waited for Gwen. It was odd that the doctor left so quickly without saying goodbye. Maybe he'd forgotten an appointment.

After several minutes passed, the doctor came back, holding a long, black frock coat. "You'll need this. We'll have frost soon, then snow. I won't have you catching pneumonia."

Feeling overwhelmed, Jeb accepted the coat and thanked him with a nod. He hated to admit not all northerners were bad, but he'd already met a handful who seemed to be good folks.

Doctor Young patted him on the back. "You're welcome. I'll help you into it when Miss Abbott arrives."

As if he'd willed her there, Gwen stood in the doorway with a clean-shaven young man behind her.

Must be Henry ...

"Good morning, Mr. Carter," she said with her ever-present smile. She must not want her brother to know they were calling each other by first names.

Jeb nodded, then stood from the bed, perched on his crutches.

"This is my brother, Henry," she said.

"I'm glad my clothes fit," he said, with a nod and a grin.

Jeb dipped his head. He could see the relation. Same nose and chin.

"The wheelchair is in the hallway," Gwen said. "I thought I would push you to the carriage, but when we get home, you'll need to walk."

Home. Coming from her mouth, it sounded natural and comfortable. Like a place they were going together— which they were—but not in the way he wanted.

There were no well-wishes as she wheeled him down the hallway for a final time. Nurse Phillips snarled. A face he wouldn't miss.

None of it mattered. The only one he cared about was the woman pushing his chair. Once again, her hair was down; soft over her shoulders. Today her dress was blue, matching her eyes, and she smelled like fresh flowers. It would have been smarter to go on hating, but it was impossible where Gwen was concerned.

Their carriage screamed wealth. Drawn by two well-groomed horses and driven by a man in uniform, who tipped his top hat in greeting as they approached. Though Jeb's own family had hurt for nothing, he knew he was on his way to a home where muddy boots most likely never crossed the floor. How would he ever fit in?

The carved wood on the interior was polished to a shine and the navy upholstery looked as though it had never been sat on. How could that be?

He hobbled to the seat with Henry's help, and then Henry and Gwen sat across from him, taking care not to hit his cast. His extended leg took up a large amount of space on the floor.

"Your coat is very fine," Gwen said.

He looked down and nodded. All this kindness made him uneasy. To make things worse, Gwen seemed uncomfortable, too. Why?

She cleared her throat. "Henry also works for Father, so the two of you will be working together. That is—he does now. He recently returned from the war."

The war?

A sudden urge to lash out arose from Jeb's gut. He was riding in a carriage with the enemy. It didn't matter that the war was over. It would never end for him. And Gwen was smiling as if she was proud of him.

If he could have, he would have screamed for the carriage to stop and hobbled his way out and down the road

—not caring how much pain he'd suffer, or lack of food and shelter. He wanted to run.

She stared at him, searching his eyes.

Did she see fire? She should.

Anger flamed from every part of his body.

"Mr. Carter? Are you in pain?"

He clamped his jaw shut, grimaced, and nodded. She'd never know how much.

"Is there anything we can do?" Henry leaned toward him.

Jeb grasped the seat with both hands to keep from hitting him.

Gwen sighed and frowned with worry. This wasn't his intent; she hadn't burned his home. But for all he knew, her brother might have.

"I don't have the pen and paper," she said. "I'm sorry, Mr. Carter. The movement of the carriage must be aggravating your leg. I hope we didn't move you too soon."

Even if she had the pen and paper, he'd never tell her his true thoughts. To ease her, he held up his hand in a gesture he hoped she would understand. Make her think he was all right.

"We'll get you into bed as soon as we reach the house," she said. "I don't want you to do any walking this afternoon."

She might not want him to, but he'd made up his mind. As soon as he was alone, he'd leave. He would never work side-by-side with a man who'd killed his family. Even if Henry hadn't set the flames that had burned his home or fired the bullets that had killed his brothers, he was one of *them*. A Yankee soldier. And nothing

Henry could ever do would stop the hate that smoldered in his heart.

He leaned back in the seat and looked out the window, taking in his surroundings. He needed to get his mind off the man sitting across from him. They were passing down a tree-lined road. The tall oaks and maples still had their leaves, but it wouldn't be long before that changed and winter set in. It wasn't likely he'd freeze to death, but he'd have to find shelter somewhere.

"We're almost home," Gwen said. "Just a little longer and you'll be comfortable. I'll have Violet, our cook, prepare some chicken soup. I know you like it."

He couldn't look at her. To see her, he'd have to look at *him*. So, he kept his eyes to the glass. With every jolt of the carriage, his heart hardened a little bit more.

And then, the final jolt.

"We're home," Gwen said. Though he could tell she was trying to be cheerful, he knew her well enough to catch the difference in her tone. She knew something was wrong with him, but she was wasting her time trying to figure it out.

Jeb waited until they stepped out, then grabbed his crutches and scooted across the seat toward the door. Just two wooden steps down and he'd be on the ground.

Henry reached to help him, but Jeb shook his head and held up his hand like a barrier between them.

"I believe he wants to do it himself," Gwen said.

"Can he?"

Jeb scowled and Henry took a step back.

"Fine. If he falls on his face, it's his own fault." Henry threw up his hands and walked away, leaving him alone with Gwen.

"What's wrong with you, John? My brother was only trying to help."

He would never allow it. Taking one step at a time, he made it down on his own.

Now, with his feet on solid ground, he looked about. The estate spread out before him; a four-level red brick home, with sculpted stone walkways, and trees and bushes planted in patterns. Fall flowers dotted here and there. He'd never learned their names. The only flowers he could name were roses and morning glories, which reminded him of his mama.

"The guesthouse is this way." Gwen nodded to the left. She touched his arm, but he jerked away. "So now you don't want my help, either?"

He shook his head. Even though he knew he'd hurt her, he had to do it. He wanted no part of their home, which included her.

The guesthouse was a miniature version of the main house. Red brick, but only two stories. When Gwen pushed the door open and held it for him to enter, Jeb wished things had been different. The house was immaculate and quiet. The perfect place to recover.

"There are five bedrooms on the first floor, so you can choose the one you like best. Although there are bedrooms on the second floor, I doubt you'll want to climb the stairs. Sarah, our housemaid, will check in on you from time to time to make certain you have clean bedding, as well as warm water in your wash basin and fresh towels. You also have your own outhouse, which is just out the back door. No steps to stumble over."

She spoke methodically. Yes, he'd hurt her.

"As for food ... for the time being, I'll have Sarah bring that as well. You can eat at the table in the dining room to your right." She pointed, without looking at him. "Since you'll need to rest, I doubt you'll want to come to the main house for dinner."

He hobbled to the center of the entryway and scanned the large room. Just like the interior of the carriage, all the woodwork was polished and shining. He could even see his reflection in the floor. Brass wall lanterns reminded him of the ones his mama had picked out for their home. He probably could have found pieces of them if he'd dug through the ash.

The large living area would have been all he needed to be comfortable. Three upholstered sofas and four over-stuffed chairs were positioned in front of a large fireplace. That would come in handy soon. They could have thrown a cot here and he would have been satisfied. That is ... if he was staying.

"I'll leave you alone now." Gwen was emotionless. "I'll ask Sarah to bring you some soup to hold you over until dinner."

He couldn't look at her.

"Or, do you want to sleep first?"

He nodded, then the door opened and closed, and she was gone.

* * *

Gwen wanted to cry. She hurried as fast as she could to the house. Without saying a word to her mother, she raced up the stairs to her room.

What happened? Why was he being hateful again? Even to her?

It was more than just pain in his leg, there was hate in his eyes. The same hate she'd witnessed the first time they'd met.

She racked her brain, trying to piece together what had happened. Perhaps it would help to write in the journal. Thankfully, she'd remembered to bring it home from the hospital.

Home – September 19th, 1865

Mr. Carter was released from Mass General and is staying in our guesthouse while he recovers.

He seemed pleased with the arrangement, until we got in the carriage.

Became irritable and would not engage in eye contact.

Would not accept help from carriage.

What had happened in the carriage? She scrunched her eyes tightly shut, recreating the conversation in her mind. At least it was a one-sided conversation. How hard could that be?

He became disgruntled after I told him about Henry. Was he angry that Henry would be working with him, or was it something about ...

The war!

That was it. He became upset at the mention of the war. Maybe her earlier feelings were correct. His anger and ill demeanor must stem from a horrific encounter while serving. After talking to Henry about it, she'd let it lie, but now, she would have to ask David his opinion. After all, he was older than Henry and far more serious about such things.

She continued writing:

Believe Mr. Carter suffers from painful memories of the war.

Will need to find a way to get him to open up and write about it.

Afraid he may try to shut me out completely.

She stared at the page. Truthfully, she believed he'd already started shutting her out and it hurt worse than she imagined anything could.

* * *

Taking the time to peek into the bedrooms, Jeb determined that he liked the one closest to the back door. It was plainly decorated in colors that suited him. Nothing bright and feminine, but earthy colors like brown and tan. A simple patched quilt covered the bed. He wouldn't be staying here, so he decided not to get comfortable, even though he was exhausted.

Since Gwen believed he was going to lie down and rest, this was the perfect time to leave. He took the case off one of the bed pillows and searched around the house for things to fill it. Anything that might help him to get by. It wasn't stealing. They'd offered him the house, so why not take what he needed elsewhere?

Limping his way through the rooms, he found candles, a box of Lucifers, an extra blanket, and even some food. A bowl of apples sat on an end table in the living room. After locating an empty jar, he filled it with water.

A twinge of guilt crept over him as he slung the pack over his shoulder and headed out the back door.

He looked from side-to-side. Since there were no other guests in the guesthouse, he assumed no one else would be about on this part of the property. All he needed to do was work his way through the trees and then come around on the far side of the lot to the main road. Then, he would follow it until he came to …

Where?

He knew nothing about Boston. Not like Atlanta, where he knew how to find the train station. And even if he found it, in his condition he couldn't hop a train. How could he have forgotten that? Maybe he could acquire a horse—*steal* a horse. And that *would be* stealing. He wondered if horse thieves were hung in Massachusetts.

How could I ride a horse?

He'd never be able to swing his left leg up and over a horse's back. It seemed he was going to have to walk west. Follow the sun.

"Where are you going, Mr. Carter?"

He'd not even gone six steps from the back door when Katherine's small voice stopped him cold.

Thinking quickly, he pointed to the outhouse.

"Oh." Her cheeks flushed and she covered her mouth. "Want me to hold that bag while you go?"

He shut his eyes and shook his head. Caught red-handed.

"I wanted to see you, even though Gwen said not to bother you. I'm really glad you're here."

A small chip of ice melted from his heart. He set the bag on the ground, motioned for her to wait for him, and took a step toward the outhouse.

"I think my sister likes you more than Mr. Finch. But don't tell her I told you."

He stopped, then turned to face her. She grinned and giggled.

And before he knew what hit him, he smiled. Gwen was right, he had a soft spot for little girls, and Katherine was no exception. But maybe his smile was for Gwen. Did she think of him as more than just a patient?

"Promise you won't tell?"

He held one finger to his lips.

"Good." She giggled again. "Go on and go, and I'll wait here for you."

Swallowing his pride, he hobbled to the outhouse. Did God send this little girl to keep him from leaving? He kept wondering why he was brought to Boston, so maybe he needed to stay a little longer and find out. Push aside his anger and allow himself to enjoy the comfort of a warm home. It was much more appealing than limping his way west.

When he returned, she was waiting as promised, but was nosing around in the pillow case.

"Were you gonna camp out?"

He nodded. Hopefully she would leave it at that.

"That sounds like fun, but Gwen says you need to rest in a good bed. I don't think you should sleep outside."

Tipping his head, he patted hers, then motioned toward the door. She opened it and he went to his chosen room. Though she said she wasn't allowed to enter, she placed his bag just inside the doorway. "Go take a nap now and I'll tell Gwen you picked the brown room."

She skipped away and he sat on the edge of the bed. After questioning his decision more than once, he took off the frock coat, pulled back the covers, and climbed into bed fully dressed. Maybe part of him still wanted to flee, but his heart rested, and he fell asleep in the most comfortable bed he'd ever been in.

Chapter 11

Gwen munched a piece of dry toast and stared out the window. Was John awake?

She'd slept little last night, going over every detail of each *conversation* she'd had with him. So sure she'd made progress, but now ...

Katherine took a seat at the table. "I told Mr. Carter it wasn't a good idea to sleep outside."

"Outside?" The girl had Gwen's full attention.

"Yes. He packed a pillow casing full of things to camp outdoors. I told him you said he should sleep in a good bed. The ground wouldn't have been good for his leg, would it?" She poured cream over a bowl of oats that Violet set down in front of her.

"No. Not good at all." Gwen rested her elbow on the table, then leaned her chin into her hand. He was going to leave. But why?

She jumped from her seat. What if he'd left in the middle of the night?

"Violet?" Gwen crossed to the stove. "Has Sarah taken Mr. Carter's breakfast to him?"

"No, Miss. She didn't want to wake him too early."

"Good. Please spoon a bowl of oats for him and I'll take it."

"Yes, Miss."

Violet did as she requested and Gwen fixed a tray to carry to John. In addition to the oats, she sliced an apple, then filled a cup of coffee, as well as a glass of milk.

"Are you sure you have time to do this, Miss Abbott?" Violet asked. "Mr. Finch will be calling on you soon."

"I'm certain. If he arrives while I'm out, please make him comfortable. Offer him some oats."

Violet's eyebrows drew down, but she nodded. Maybe it was an odd request, but Gwen didn't have time to argue or explain. She needed a good excuse to go to the guesthouse to make certain John was still there.

"Tell him good morning for me," Katherine said with a mouthful of cereal.

"Be glad mother didn't see that," Gwen scolded, then followed her words with a smile.

After covering the tray with a towel to keep the oats warm, Gwen bustled out the back door and walked hastily across the property to the guesthouse. What would she do if he was gone? Send someone after him?

"What was he thinking?" she muttered under her breath. "Foolish, foolish man!"

Resting the tray on one arm, she managed to open the front door, too worried to stop and knock.

It was nearly nine o'clock. A late morning by anyone's standards. The house was silent.

Tiptoeing across the floor, she eased her way to the brown room. It would have helped if Katherine had added the small detail of his intentions to sleep outside before this morning.

A soft snore met her ears, and she breathed a relieved sigh.

"John?" she whispered loud enough to stir him, but hopefully not so loud as to startle him.

His eyes remained closed. Entering his room, she set the tray on a small round table in the corner. It suddenly occurred to her that it might be improper to be here. When he was in the hospital, she was considered a nurse in many ways. No one thought anything of her being in his room. But this was no hospital.

A wooden rocker was positioned beside the bed, so she sat and waited. She noticed the tiny porcelain hand resting on the oak bed stand close to the headboard.

How did his sister die? So much pain in this poor man's life.

Albert wouldn't be arriving for another hour. She wasn't pleased about having to see him mid-week. But since the New England Museum of Natural History was only opened on Wednesdays from noon until two o'clock, she'd made an exception from their usual Saturday outings. He assured her that she would find the museum interesting. Since she had to miss an entire day of school, it had better be remarkable.

Minutes ticked by. There was something lulling about his gentle snore. She studied his face; no trace of anger or hate. Even through his thick beard and mustache. What did he look like beneath that face full of brown hair? If he didn't trim the beard soon, he'd begin to look like her grandfather. No young man should have so much facial hair.

His oats were getting cold.

"John?" She leaned toward him. "John, you need to wake up."

As his eyes opened and met hers along with the bright, sun-filled room, he blinked hard several times. For an instant, it looked as though he was about to speak. Then he licked his lips and pushed himself up on his elbows, questioning her presence with his eyes. Eyes no longer full of hate. What had changed? Again.

"I brought breakfast. Oats, an apple, coffee, and milk. I hope you're hungry."

He nodded, so she got the tray and positioned it on his lap.

"Would you rather get out of bed and eat at the table?"

He shook his head and began eating.

Oh, fiddle! I forgot the pen and paper.

Maybe she wouldn't need them. "John—I'd like to know. Were you planning to leave yesterday?"

His spoon hovered in midair and then he nodded.

"But, why?" What a silly thing for her to ask. Without the pen and paper, a simple nod or shake of the head wouldn't give her the answers she needed. "Oh ... never mind. I'll come back later this afternoon and bring the paper and pen so you can write. Whatever the answer might be, I'm glad you changed your mind."

He stopped eating and just sat there, staring at her. At least he wasn't frowning.

"John—I care about you. I don't want to see you hurt. Until your cast is off, you have to be careful. So, please, stay in bed today as much as possible. Sarah will bring your lunch, then I'll come by and see you before dinner. I have to go out."

She stood and walked toward the door. "Promise me you won't try to leave again."

He nodded, then dipped his spoon into the oats.

Leaving him was harder than she thought it would be. But she couldn't hover over him like a mother tending a baby. He wasn't her baby, and truthfully, he wasn't her *anything*.

Though not yet ten o'clock, the moment she walked into the house, she heard Albert in the kitchen talking to Violet. No—*scolding* Violet.

How dare he?

"Oh, there you are," Albert said as Gwen entered the kitchen. "This woman is trying to feed me. I told her that I don't care for oats and she keeps insisting that I sit down and eat. You really should speak to your parents about her behavior."

"Miss Abbott." Violet rested her hands on her hips. "You told me to offer him oats. I was doing as you asked."

"Yes, I know, Violet. Thank you." Gwen took Albert's arm and led him down the hallway. "You shouldn't have scolded her."

He pulled his shoulders back and peered down his nose at her. "Why did you ever tell her to feed me oats? I despise oats."

"I wasn't aware." She could easily make a list of the things *she* despised at that very moment.

"And what is this I hear about that man from the hospital staying in your guesthouse? Hmm?"

Katherine must have told him. But where did she go? Seems she'd spilled the beans and fled, leaving Gwen to pick up her mess.

"He had nowhere to go. Father, as you know, is charitable. Mr. Carter is going to work for him. He's quite good with writing and figures."

Albert crossed his arms. "You are referring to calculations, aren't you?"

"What other kind of figures would I be referring to?"

After sucking in a huge amount of air, he shook his head. "You aren't that naïve, Gwendolyn."

When his implication sunk in, she couldn't have been more offended. But Albert was good at offense. It was his talent. And why was it that her father insisted they court? Steam crept up from the bottom of her toes.

"Shame on you, Albert. Mr. Carter is a decent man."

"How do you know this? The man is mute. You have no way of knowing what's going on in his mind. I'll have you know that I don't approve of him being here."

Katherine must have talked a lot while she was gone. Or maybe it wasn't Katherine. Could Henry have told Albert about John? No matter. Albert would not dictate who her father had already approved to be here. "It's not your concern, Albert."

"Oh, but it is. Or have you forgotten that we have an arrangement?"

"Arrangement? We're courting. That's the extent of our arrangement."

A devious smile curled the corners of his lips. "Speak to your father. You may find that it's more." He took her by the hand. "Now then, let's be on our way. I thought we would ride about the city before going to the museum, while the weather is still fine."

She was at a loss for words, and he seemed to know it. He gloated, walking tall and proud as he escorted her to the carriage. No chaperone. What did he arrange with her father? And why was she never advised of their *arrangements*?

Tonight she would speak to him before Albert had the chance to tell him that he needed to remove John from the guesthouse. She would never let that happen.

* * *

Jeb couldn't deny that he was glad to see Gwen's face when he opened his eyes. He loved seeing her with her hair down, dressed in gowns that complemented her appearance. But what he saw in her was more than outward beauty. Her heart was pure and good. She was more giving than any woman he'd known before, except for his mama. Gwen was the kind of woman he'd always imagined bringing home to meet her. It was sadly impossible. His mama was dead and Gwen was out of reach. If he didn't learn to accept those facts, he might become the crazy man everyone already thought he was.

The breakfast was good and filling, yet he needed to get up and move. Not to leave—he wouldn't break that promise—he'd just go out to wash and use the outhouse.

His body was stiff and sore. Not the intolerable pain he'd dealt with after his accident—something slightly more manageable. In many ways, he felt good, but being crippled limited him. As long as he didn't see Henry, he could control himself. And most likely her other brother had served in the war, and he would prefer not to encounter him. Her folks were another matter.

Eventually he'd have to meet her daddy. He'd be working for him.

My luck he'll be a retired General.

Not likely. He doubted the Yanks would draft a prominent store owner. Abbott's Department Store had to be something special for them to afford a place like this.

After tending to business, he returned inside and went to the wash basin. Even though he didn't see her, Sarah had to have come in. The water was warm.

Did Gwen tell 'er to put this here?

He moved a chair up to the dressing table. A wood-framed mirror sat atop the table next to the wash basin, and arranged beside it were all the things he needed to shave. Including scissors. Looking in the mirror, he understood why. His beard was lengthy and completely unkempt. His mama would have fussed. She liked all of her boys clean shaven.

Maybe Gwen wanted to see his face. She might not recognize him. He chuckled at the thought. But it would be hard to fool her with crutches under his arms.

After clipping the thickest parts of his beard, he prepared the shaving soap and dabbed it on his face with the wood-handled brush. The bristles were soft and pliant. Expensive.

Leaving a straight-edge razor in his room showed trust. He could easily kill a man with a single swipe, and if he wasn't careful he might bloody himself.

Each stroke of the razor revealed a bit more of his face, taking years from his appearance. He wiped away the remnants of the soap and pressed the tip of his finger against a small nick under his chin. Not too much blood.

After cleaning up the mess he'd made, he returned to his bed. The house was too quiet. He was even beginning to miss Nurse Phillips. How would he ever occupy his time?

A similar Bible to the one from the hospital sat on the table in the corner of his room. Gwen told him he should read it, so why not now?

After getting comfortable in bed, he opened the book and started at the beginning. Maybe he'd have it all read by the time he was well enough to leave.

* * *

Gwen had seen enough skeletons. Yes, she found them interesting and maybe Albert's intentions were good, but skeletal remains of birds and mammals were a bit disturbing. He'd told her that he thought they would benefit her research, but the only research she wanted to do right now was get into John Carter's mind.

She couldn't stop herself from worrying about him leaving, even though he promised he would stay. It was hard to trust a man she'd only known a few weeks. She couldn't even trust Albert and she'd known him for more than ten years. Could any man be trusted?

They were nearly home. Fortunately, he took the seat across from her in the carriage.

"Gwendolyn ..." He reached for her hand. "I wouldn't have minded if you'd worn the same fine dress you wore to the theatre. It would have been appropriate for the museum."

She patted her pink, cotton skirt. Nothing close to the silk he referred to. Although it wasn't the *fabric* he'd admired in the dress. As he'd said, she wasn't naïve.

"This dress is more comfortable. Don't you like it?"

"Anything looks lovely on you. But—there was something more to that dress that I find appealing. I hope I shall see you in it again soon."

His thumb worked across her skin as if he were digging for treasure. She pulled her hand away. "Albert, we're almost home."

He frowned. "I shall see you on Saturday. Perhaps you'll wear the gown?"

Never.

"It needs some repair." She hated to lie, but ... "I stepped on the hem when I was going to my room. I haven't had the opportunity to fix it."

"Oh." His shoulders drooped.

The carriage stopped. "We're home." She stood and didn't wait for him to open the door. Stepping down, she felt his hand on her shoulder.

"Gwendolyn, why didn't you wait for my assistance?"

"I'm sorry, Albert, but I need to tend to personal matters." It had become her best reason for escaping from him.

"Very well. I shall see you Saturday." He waved to the driver to go on and pulled the door closed.

The carriage drove away, and she was relieved to be alone. Her feelings for him weren't improving ... quite the opposite.

Even though she needed to speak with her father, he wouldn't be home from the store until dinner time. Still two hours away. This gave her a good excuse to check on John before returning to the main house.

She knocked on his door.

And just how could he tell me to come in?

She pushed the door open. "John?" She called down the hallway to him. "I hope you're not sleeping." If he *was* sleeping, she probably woke him.

Cautiously, she peeked into his room, then smiled seeing his face buried in the Bible. "I see you took my advice."

He raised his head and she stumbled backward.

What?

The rate of her heart increased to double its normal pace. Maybe triple. His face was smooth. Clean shaven. More handsome than she ever could have imagined. He had high cheek bones, and a well-shaped mouth. But her eyes were still drawn to his bluer than blue eyes.

Oh, my ...

He cocked his head and raised his brows.

"J—John. I scarcely recognized you. You gave me a fright."

Untrue. He was less frightening than the first time she'd seen him. No doubt he saw through her lie.

He's probably laughing at me this very minute.

He motioned for a pen and paper, and she slapped herself on the forehead. "I—I forgot. I'll be right back."

Thank goodness she had an excuse to leave. She bustled back to the main house. She needed a drink of water. Her throat was drier than a desert. How could seeing him this way affect her so?

Her mother was at the foot of the stairs. "Did you have a nice time with Mr. Finch, my dear?"

"Lovely," she muttered and hurried up the stairs.

"That's wonderful!" Her mother's pleased cry carried Gwen all the way to her room.

Grabbing the writing tools, she hastened back down the stairs.

"Are you all right, my dear?" Her mother hadn't moved from the base of the stairway.

"I'm fine, Mother. I'm working on my research."

"Dinner will be at five o'clock."

She nodded and went on her way. Dinner was always at five o'clock.

Now, stop acting like a child, and breathe.

Realizing she'd neglected to get a drink of water, she stopped by the kitchen and poured a glass from a pitcher Violet kept fresh and filled. She downed it quickly, refilled it, and drank again. Now she was ready.

* * *

Jeb chuckled aloud the moment he'd heard the door slam shut. The look in Gwen's eyes was one he would never forget. They'd popped open wider than a dinner plate. And though she'd stumbled, at least she hadn't fallen and hurt herself.

Shaving had been a good idea. The best he'd had in a long time.

He set the Bible on the bed stand and waited for her to return. Already in the book of Exodus. The story of Moses had always been a favorite. And now more than ever he knew all about mistaken identity.

The door creaked open. He rubbed his hands over his smooth face, then wiped away the grin. It wouldn't be wise to let her see just how much she'd pleased him.

She loudly cleared her throat and then entered the room, waving the paper.

"I got it." She pointed to the rocking chair. "Mind if I sit?"

He shook his head. He wanted her here.

After glancing sideways at the Bible, she picked it up and handed it to him. "How far did you get?"

She set the paper down, dipped the pen, and then placed it in his hand.

MOSES

"Oh. As a baby, or is he already grown?"

JUST PARTED RED SEA

"I love that part." She twisted a strand of her long hair around her finger. Must be nervous. Did a shave make that much of a difference?

He rubbed his chin, then wrote:

DO YOU LIKE IT?

Her head bobbed up and down. "Very much. You're a handsome man, John Carter." She swallowed hard.

YOU'RE NERVOUS

"No. It's just that ..."

YOU'RE VERY NERVOUS

"Yes. I am. I have to admit that you confuse me. One minute you're hateful and the next you're ... *shaved.*"

He covered his mouth, hiding a laugh.

I'LL NEVER HURT YOU. DON'T BE AFRAID OF ME

"Then, I want you to answer my questions. No matter how hard it might be."

He shifted his body and scooted back, resting against the headboard. Some things he would never tell her, so in order to appease her, he might have to create more lies.

ASK

"Were you in the war?"

He nodded.

She let out a long breath. "Did something awful happen to you?"

Another nod.

"Is that why you can't speak?"

These questions weren't so bad. So far, he hadn't lied. After all, she didn't ask what side he'd fought on. Again, he nodded.

She looked at her hands and twisted her fingers together. "Did your sister die during the war?"

Why'd she hafta bring up Anna?

Slowly, he nodded.

"How?"

Gripping the pen until his knuckles turned white, he answered.

BURNED

Gwen's hand flew to her mouth, covering a gasp. Tears trickled down her cheeks. "Oh, John. I'm so sorry." She placed her hand over his, and he loosened his grip on the pen.

Her skin was softer and warmer than a rabbit pelt.

Then without a second thought, he wiped away her tears.

She grasped his hand. Not in anger, but with affection. His heart beat out of his chest. What was he going to do? He was falling in love with her. Falling to his death, it would seem. He could never have her.

"I'd better go." She pulled her hand to herself, sniffled, and stood. "Thank you for being honest. I know it wasn't easy telling me."

He wanted to reach out to her. Wanted to hold her. The ache in his heart grew as her footsteps faded away. This was a wound that could never be healed.

Chapter 12

Gwen poked at the meat with her fork. Even though roast beef had always been a favorite, she couldn't eat, unable to erase John's image from her mind. Such a tormented soul, and yet he possessed an unexpected gentleness. The way he'd wiped away her tears ...

"Gwen?"

Her mother's voice startled her and she dropped her fork, sending it clanking to the floor.

"Gwen, dear? Are you ill?"

"No, Mother." She bent sideways and picked up the fork. Sarah was there almost instantly, handing her a clean utensil. "Thank you, Sarah. Oh—Sarah—have you taken Mr. Carter his dinner?"

"Yes'm," she replied with a grin. "I figger I scared him. You din't tell him I was colored, did ya?"

"No." She never gave it a second thought. Sarah had been with them for three years and was as much a part of their staff as Violet, or their carriage driver, George. Her skin color didn't matter to them. "Was he hateful?"

"No'm. He wadn't hateful. After his eyes was back in his head, he took the tray from me an smiled." She chuckled and held her hands against her belly. "Man shore knows how to eat."

"Thank you, Sarah." Gwen scolded herself for not telling him. Maybe wherever he came from, they didn't employ Negroes.

"You certainly worry yourself over that man." Her father wiped the corner of his mouth with a napkin.

"He's been terribly hurt, Father." Gwen took in her family. Everyone at the table was enjoying their meal, dressed in expensive dinner clothes, eating off fine china, and drinking from crystal goblets. Aside from a baby that her mother had failed to carry to full term, and all of her grandparents, Gwen didn't know what it was like to lose family. John had nothing. No family, no *things*. She had everything.

"Don't let your heart get in the way of good sense." David shook his finger at her.

"Yes, Gwen," her mother added. "It's not wise for you to spend so much time alone with him. Now that he's living here, it would be best that you're chaperoned when you see him."

"Why? I'm still working on my research—my journal. Doctor Young expects a full report."

"I agree with your mother," her father said. "Don't go to his room alone. Sarah can accompany you when you do your *research*."

"Don't you trust me?" Her stomach twisted in knots. Her hands were being tied and she didn't like it.

"I trust you. But I don't know the man. How can you expect me to trust *him*?"

She set down her fork and pushed her plate away. Her appetite was completely gone. "After dinner, why don't you go with me to the guesthouse so you can meet him? I'd have him come here, but it's not wise for him to do a lot of walking." Besides, she wanted to talk to her father about Albert. He was the one he shouldn't trust.

"I should have already met the man. He's living in my house, after all."

"I'll go with you," David said.

"Good luck," Henry huffed. "Gwen may find him trustworthy, but I've never seen a man with so much hate behind his eyes."

"He's nice!" Katherine blurted out. "He made me a flower."

Gwen sat back and listened to her family argue about the good and evil sides of Mr. Carter. If she defended him too much, her father would accuse her of having feelings for him. And the truth of the matter was; she did.

As dessert was served, the mood around the table softened. It was settled. Her father and David would go with her to the guesthouse and meet John, but her mother would wait until after they approved of him.

* * *

Much better than hospital food. Jeb lifted his plate and licked the last bit of roast beef gravy. He'd already slopped up most of it with his bread, but he wasn't about to let even the tiniest bit go to waste. With a belly full of roast, carrots, potatoes, bread, and plum pudding, he set the plate on his bed stand and rested his head against the pillows. Content.

He hoped Sarah hadn't noticed his shock when she'd brought the food. Seeing a Negro working for a white northern family was surprising. But Sarah was no slave. Freedom was evident on her smiling face.

And where was Gwen? Had he scared her away completely?

The creak of the door was followed by heavy footsteps and muffled voices. *Men's* voices.

Jeb repositioned himself and waited.

Gwen's dainty hand rapped on the doorframe, then her sweet face appeared. "John? My father is here to meet you—and my brother, David, as well."

Though he knew the time was coming, was he ready to face them?

Both men walked into the room with an air of confidence. Shoulders back, chins up. Obviously showing him who was in charge. After meeting Henry, he would have recognized David anywhere. Undoubtedly brothers. And the elder man was the cloth they'd been cut from. Tall, medium stature, light-colored hair, but a darker blond than Gwen's.

Gwen positioned herself between him and her family. She was nervous earlier, but now sweat beaded on her brow. He hated causing her so much distress.

"Father, David, this is John Carter." She motioned toward him with her hand. "Mr. Carter, this is my father, William Abbott, and my brother, David."

After Gwen took two steps back, her daddy approached him. He assessed Jeb from head to toe and then crossed his arms over his chest. "Mr. Carter, I can see by your clean plate that you approve of the food. Can I assume you're ready to start earning your keep?"

He wasted no time with small talk.

Jeb nodded.

"Good. You can accompany Henry to work next week, starting on Monday. And from what he tells me, you don't always have a pleasant disposition. I expect you to act properly and treat my other employees with respect. And even though Henry will be guiding you on what you are to do, you will answer to me. Are we clear?"

Even if he hadn't served as a military officer, he acted like one.

Jeb nodded again, looking him straight in the eye.

David stepped forward and unlike his daddy, extended his hand. Jeb had no choice, but to shake it. Refusing the handshake of Mr. Abbott's son would be disrespectful and he might find himself on the street.

"I'll also be working with Father, until I leave for Washington," David said. "General Sherman has recommended me for an advisory position to President Johnson. I'm to be there in December when Congress reconvenes."

Jeb's chest tightened and it was all he could do to keep his face emotionless. David could have spoken any other name—mentioned the devil himself—and it wouldn't have ignited Jeb's rage. Hate wasn't a strong enough word to describe his feelings for Sherman, and Gwen's brother knew him personally.

"Is there something wrong, Mr. Carter?" Gwen stepped up to him on the other side of the bed, and pointed to his hand.

Jeb hadn't realized that his hands were shaking. His breathing became rapid. If only they'd leave.

"Father, I believe Mr. Carter needs to rest." Gwen's brow wrinkled with concern.

Mr. Abbott nodded and motioned his head toward the door. "David, let's leave him for now."

"I'll check on you later," Gwen whispered.

He clenched his jaw, and gave a single nod. He could tolerate *her*, but how could he ever be in a room with these men? Work beside them? He had until Monday. Five days to get his head on straight.

* * *

Gwen knew John well enough to see the instant change in his demeanor. He'd handled her father well enough, but something sparked with David. The tension in John's body was worse than ever. And when his hands began to tremble, she assumed something horrible was going on in his mind. Sooner or later, she had to know the cause of his pain. There was more to it than the death of his sister.

"I'll speak with you in my smoking room." Her father's harsh tone meant business.

"Yes, sir." She followed him down the hall to the large double doors.

David grinned at her and then went on. Yes, he knew that tone, and was probably already aware of what her father intended to speak with her about. It seemed that every man in her life knew what was in store for her before she did.

Her father crossed to his desk, grabbed his pipe, filled it, and sat. Once he lit it, he'd be ready to talk.

A puff of smoke drifted over her head as she took a seat close to him. This wasn't how she'd imagined their encounter. It was her intention to speak with him about Albert, but now things were upside down. Hopefully, she'd be able to say her peace.

"I'm concerned about that man." He puffed again.

"Mr. Carter?"

"Of course, Mr. Carter. What other man would I be concerned over?"

Perhaps Albert Finch?

That discussion would come later. "Father—he's troubled ..."

"And that's what concerns me. If his mind isn't right, I don't know that I want him here."

Her heart thumped, faster and faster. "I assure you, he's a good man. I've seen that myself. And look what he did for Katherine. He's sweet to her."

"A paper rose does not make a man *sweet.*" He shook his head and fidgeted with papers scattered about on his desk.

"Please ... we've come so far. I honestly believe he had something terrible happen to him in the war. David's mention of General Sherman appeared to have upset him. I know that in time I can get to the bottom of his troubles. I can help him."

Rising to his feet, her father crossed to her and cupped her cheek with his hand. "My soft-hearted girl. Your brother said it well. Don't let your heart get in the way of good sense."

"He won't hurt me. I'm certain he won't."

He took a step back and crossed his arms. "I'll allow him to stay as long as you assure me that you'll take someone with you whenever you see him. And once he starts working, I'll make up my mind as to what kind of a man he is. I can tell a lot about a man by his work ethics."

Her heart calmed. He wasn't going to make him leave. "I promise I'll take someone with me." She'd do whatever it took to keep him there.

Her father returned to his seat, leaned back, and inhaled the pipe. As he blew a ring of smoke into the air, he sighed. "Now for the other matter."

"Other matter?" A lump rose in her throat.

"Yes. Regarding Mr. Finch."

Remembering Albert's sly grin, her heart once again increased its pace. "Mr. Finch?"

"He came to see me yesterday at work. After apologizing for interrupting me, he explained that the matter was urgent, so of course, I listened."

She closed her eyes and prayed that it wasn't what she feared.

"He is completely smitten with you and has asked for my permission to marry you. Now, I know that you've not courted long, but the poor man is ... *anxious* to say the least. He loves you, my dear, and will be a fine husband."

She didn't dare say the words she wanted to say. And if she screamed, it would only upset her father. But she couldn't accept this without speaking her mind.

"But, I don't love *him*."

"Gwendolyn, we've had this discussion before. He loves *you*, and you will undoubtedly learn to love him. I told him that you will be agreeable. It will be up to him to choose *when* to propose."

Oh, Lord. I can't breathe.

"One other thing, my dear. I would like you to consider a double wedding with your brother and Miss Clayton. I've already discussed it with David and he thinks it's a fine idea."

Now, not only could she not breathe, but she couldn't speak. David and Martha were getting married on December second, just before he left for Washington. That was little more than two months away.

"You're pleased?" He leaned toward her, studying her face.

Building up courage, she squeaked out the words, "What if I don't want to marry him?"

He inhaled deeply, puffing out his large chest. Rising to his feet, he towered over her. "You will not shame this family. I've given my consent. He's a decent man with the means to care for you at the level you've grown accustomed to. There are times in our lives that we all have to do things not of our choosing."

"What you're referring to is my entire life! All the years ahead of me that will be spent with a man I can scarcely tolerate! He doesn't love me. He simply sees me as a vessel to satisfy his primal urges!"

The fury in her father's eyes prompted her to cover her mouth. Had she truly spoken her thoughts?

"Gwendolyn ..." He gripped his lapel and faced her squarely. "Don't raise your voice to me. And—the things you spoke of should never be said. All that I can say regarding that matter is that you're a lovely woman and Mr. Finch sees that. How can you fault him for noticing your beauty?"

Thankful that his admonishment was gentle, she calmed. "Admiring my appearance is not love."

"Noticing beauty is the beginning of love." He, too, had calmed. "Give the man time. Do you honestly believe I would have you do something that would bring you harm? I only want what's best for you."

He extended his hand and brought her to her feet. And then, as he had done for as long as she could remember, he pulled her close and stroked her hair. "This is for the best, my dear." After kissing her on the forehead, he sent her on her way.

This was the arrangement.

She trudged up the stairs to her room, laid face down on her bed, and cried until no more tears came.

Chapter 13

These were not the eyes Jeb wanted to see when he woke up. Blue just like Gwen's, but unkind.

"Good morning, Mr. Carter," Henry said. "Or shall I call you, John?"

He'd prefer he not speak at all.

Feeling vulnerable, he pulled the covers up to his neck and stared at Henry.

"You look uneasy ... *John.*"

Jeb would not be intimidated by him. He scooted himself up in bed, lifted his head, then shook it from side to side.

Henry leaned back in the rocking chair, then pushed off with his feet to get the chair moving. "I believe we started off on the wrong foot—so to speak."

You don't know the half of it.

"Since we'll be working together, I'd like to be friends. For Gwen's sake. You see, I know that she cares for you, and though I honestly don't know *why* she does, I love my sister and will help her however I can."

He stopped rocking and leaned forward, locking eyes with Jeb. "If you ever harm her in any way, you'll answer to me. Not my father ... *me*." He glared, long enough to get his point across, then leaned back. "That being said, I have something for you."

He crossed the room to the table, then came back and extended a stack of folded clothes. "These are new. Since my clothes fit you, these should as well. I also took the liberty to purchase underdrawers and a new pair of boots. Gwen has already altered the trousers for your cast. Don't worry. I'm not out any money. Father started an account for you. You'll be working off the debt. You can't be expected go to work in the same clothes day after day."

Jeb nodded and set the bundle aside. It would be good to have clean clothes to wear. He just wished Gwen had brought them, not Henry.

"I have to be honest, John. It's odd that you can't speak. I never know what you might be thinking."

You don't wanna know.

"Well, then. Sarah should be here soon with your breakfast. Enjoy the few days you have remaining to rest. Father intends to keep you busy. How else do you think he made his fortune?"

Henry left without another word, leaving Jeb pondering every remark. He wanted to believe that Henry was genuinely eager to help him, and simply concerned about his sister. But there was something more to it. Henry didn't trust him. And why should he? He'd treated him as poorly as he had Nurse Phillips.

Monday, Henry would take him to work. Jeb's daddy had taught him the importance of doing his best at all times, so he wouldn't let him down. He'd work hard and show these northerners that he was worthy. More than anything, he wanted to prove that he was just as good as Albert Finch.

The day went by without any other encounters, and except for Sarah, he saw no one. He tried to ask her about Gwen, but found that she was unable to read, so the paper and pen Gwen left behind did no good. Pretending to be mute was becoming more and more inconvenient.

His stomach rumbled and he wondered what Sarah might bring for supper—or *dinner* as they called it. When the door opened, his mouth watered in anticipation.

"I brung sumthin' you might like," Sarah said with a wink. She set the tray of food on his small table. He preferred eating in his room rather than at the large dining table.

Lifting his nose in the air, he sniffed.

Ham?

He wasted no time tucking his crutches in place, and hobbled to the table.

Sarah chuckled as she removed the cover from the plate. Yes, it was ham. And peas, and biscuits with preserves, and ...

"Hello, John."

Gwen?

Sarah tittered even harder, then left the room. She scooted a chair close to the door, then sat.

Odd.

"Sit down and eat," Gwen said. "I won't stop you."

He sat, but nodded toward the door and questioned her with his eyes.

"Oh. You want to know why Sarah stayed?"

He nodded.

Gwen's eyes shifted downward. "My parents don't want me to be alone with you." She lifted her face and met his gaze. "But at least they didn't ask you to leave."

This shouldn't surprise him, but it made things inconvenient, and not nearly as enjoyable. The time he spent with her was the only time in his day that he felt alive. And he didn't want her to stop telling him what she was thinking because someone else was listening.

Sarah started to hum.

Gwen grinned. "I believe she's trying to tell us that she's not going to eavesdrop."

Just as he'd hoped.

He picked up his knife and cut the ham, then spread some of the strawberry preserves on one of the biscuits. He pointed to the other biscuit.

"No, thank you. I've already eaten. You go on ..."

Before taking a bite, he bowed his head and closed his eyes. How he'd gotten out of the habit of saying a prayer before eating, he didn't know. But it was time to change that. A silent prayer was better than none at all.

When he lifted his head and opened his eyes, she smiled at him.

"Amen."

He nodded.

She tilted her head and stared at him, but then blinked rapidly and shifted her gaze. Having her so close made his stomach flip, so he decided to eat and hoped the distraction would ease it.

"You've become comfortable with Sarah, I see." She kept her voice low.

He matched her smile and nodded. Smiling for Gwen was easy now and honestly felt good.

She brightened and laughed. "Medically speaking, did you know that it takes fewer muscles to smile than it does to frown?"

He shook his head.

"It's true. So, as your caregiver, I suggest that you smile more. Reserve your strength for walking."

This was what he admired about her. Not only was she kind, but she was smart, and had a sense of humor unlike anyone else.

"About Sarah ..." She moved in close, speaking even softer. "We brought her here three years ago. On the Underground Railroad. Isn't that wonderful?"

Another sign of a charitable heart. Northern abolitionists helped the slaves escape. He understood why, but northerners needed to know that not all slave owners were brutal. Freeing the slaves wasn't what enraged him about the war. He'd fought to protect his home, but what good had it done?

Again, he nodded. Would she be so kind if she knew that his family owned slaves? But all that was in the past.

"She believes all of her family died. She had no one left, but now she has us. I'm sure you've found that she's cheerful. I don't know how, after all she's been through."

He continued eating, listening to every word. He and Sarah had more in common than he realized.

The tune Sarah hummed changed.

Amazing Grace

"I think that has a lot to do with it." Gwen nodded toward the door. "Amazing Grace. Sarah has faith in God. She likes hymns."

So did he. They used to sing that song in church. What had happened to his faith? The soldiers may have burned his home to the ground, but had he allowed them to reduce his faith to ashes? Raised in a Christian home, he'd been taught to love, and to *turn the other cheek*. Is that what he needed to do now? Set aside his anger—his hate—and *love?*

"Tell me what you're thinking, John." She stood from the table, got the paper and pen, then sat down again.

The thoughts going through his head could fill a book.

GLAD YOU HELPED SARAH

"And now, I'm helping you." She said the words as if it was her duty. No, he had to mean more to her than that.

AND WHEN I LEAVE?

She licked her lips and swallowed hard. "Then I imagine I'll have to find someone else to study."

He had to push harder—had to know.

Setting the pen down, he reached out and took her hand. Her breath hitched, but she didn't pull away. His heart pounded watching confusion cover her face.

"John ..." Her hand trembled in his. "I can't ..."

Slowly, she removed her hand from his grasp. "I'd better go." Tears glistened in her eyes and he wrote quickly.

PLEASE DON'T CRY

"It's all I've done lately."

With those words hanging over his head, she fled the room. What did she mean? Was he the cause of her tears?

* * *

None of it was fair.

Gwen shut the door to her room and returned to her bed, once again dampening her pillows with tears. Her heart tried to tell her the truth. She'd ignored it over and over again, convincing herself he was her patient—someone she was helping. Nothing more.

And now, she was destined to marry Albert, but her heart was already taken. Held by a man she could never have.

She was an Abbott. A woman of social rank. One of the highest on Boston's scale of elite. She'd give it all away if only she was allowed to follow her heart. To do that, she would have to defy her father and break her mother's heart.

I can't ...

John Carter had been in her life for scarcely a month. Her family had surrounded her with love and support for her entire life. She couldn't betray them.

Can I change my heart?

Sitting on the edge of her bed, she dabbed her eyes with a handkerchief. Both men were good looking, that was undeniable. Maybe she was being too hard on Albert. After all, he was a man, and as her father told her, one who found her attractive. Should she fault him for that? And John was someone passing through her life, never meant to take permanent residence.

There was only one solution. Limit her time with *Mr. Carter.*

Tomorrow she'd be with Albert and she would try to see him through different eyes. And next week, Mr. Carter would be occupied with work. He wouldn't need her. She would keep her distance and when she chose to see him it would be for the purpose of checking on his physical well-being. Something she could report in her journal.

She would sit at the table in the corner of his room, not in the rocking chair. The further away from him, the better. Anything to keep her from having to look into his blue eyes. She was a student of medicine and he was her study. Nothing more.

So why was all this logic piercing her heart?

Chapter 14

Eight in the morning and Jeb was dressed and ready to go. He limped his way over the stone path to wait for the carriage. And right on time, the three Abbott men approached from the main house.

He should be anxious about his new job, but felt nothing. There had been no sign of Gwen for the entire weekend. Why didn't she come to see him?

All he could think about were her tears. He shouldn't have held her hand. He'd crossed the line.

"Good morning, Mr. Carter," Henry said with a bow of his head.

Jeb bobbed his head at Henry, then acknowledged the others.

"I hope you're ready for a long day," Mr. Abbott said. "Although you'll be at a desk for most of it, I don't want you harming your leg. I can't have you in my guesthouse forever."

Not sure how to take Mr. Abbott, Jeb chose not to look at him. Maybe he was an inconvenience, but he planned to prove that he had brains.

The enormity of Abbott's caught him off guard. Mr. Abbott explained to him the concept of a departmentalized store, and Jeb found it fascinating. Rather than everything mixed up randomly, shelf after shelf, there were separate departments for linens, clothing, and dry goods. And the clothing was separated into different areas; women's, men's, and children's.

As Jeb hobbled behind Mr. Abbott, listening to every word, he had a new respect for the man. And William Abbott took pride in his accomplishment. Pride well earned.

They went through a set of swinging doors and Jeb's eyes popped. Crates lined the walls, stacked from floor to ceiling. Shelves filled with partially opened boxes covered row after row as far as he could see. Everything was illuminated by the sunshine pouring through windows at the top of the walls, just below the ceiling.

"And this is where we begin." Mr. Abbott sighed heavily. "Inventory."

Jeb scratched his head. *Overwhelming.*

Henry and David stood behind him, chuckling.

"Told you Father would work you hard," Henry said.

"Work *us* hard," David interjected. "Mr. Carter will be doing the paperwork, but we'll be the ones climbing the ladders to reach the merchandise."

They continued on to the back of the stockroom and Jeb was directed to a large oak desk with a padded wooden chair. The desk was neatly arranged with an in-

ventory journal, additional paper, pens, ink, and a glowing lantern.

Mr. Abbott motioned for him to sit. This would be his
work station, and where he would prove his worth. "You
will work until noon, at which time lunch will be
brought to you. You'll have thirty minutes to eat, then
you'll work until four o'clock. Mrs. Abbott insists that
we're home for dinner at five."

He nodded. Honestly, this was much better than staring at the walls of his room. And having reached the
book of Numbers in his Bible, he was having a hard time
staying interested.

After telling Henry and David to look after him, Mr.
Abbott excused himself.

It didn't take long before Jeb figured out more than
one way of making his job easier. Even though the store
was arranged in departments, the inventory had no organization. Merchandise was placed on the shelves according to when it arrived at the store.

He rapidly jotted down his thoughts.

*MERCHANDISE SHOULD BE SORTED IN
STOCKROOM BY DEPARTMENT. WILL MAKE
COUNTING EASIER.*

Henry and David looked at him, then at each other.

"I've been saying that all along," Henry said.

"No, you haven't." David grinned. "All we've ever done
is shove boxes down the line as new merchandise comes
in. No sorting at all. His idea is brilliant."

Brilliant? No. It just made sense. To Jeb, it was simple.
Why hadn't they thought of it themselves? With the large

amount of inventory, how did they ever find anything without organization?

David patted Jeb on the back, while looking at his brother. "Admit it, Henry."

Henry's mouth twitched, then formed a smile. "It's brilliant."

Jeb set about listing all of the various categories of merchandise. He then made large signs for *the boys* to label the shelves. Once that was done, David and Henry enlisted the help of several store clerks and began the long process of moving, sorting, and arranging boxes. In the end, it would be much easier keeping up with inventory and seeing which items should be ordered.

While they sorted, Jeb counted some of the smaller merchandise and posted the results in the journal.

When Mr. Abbott came to check on their progress that afternoon, Jeb enjoyed watching him take in the newly organized stockroom. His mouth dropped open, staring at the shelves. He then rubbed his chin. "I'm speechless."

Jeb chuckled.

That's my job.

"It was all John's idea," Henry said, wiping his brow. He'd worked up quite a sweat climbing up and down the ladders.

"Mr. Carter?"

Jeb scribbled a note.

MADE SENSE

As Mr. Abbott's head bobbed up and down, scanning the room from shelf to shelf, he stood a little taller. "Yes, Mr. Carter, it most certainly does."

Jeb refused to gloat. More than anything, he was glad to help. He'd always had a gift for common sense, so it felt good to put it to use.

The ride home was more enjoyable than the ride going to work. He listened as the men chatted about their day and all that was accomplished. Though he couldn't speak, they spoke *of* him, which included him in the conversation.

As he exited the carriage, he turned and headed toward his room.

"Where are you going, Mr. Carter?" Mr. Abbott asked.

Jeb pointed to the guesthouse.

"Aren't you hungry?"

He was starved, so he nodded. Wouldn't Sarah be bringing his meal?

"Then come with us." Mr. Abbott pulled his watch from his jacket pocket. "We have five minutes. Mrs. Abbott insists we're on time."

Jeb hesitated.

"C'mon, John," David said. "Father's telling the truth. Mother doesn't appreciate tardiness."

He looked at Henry. When the man smiled and jerked his head toward the main house, Jeb knew all was well. In one day, he'd proved himself.

"Gwen will want to hear all about your day," Henry said. "She may want to write about it in her journal."

Gwen ...

In all the busyness of the day, he'd set aside his worries about her. But now, knowing they would be at the same table, his stomach flipped. What would he say to her?

Nothing. After all, he was mute.

* * *

John?

Gwen lost her breath the moment she saw him at the dinner table. For a brief second, their eyes met, but she quickly looked away. She'd done well over the weekend, concentrating solely on Albert. And now ... why was John here? That is ... *Mr. Carter.*

To make matters worse, he'd been seated in the chair beside hers.

She swallowed the frog that had lodged itself in her throat, raised her chin, and glided across the floor to her place.

John attempted to rise and help seat her, but Henry motioned for him to stay and helped her himself. Why the chivalry? Henry *never* helped her with her chair.

Katherine was already at the table on the other side of John, giddier than ever. Was there a secret everyone in the family was aware of that she'd not been privy to? Gwen frowned and pulled her chair closer to the table.

"Why so glum, dear?" her mother asked.

"I'm not. I just ..." Gwen felt John's presence beside her, certain his eyes were on her.

"Aren't you happy to see Mr. Carter?" her father asked. "If he could talk, he would tell you about his successful day at Abbott's."

She shifted her body just enough to view him from the corner of her eye. It was all she could bear. "It went well?"

"Better than well," David said. "Your *patient* is brilliant. You should see the stockroom."

They told her in detail how John had reorganized the inventory. Their mood was cheerful and it seemed John was at ease with every one of them. She was the only one at the table who was uneasy.

Gwen just happened to be on John's left, and while readjusting her legs, she accidentally bumped his cast. A large grunt from him ripped her heart wide open. The last thing she wanted to do was hurt him.

"I'm so sorry, John. Um—*Mr. Carter.*" Everyone was looking at her. She couldn't do this. Before bursting into tears, she pushed her chair back and hurried from the room. She didn't stop until she reached her bedroom.

Rather than throwing herself on the bed, she paced. It was the only way she could determine how to fix the mess she was in.

"I'll starve to death," she muttered. "I can't eat at the same table with him."

Pace. Pace. Pace.

Considering herself an intelligent woman, she'd always been able to figure out anything she set her mind to. There had to be a solution. She thought she'd already decided what to do. Focus her attention on Albert—which she had done all weekend—and limit her interaction with John.

"*Mr. Carter.*" She clenched her fists. Why was it so hard to erase his first name?

"A-hem ..."

Gwen's entire body shook, startled by Sarah who stood in the doorway.

"Miss Gwen? Can I talk to you?"

"Sarah—of course. Come in."

Gwen sat on the edge of her bed and Sarah pulled up a chair.

"Miss Gwen, I's thirty years old, and I's seen many things. I's *heard* things, too." She folded her hands in her lap, but leaned in toward Gwen.

Had she been listening to her conversation with John? "Heard things?"

Sarah nodded. "But it don't matter none. What I do better than anythin' is understan' when folks is hurtin'. And you're hurtin', ain't ya?"

Gwen's chin quivered and the tears came.

Sarah stood and sat beside her on the bed, encircling her with one arm. "Go on an cry, Miss Gwen. Then talk to me."

After blubbering for several minutes, Gwen blew her nose on a handkerchief and did her best to relax. "I can't talk about it, Sarah. It's something I need to take care of myself."

"Sometimes it heps to talk."

"Not this time. I know what I have to do, but it's very hard."

Sarah patted Gwen's knee. "You're a smart girl, but smarts don't always matter when it's your heart what's mixed up."

Gwen pulled back and stared at her. How did she know?

Sarah chuckled. "I understan' better than you know."

Gwen folded into herself, holding her face in her hands. Sarah gently rubbed her back, attempting to calm her. "It will just take time." Gwen mumbled the words through her fingers.

"Yes'm. Everythin' in time. But if you change your mind, you come talk to me."

"I will."

"Now, then. You best go down an eat your supper. Your mama sent me to check on you. They's worried 'bout you."

Sarah gave her a quick hug, then left the room.

Could she face them now with swollen eyes and a red nose? Her stomach grumbled. She needed to eat.

"You'll be twenty in less than three weeks," she scolded herself, standing. "Stop acting like a child."

Throwing her shoulders back, she wiped her eyes one final time, then headed down the stairs.

* * *

The happiness Jeb felt after his successful day followed Gwen out of the room. Knowing she was about to cry again tore him apart. What was wrong with her? The only conclusion he had was that he'd messed up everything with her. But until he could *speak* with her alone, he'd never know.

Good. She's comin' back.

Gwen brushed by him and took her seat. Yes, she'd been crying. If only he could reach out and touch her.

That's what caused this mess to start with. What was I thinkin'?

"Forgive me for leaving so suddenly," she said. "I wasn't feeling well."

"Are you all right now, Winnie?" David asked. The concern in his eyes was apparent.

He called her Winnie. I like that.

"Yes, I'm fine. And I'm hungry."

The mood at the table improved with Gwen's return. Her family reminded Jeb of his. Everyone cared about each other. And even though there were arguments, at the end of the day they were a family, and nothing stopped their love.

But he wasn't a member of this family and never would be. So no matter how good it felt being here, it wasn't going to last.

Through the rest of the meal, Gwen wouldn't look at him, or speak to him. Had it not been for Katherine, he might as well have been invisible. She spent time between bites of food telling him how excited she was about Christmas. She went into detail about all their family traditions, as well as what gifts she hoped for. She'd have rambled all night, but her mama finally told her to hush and eat.

Jeb didn't mind. Katherine kept his mind off the woman on his other side.

"Can I walk home with Mr. Carter?" Katherine asked her mama.

"May I," Mrs. Abbott corrected her.

"May I walk home with him?"

"Yes, you may. But only to his front door. Mr. Carter needs some rest. He's had a long day."

Mrs. Abbott smiled at him. She was a beautiful woman and Gwen resembled her, but Gwen was something more. How he wished the smile had come from Gwen.

With Katherine by his side, he waved his *goodnight* to everyone at the table, then headed home.

"Gwen's confused," Katherine said, causing him to stop on the path.

He tipped his head and stared at her.

She raised her brows and somehow looked like a woman much older and wiser than her nine years. "She *had to* see Mr. Finch this weekend. But she likes you, and I think she'd rather spend time with you. So, she's confused."

Was that why she was cryin'? This little girl knew more than the adults at the table.

"I think she went to her room to figure it out. She does that sometimes."

He nodded and began walking again.

"I like you better, too. So, if she marries Mr. Finch, then maybe I can marry you. But you'll have to wait for me to grow up."

He bent down, looked at her face-to-face, and gave her a huge smile. One day, she would capture a lucky heart.

Her cheeks flushed red and she walked with him the rest of the way home.

Standing in the doorway, he watched her skip back.

If Gwen marries Albert, I might just have to wait for you.

He shut the door.

Please, God, don't let that happen.

His silent prayer repeated in his mind until he lay down and drifted off to sleep.

Chapter 15

As Gwen walked in the front door of Massachusetts General, it seemed like much longer than one week since she and Henry had taken John home. Her life had been a whirlwind ever since. Between entertaining Albert and trying to avoid John, nothing was as it had been. Fortunately, Albert didn't propose over the weekend. That would have added even more stress.

It was time to check in with Doctor Young.

Clutching her journal to her chest, she walked to the second floor. Nurse Phillips was coming toward her. Preparing for the usual scowl, Gwen stood tall and breathed deeply. She wouldn't let the woman upset her.

"Miss Abbott?"

Oh, dear. I didn't expect her to speak to me.

"Yes. May I help you?"

Nurse Phillips crossed her arms over her chest and one side of her mouth curled upward, which made her look a bit like a snarling bulldog. "How's Mr. Carter?"

"Umm ... Mr. Carter is well. He was here earlier today. Didn't you see him?"

She shook her head. "Just got here. He still throwin' things?"

"No. Well—not that I know of. He's working now—for my father."

Nurse Phillips rolled her eyes. "Figures." She continued on down the hall without another word.

Strange woman.

That was probably the most uncomfortable conversation she'd ever had.

She continued on to Doctor Young's office.

"Miss Abbott." Dr. Young took her hand and led her to a chair. "I'm so pleased to see you."

"It's Tuesday. I always come on Tuesday afternoon."

"Yes, but I thought that since Mr. Carter was in your care, you'd stay home. You weren't here last Thursday."

After explaining that she had to make up some schoolwork because she'd missed Wednesday's classes, she asked him about John's appointment.

"He appears to be well. Getting around splendidly with the crutches. And I'm pleased that he's working for your father. From what your brother told me, he's doing well at Abbott's."

"Yes, he is." She placed the journal on his desk. "However, I've not been doing well at keeping up with my journal. I'll do better. I do believe I know what's troubling him."

"Yes?" Doctor Young peered at her over the top of his glasses.

"I don't know specifically, but I know that he was in the war. And that his little sister died. Horribly."

She didn't even like to think about it. A five-year-old burning to death would give anyone nightmares.

"Go on ..." He leaned back in his chair and folded his hands together, resting them on his belly.

She opened her journal and traced her fingers over some of the entries. Then she lifted her gaze and looked directly at the doctor. She didn't need the journal to remind her of her time with John. "Katherine makes him smile. And he's smiled for me a time or two. I believe he's more comfortable with my brothers now, and if all goes well he may retain his employment even after the cast is removed. Which, I feel is a very good thing."

Was she rambling? In many ways she could talk endlessly about John.

"You care for him."

Gwen blinked hard, staring at the doctor. "Of course I do. He's ... my patient."

"A caregiver's eyes don't normally sparkle when they speak about their patients."

She shifted her eyes downward and affixed them to the journal. "Sparkle?" She enjoyed talking about him and how well he was doing. But talking about him, made her want to be with him and learn even more. That couldn't be part of her plan.

He chuckled. "Yes, accompanied by a nice shade of rose-colored cheeks." He tapped on the page. "I'm a doctor. I'm quite capable of making a diagnosis."

After shutting the journal, she stood. Was she this transparent at home? If so, then that was even more of a reason to keep her distance from John. And heaven forbid if John and Albert were ever in the same room. The thought made her shudder.

"Do you have another patient for me to tend?" She held the journal close.

"None specifically. Today you'll join me on my rounds and take notes." He stood and walked toward the door. "Don't fret, Miss Abbott. Your secret is safe with me."

She followed him out the door.

* * *

Gwen listened to the non-stop conversation at the dinner table, but couldn't bring herself to participate. Not with John sitting beside her. Fearing that she'd say the wrong thing or ask the wrong question, it was easier to remain silent. Just like him.

"Doctor Young said that John's leg is healing well," Henry said. "But the soonest they'll remove the cast is the end of November."

"Convenient for him," David said with a chuckle. "By then, we'll have all the inventory counted."

The end of November.

Just before she was supposed to marry Albert. And then, would John leave?

She forced herself to look at John and caught the wiggle of his brows over David's remark. He wasn't the angry, hateful man she'd encountered when he first came to the hospital. But even when he smiled, a hint of sorrow remained in his eyes.

Oh, goodness ...

She forgot to shift her gaze and now their eyes met. He smiled a sad, questioning smile. How was he able to say so much with silence?

'Tis my happiness that renders me silent ...

Was her silence meant to keep her happy? If so, then why was she miserable?

It was settled. Tonight she would go to his room. To write in her journal, of course. Surely, Sarah could accompany her.

* * *

Jeb had just finished cleaning his teeth when the door creaked open. Hoping that it might be Gwen, he wiped his mouth with a clean wash cloth, then hobbled back to the bed. It was good that he hadn't undressed.

His heart sunk when Sarah peered through the doorway.

"Don't look so sad," Sarah whispered, then grinned. "I din't come alone."

Gwen marched through the door, clutching her journal. Without saying a word, she went straight to the corner table and prepared to write. She'd even brought an extra pen and ink and didn't bother picking up the set next to his bed. Was she *that* determined to keep her distance from him?

"I'll be right outside the door," Sarah said and started humming.

Jeb cleared his throat. How else could he get her attention?

She ignored him and dipped her pen.

He could play this game. Sometimes using tried and true methods got the best results. Taking a pillow from the bed, he threw it. Perfect aim.

"Oh!" She jumped to her feet. The fire that came from her eyes could have ignited the room. Maybe it wasn't such a good idea. Not such perfect aim. He hadn't meant to knock over the ink bottle.

"John Carter! What were you thinking?"

All he could do was shrug. At least he'd gotten her attention.

"If that ink had spilled on my dress, mother would have been furious."

Sarah rushed into the room. "I'll clean it up, Miss Gwen."

"It's all right, Sarah. Only a little spilled. The bottle was almost empty." Gwen left the room.

Why'd she leave? Stupid, stupid idea.

"Throwin' things again, Mr. Carter?" Sarah shook her finger at him. "There are other ways to get a woman's attention."

Maybe Sarah was on his side. He'd barely had time to smile at her before Gwen came back in the room. She held an old rag in one hand which she used to dab up the ink.

"All better," she said to Sarah, then sat back down.

Sarah left the room and Gwen returned to writing.

He wanted to scream *talk to me*, but that would spoil everything. He cleared his throat.

"I'll be right with you, Mr. Carter. I'm logging your progress in my journal."

Ouch. That was cold.

He grabbed the paper and pen from beside his bed. New plan. Write a note.

PLEASE TALK TO ME

She wouldn't even look at him. So, he blew on the words until the ink was dry, then wadded the paper and threw it at her. It bounced off her shoulder and landed on the floor beside her.

Her head turned. She bent down, picked up the paper, and smoothed it. Her shoulders rose and fell as she inhaled and then let her breath out slowly.

She stood and walked toward him.

Please, sit in the rocker.

"Mr. Carter ..."

His hand flew over the paper.

JOHN

"*Mr. Carter*, you have to understand. You're my patient. Nothing more."

He wouldn't believe it. Hundreds of questions went through his mind. What was the most important?

DID I UPSET YOU?

"No. But you shouldn't have thrown the pillow. I thought we'd gone beyond that."

So did he.

NOT THE PILLOW

WHEN I HELD YOUR HAND

She finally sat, but then drew back. "It didn't make me angry, but you shouldn't have done it. You know that Albert and I are courting."

I'M SORRY

"Don't be sorry. But it can't happen again."

Sarah's humming seemed to be getting louder.

IT WON'T. I WANT YOU TO COME AND SEE ME.

"I can't come as often as I used to. Besides, you're being kept busy at the store and my weekends are set aside for Albert. At least you're eating at the main house, now. We'll see each other then."

WILL YOU TALK TO ME THERE?

"I'll try. But please understand—it's not proper for me to call you *John*. I'm afraid I allowed myself to become too familiar with you."

He shook his head.

"It was my doing. Please forgive me if I hurt you."

If she was the one who'd hurt *him*, then why did *she* look so sad? She was the one who'd been crying.

I'M FINE

WORRIED ABOUT YOU

It wasn't entirely true. He wasn't fine, but he didn't want to be the cause of her sadness.

She tipped her head, then nervously worked her bottom lip with her teeth. "You have such a big heart, John Carter."

Rising from the rocker, she returned to the desk, wrote a few more lines, then blew on the ink and closed the journal.

"Goodnight, Mr. Carter. I hope you'll sleep well."

Leaving already? She'd not even stayed ten minutes.

He couldn't stop looking at her, wanting to say so much.

"I'll see you at dinner tomorrow."

And then she was gone. He laid down flat on the bed and stared at the ceiling. Why did he ever start this charade? Silence was killing him.

Chapter 16

Jeb's routine was set. He worked Monday through Friday, and on the weekends he stewed over Gwen. Knowing she was with Albert was unbearable. And she never came to see him anymore. The only time he saw her was at dinner, and he couldn't write at the dinner table. It wouldn't be appropriate. Besides, the things he wanted to write could never be seen by her family.

He'd returned to reading the Bible. Once he made his way past the *of the people's*, the book of Numbers became more interesting, but even then, he couldn't stay focused. His mind was too cluttered, wondering what Albert and Gwen were doing.

"I ain't heard you turn a page since I been in your room," Sarah said. She'd come in to sweep the floor and dust the furniture. "Your eyes ain't closed. I know you ain't sleepin'."

He lowered the Bible and looked at her, then sighed with a frown. Since Sarah couldn't read, he had no way of communicating with her.

"Would it make you feel better knowin' I seen that same look on Miss Gwen's face?"

He shook his head. He didn't want Gwen to be unhappy.

Sarah put aside the broom and sat beside him in the rocking chair. After fidgeting with her apron, she scrunched her eyes shut, shook her head, then slapped her hands against the arms of the chair, popping her eyes open wide. "I just gotta say sumthin'."

I can see that.

She leaned in. "I know."

What did she know? That he was in love with Gwen? He suspected she sensed something between them.

"You can stop pretendin' with me, Mr. Carter. I knows your secret."

He splayed his hands wide, questioning her with his eyes.

"Talk to me, Mr. Carter. I knows you can."

It was worse than a slap in the face.

How could she know?

She couldn't.

He scooted fully upright, then looked toward the door.

"Don't you worry none. No one will come in. 'Sides, that door squeaks so loud, we'd hear it."

He still couldn't bring himself to speak. Maybe he'd forgotten how. Truthfully, he was afraid.

"You talks in your sleep. An I ain't never heard no man from Boston talk like you do. You's from the south, ain't ya?"

He closed his eyes. Memories of nights sharing a room with his brothers came to mind. They'd laughed at him over things he'd said while sleeping. He never thought ...

"Please, don't tell." His words barely came out, scratching across his throat like an unswallowed piece of food.

Her face lit up like the sun. "Oh, I won't, Mr. Carter. I's just glad we can talk. I understan' why you don't talk. I knows what it's like to be scared a the folks 'round you."

Using his voice felt unnatural, and his insides churned; nervous that he'd be caught. "I never meant to come to Boston. Hopped a train I thought was goin' west."

"The good Lord brought you here." She jerked her head into a nod, making her words a proclamation.

"Why? I don't belong here."

"One day you'll look back an know why. Sometimes the pieces of our lives don't make no sense. But God knows what He's doin."

He wished he had her faith. Even after all she'd been through, she seemed to be at peace with her life.

He rubbed his dry throat with his hand, which prompted her to get him a glass of water. After gratefully downing every drop, he was ready to speak again. "I'm gonna leave when my leg heals."

She chuckled.

"Why ya laughin'?"

"I's sorry, Mr. Carter, but hearin' yo' southern talk tickles me. If Miss Gwen heard how you talk-"

"She can't." He reached out and grabbed her hand. "If she knew I could talk—and talk like this—she'd never forgive me."

Sarah's face instantly changed; filled with compassion. "Oh, she'd be hurt, but once she thought it through, she'd understan'. Miss Gwen loves you. She don't know it yet, but I reckon it's why God brought you here. She needs you and you need her. Albert Finch don't need no one. It would do the women of Boston good, if that man never married."

He stared at her. Speechless. Could it be true?

"Mr. Carter, don't look so surprised. You've seen it, too. I knows you have." She grinned. "I reckon you should know that Friday is Miss Gwen's birthday."

He still couldn't speak. His heart was in his throat.

"Give yo'self a good shave before you go to dinner Friday night. I din't put that razor in your room for nothin'."

"You?"

"Course it was me. I's told to take care of you. Heppin' you, hepped Miss Gwen see the light." She stood, taller than ever. "Next time, you can tell me your story."

Picking up the broom, she left him to his thoughts. He had a lot to think about.

* * *

Twenty years old. Gwen *had* to marry Albert. It was as her father said; men don't want women declining in years. If she didn't marry Albert, no man would want her. But maybe she didn't need a man in her life. If she was allowed to finish her education, she could easily obtain employment. Then she wouldn't need a man. She could support herself—make her own way.

Sifting through the dresses in her wardrobe, she contemplated which to wear. Her hand rested on the lavender dress that Albert loved. Should she?

She was shocked when her mother moved dinner to five-thirty. She said she wanted to be certain Albert had plenty of time to reach their home for dinner. She'd have set it even later if not for the fear of darkness making his return home difficult. And staying in the guesthouse for the night was out of the question. Not with John there.

Her stomach fluttered. Albert and John were going to meet and she would be there watching it unfold.

In the two and a half weeks since her last private conversation with John, she'd spent more time with Albert than she cared to remember. He'd stopped pushing for her affections, but that wouldn't last long. After all, according to her father, he would be her husband soon enough.

She'd succumbed to holding his hand and endured the kisses that had ultimately chapped her knuckles. Did her lips have the same torment awaiting them?

"Yes, dear," her mother said, entering the room. "Wear the lavender. I know Mr. Finch likes it."

"Will he like it as well without the corset?" She wasn't about to wear that torturous undergarment. Not with birthday cake to look forward to.

"Why not wear it? After all, you're now twenty. There's no longer a trace of a young girl in your figure. Wear what is fashionable."

Gwen pulled the dress from the wardrobe and draped it across her bed. "I'll wear the dress, but no corset. It's my birthday and I want to enjoy myself."

Her mother gave her a look of disappointment, then threw up her hands. "You'll look lovely no matter what undergarments you wear. Though I doubt the dress will fit the same without it."

Gwen hoped it wouldn't fit the same. She wanted to be comfortable, not bound like a trapped animal. Besides, she'd read in her medical journals that corsets could cause digestive difficulties. So, her decision was not simply for comfort, but for her good health, which was more important than pleasing Albert Finch.

After helping with her dress, and giving a pronounced sigh after seeing it on, her mother left the room.

Gwen stood in front of the mirror. Much better. Her breasts didn't look like grapefruits ready to burst out of their rinds. Still, she wished she wasn't showing so much flesh.

Once again, her mother brought the pearls for her to wear. Rather than putting her hair up, Gwen opted to leave it down. Partially to keep her neck warm. But if she wanted to be honest with herself, everything she was doing was to impress John, not Albert.

A silly thing to do when the two men are about to meet each other.

Just when Gwen was about to descend the stairs, Sarah hurried toward her, waving one hand and motioning her back into her room.

"What is it, Sarah?"

Sarah pushed the door closed. "I brung you sumthin'. It's from Mr. Carter." From beneath her apron, she produced a bouquet of paper roses.

Gwen stumbled back to the bed and plopped down. Her heart raced and tears formed.

"Miss Gwen?" Sarah moved to her side, setting the gift on her bed stand.

Gwen reached for the flowers. "They're beautiful. It had to have taken him a long time."

"Yes'm. He's been workin' on 'em every night."

"How'd you know they were for me?"

Sarah shook her head, frowning. "An who else would they be for? 'Sides, I told him it was your birthday."

Gwen wrapped her arms around Sarah's neck and hugged her tight. "Thank you, Sarah."

"You best wipe those tears. Be shore to make the time to thank him." She raised her eyebrows and peered into Gwen's eyes, making her point.

"I will."

Gazing at the intricacy of the flowers, she hesitated putting them down. But she couldn't hold them forever. The good thing was, they would never die, just like Katherine's rose.

"You ready for this?" Sarah asked.

How did Sarah see into her heart and mind?

She nodded without saying a word and they descended the stairs together.

Albert was waiting at the bottom.

Upon seeing her, his eyes widened and he his face lit with excitement. Yet as she reached him, his expression changed. He glanced at her bosom and the confusion in his eyes prompted her to giggle, but she quickly stifled it.

Sorry, Albert. Not quite so much to see this time.

"Gwendolyn." He took her hand and raised it to his lips. "You look—lovely."

"Thank you, Albert."

Sarah scurried past them and went down the hallway toward the kitchen.

"And may I be the first to wish you a very happy birthday." He caressed her hand, then kissed it again. She would need to use additional lanolin cream tonight.

"Thank you, Albert."

He grinned and extended his arm. "I'll give you your gift shortly."

"That's very kind of you, Albert."

Her vocabulary seemed to be limited when it came to Albert. Maybe it had something to do with the fact that all he was ever interested in was her appearance. She tried to recall a time when they'd had an intelligent conversation. Nothing came to mind. John, on the other hand, spoke far more intelligently with utter silence.

And there he was, already seated at the dinner table in his usual spot. Leg extended; crutches close by. Her entire family was there, waiting for her before sitting themselves.

John met her gaze, then shifted his eyes to Albert, who appeared oblivious to anyone in the room but himself. He paraded her to the table.

Happy birthday wishes rose up almost in unison. Her mother motioned for them to sit on the opposite side of the table from John. Not her usual chair. Though she understood her intentions, this arrangement made things even more difficult. Now she would have to look at him across the table through the course of their entire dinner.

Albert pulled out her chair and she sat, keeping her eyes affixed to the table. Much easier that way.

"Oh, Mr. Finch," her father said. "You've not met our houseguest, Mr. Carter."

John attempted to rise.

"Don't bother, Mr. Carter," Albert said. "I'm aware of your impairments."

John nodded and sat fully, then caught her eye. What she saw was more pain than ever, and not of the physical kind.

She wanted to thank him for his thoughtful gift, but she wasn't about to do it in front of Albert. For now, she smiled at him, and his expression eased. Why was her heart beating out of her chest? Why did she want more than anything to go to him and have everyone else in the room disappear?

"Gwendolyn?" Albert waved his hand in front of her face.

Entranced, she shook her head. "Yes?"

"Your father is preparing to say the blessing."

She glanced around the table. Everyone had their heads bowed, except for her and John ... and Albert.

"Oh," she whispered. "Forgive me, Father." She folded her hands, bowed her head, and closed her eyes.

As her father prayed, her mind wandered with her own prayer.

Lord, help me make it through tonight. Ease John's pain, and please make Albert behave.

"Amen." She said the word louder than usual.

Katherine giggled until she was hushed by their mother.

Since it was Gwen's birthday, she'd selected the menu for the meal, and with Sarah's help, Violet made the best fried chicken in Massachusetts. Along with mashed potatoes, green beans, and hot rolls, no one would leave the table hungry.

She caught John licking his fingers and grinned. At least he knew how to eat fried chicken. Sarah had always said it had to be done with fingers, not a fork. Albert sat rigid through the meal with knife and fork appropriately positioned, sawing and prodding his chicken leg. He cast a look of disapproval at John, but fortunately, John hadn't noticed.

The most intriguing part of the meal was when David told Albert about John's success at the store. John sat listening with a gracious smile, while Albert's temperature rose. She felt the heat of his body next to her and marveled at the way the corner of his mouth twitched when he heard something he didn't like. He wore jealousy like an ugly, green cloak.

When Violet brought out the cake, Katherine clapped her hands together. "I want lots of icing!"

"Now Katherine," their mother scolded. "Mind your manners."

Gwen laughed. "It's all right, Mother. She can have some of my icing."

Violet cut slices of the frosted white cake and passed them around the table.

"Aren't you going to make a speech, Gwen?" Henry asked, while swiping a finger-full of icing from the edge of his plate. He then popped it into his mouth. "Delicious."

"A speech?" It was the last thing she wanted to do. "Please ... no."

Albert scooted his chair back and stood. "Since Gwendolyn is reluctant to speak, I would like to speak on her behalf."

Oh, my dear Lord. I should have spoken.

Albert cleared his throat and puffed out his chest. At any moment, she expected peacock feathers to fan out from his behind. "All of you are well aware of my courtship with Gwendolyn, and tonight I would like to take it one step further."

I'm going to be sick.

"Tonight, Gwendolyn's life has reached two decades. In another year, I, too, shall reach the ripe age of twenty. We cannot waste another day."

After grunting several times, Albert kneeled on one knee at her feet.

No. Not here. Not in front of John.

From his jacket pocket he produced a small box, opened it, and held up a ring. "Gwendolyn, I adore you. Please say you'll be my wife."

The silence in the air smothered her. Her chest was tighter than when it had been bound in the corset. She didn't dare look at John, but she knew that every eye in the room was on her, waiting for her answer.

Her father cleared his throat.

I know, Father. I know what I have to do.

She couldn't manage a smile, but forced her words. "Yes, of course. I'll marry you, Albert."

The silence erupted into laughter and cheers, as the proud peacock placed the ring on her left hand. A single ruby sparkled in the candlelight.

He pulled her hand to his face and kissed it, then waved it in the air for all to see. "The future Mrs. Albert Finch," he proclaimed. "And the mother of my heirs."

Lifting her to her feet, she was immediately surrounded by her family with hugs and well-wishes. Katherine gawked at the ring, then giggled when Albert told her not to touch it.

Gwen glanced across the room. Sarah was wiping her eyes and walked out. And when Gwen finally turned her head to look at John, his seat was empty.

"Where's Mr. Carter?"

"He went to his room," her mother said. "He looked as though he didn't feel well. I hope he's not coming down with something."

"It's a shame," Gwen whispered. "Perhaps someone should look in on him."

Albert took her by the arm. "Not you. Let someone else go. Tonight we're celebrating."

"Yes," her father added. "Everyone have a seat and eat your cake. Violet is preparing tea. We'll toast the fine couple."

Gwen poked at her cake with a fork.

The fine couple?

She didn't want to celebrate. As soon as Albert was gone, she intended to check on John. Though she doubted he was ill. His malady was one she shared.

Chapter 17

Gwendolyn, I adore you.

The words sickened Jeb. Albert Finch was not only arrogant, but the way his eyes moved over Gwen made him want to poke them out of his face. He looked at her as though she was part of the meal and was ready to take a large bite.

She deserves more.

He simply couldn't stay and watch him gloat over his prize. Gwen would understand. After all, *she* had a heart.

Closing his eyes, he pictured her. She looked beautiful tonight, but uncomfortable. The dress was unlike anything she'd worn before. He'd counted at least a dozen times that she'd fidgeted with the pearls at her neck. What had made her so uneasy? Him, Albert, or something else?

Even though he knew she and Albert were to be married, he'd always hoped that what he believed she felt for *him* would change her mind.

Stupid idea. I ain't got nothin' to offer her.

Sarah had been kind enough to bring warm water for him to shave before dinner. Little good it did. Gwen rarely looked his way. Maybe he should grow the beard back. It was easier to hide behind.

The room was cold and he couldn't stop shivering. The fire in the living area had died down, so he hobbled out of his room to add another log. The warmth from the flames felt good against his cold hands as he held them up to the fire.

There was no need to go to bed. He'd never be able to sleep. Instead, he made himself comfortable on the sofa and covered up with a blanket that was draped over the armrest.

The fire danced before his eyes. Mesmerizing, but so deadly.

The squeak of the front door brought him out of his trance.

"John?"

His heart leapt at the sound of Gwen's tentative voice.

Alone? Why's she alone?

She was bundled in a heavy wool coat, with a scarf wrapped around her head. And though she shut the door quickly, the cold night air swept through the room.

Unwinding the scarf, she approached him with caution. She stood beside the sofa, looking down at him, frozen to the floor.

He patted the spot beside him.

"I shouldn't."

He patted again.

With a heavy sigh, she finally sat, as far from him as she could on the small sofa.

"I—I wanted to thank you for the beautiful roses. They were the finest gift I received."

He pointed to her ring and questioned with his eyes.

She looked down and away from him. Then her shoulders jerked forward and she began to sob.

What could he do? He didn't dare touch her.

"I don't want to marry Albert," she cried. "Can you imagine what my life will be like as his wife?"

He could, but he didn't want to. He needed to talk to her, so he mimed writing.

She sniffled and nodded rapidly, then went to his room and brought back his writing tools. He scribbled quickly.

DON'T MARRY HIM

"I have to. If I don't, it'll hurt my family."

BUT YOU DON'T LOVE HIM

She cried even harder. "It doesn't matter."

His heart thumped. She had to know how he felt.

Putting away all sense, he set aside the paper and reached out, brushing her cheek with his hand.

She looked at him through her tears, then blinked, causing droplets to fall down her face and across his fingers.

"John—I ..."

With one finger tucked under her chin, he drew her close. His heart took over and his lips met hers.

She didn't back away and kissed him fully, as his hand moved behind her head, holding her firm.

When they parted, she stared at him, breathing with slow, steady rhythm. "I love you."

Vowing never to shed another tear, something came over him when she spoke what he'd wanted to hear. Tears filled his eyes.

He picked up the paper, and as he wrote, teardrops fell.

I LOVE YOU TOO

He smiled at her, believing that since they'd proclaimed their love, all would be well. But instead of returning his smile, she burst out crying, harder than before.

"You can't love me. It's not fair to you. We can never be together."

WHY?

"Father won't allow it. I have to marry someone of stature."

SO I'M NOT GOOD ENOUGH

She placed her hand against his cheek. "You're better than all of them. But you have to understand."

I DON'T

She stood, breathing hard. "I know nothing about you. I don't even know where you come from, or who your family was. How can you expect Father to approve of us when we don't know who you are?"

His hand rested against the paper. If she knew who he was, it would confirm everything she said. They'd never allow it.

"I don't understand my feelings. I want to be with you, but I can't. I came here tonight to thank you for the gift, and also because I knew you were hurting. Albert ... means well. But he sometimes comes across poorly."

Poorly? She's too kind.

HE DOESN'T DESERVE YOU

"Maybe I don't deserve *him*. After all, I kissed you willingly. I've already betrayed him and I'm not yet his wife."

He beat his finger against his words already written.

DON'T MARRY HIM

"I can't come to you again. It's hard enough seeing you every night at the dinner table. I know I shouldn't have come, but ... I'm sorry ..."

She rushed out and the door slammed, crushing his heart.

Wadding up the paper where he'd written his love, he threw it in the fire. Burned, like everything else.

* * *

Not wanting to risk anyone in the house seeing her, Gwen stumbled up the stairs without a lantern. As many times as she'd climbed them, she knew each step by count, not to mention that some had a unique squeak. With tear-filled eyes, the lantern wouldn't have done much good anyway.

The ache in her heart was unbearable. How would she ever overcome this pain?

She lay upon her bed, fully clothed, and let the tears flow.

He loves me.

The feel of his kiss lingered on her lips. No other man had ever been allowed. To share, for a brief moment, the same air. She hungered for more, but only from him. It was a hunger that could never be satisfied.

But what was it exactly that she loved about him? She scarcely knew him. And yet, once she got beyond his hardened heart, she found a gentle man. A man with a soft touch and a loving soul. Though she didn't know where he was from, or who his family was, maybe she knew him better than she first thought. Good character, intelligent, spiritual, and more handsome than any man ever should be.

Using her common sense, she weighed his qualities against those of Albert. Albert lacked character, his intelligence was questionable, and though he sat beside her at Sunday services, she wasn't certain about his spirituality. And maybe that wasn't her place to judge. Only God could see into a man's heart.

As for Albert's looks, the more she got to know him, the less handsome he appeared.

Lord, I'm doomed.

Twenty years old and she already had one foot in the grave. Maybe having children would help. She and Albert were bound to start a family right away. She loved babies and would love her own even more. Her days would be spent tending them and Albert would be away working. Children would give her somewhere to put her love, and in time she could forget John Carter.

She had to.

Chapter 18

Days ticked by too slow for Jeb. Ever since that night, he couldn't forget the taste of her. And when they were in the same room together, the air hung heavy around his shoulders, making breathing difficult.

On the rare occasion that he'd catch her eye, he knew she felt it, too. But her loyalty to her family would keep her bound to Albert Finch.

She never laughed like she used to and he missed their time together. But November had come. Soon his cast would be gone and so would he.

With inventory complete, he was now assigned to quality control and stock orders. Business had picked up now that Christmas was only a little more than a month away. He kept his desk in the stockroom, which suited him. Anything was better than having to see all of the smiling faces of shoppers. Smiles that he couldn't return.

Was his heart hardening again?

Saturday. Where was Albert taking her today?

Why should I care?

The fire roared before him. Having the cast on his leg gave him a good excuse to stay here, comfortable on the living room sofa, reading. Since no one visited him, he had plenty of time to read and was already in the New Testament. Much more uplifting than the Old. He needed it.

A knock on the door stopped his reading.

Unusual for a knock. Sarah came in without announcing herself and Gwen didn't come at all. So, who would be knocking?

He hoisted himself onto the crutches and limped to the door. Peering out the window, he saw Katherine's small figure, shivering in the cold. Flurries of snow whipped around the poor child. At least it hadn't covered the ground. He wasn't ready for that.

He pushed the door wide and she stepped inside, but remained in the entryway.

"I'm not supposed to come in. Father says it's inappropriate."

Inappropriate or not, he doubted he'd want her frozen.

He shook his head at her, then motioned to the fire. When she didn't budge, he pointed a stern finger. This time, she moved.

"I'll sit to get warm, but don't tell Father." She started giggling. A giggle he'd grown to love. "Guess you can't, can you?"

Always the mute jokes. He'd brought them on himself.

She brushed a bit of snow from her coat, then sat on the sofa and looked around the room.

"You'll need a Christmas tree."

No, he wouldn't. He'd be gone long before Christmas.

"Father always puts one in the main house, and if we have guests, he puts one in here, too. I love Christmas."

He smiled and nodded. She'd told him many times before.

"Mr. Carter?" Her mouth twisted and she hesitated. "I wish *you* were marrying Gwen. She doesn't smile much anymore. And I know she misses you."

Words from the mouth of a child. Life was so simple for children.

"And Mr. Finch smells funny. Gwen says it's *cologne*. It's supposed to smell good, but I think he smells like a skunk."

Maybe he *would* marry this child one day.

"Anyways, I'd rather have you for a brother than him. I like you a whole lot more. Why did Gwen say she'd marry him, when I know she doesn't want to?"

He shrugged and smoothed her hair.

"It's not too late, Mr. Carter. Until she says, *I do,* you can change her mind."

He sadly shook his head. Gwen had made up her mind and nothing would change it. Besides, it was for the best. This way, he never had to tell her the truth. He'd be gone, she'd marry Albert, and they'd be none the wiser.

"I wish you could talk. If you could, you could tell her not to marry him." Her little body seemed to fold into itself, then her head tipped to the side. "Why don't you write her a love letter?" She covered her mouth and snickered.

Again, he shook his head. He'd already tried. It may not have been a letter, but he couldn't have spelled out his feelings any plainer.

She hopped off the sofa. "I better go back. If I'm gone too long, Mother might come looking for me."

He took her hand and gave it a gentle squeeze. Then he warmed to the core when she leaned over and kissed his cheek.

With a sad smile, she walked away.

She wanted him for a brother. He'd give anything to be part of her family, though none would ever replace the family he'd lost.

He'd just picked up the Book again when a blast of air chilled him from the door opening wide. Turning his head, he watched Sarah bustle in.

"Least down south we din't have snow!" She shuffled across the floor and stood in front of the fireplace. "It ain't s'posed to snow 'til December. Least it ain't stickin'."

He stared into the flames, setting aside the Bible.

Sarah stomped her feet a few times, then faced him with her hands on her hips. "Cat got your tongue?"

He chuckled. She was the only person he ever spoke to. "Sorry. I forgot."

"What? That you have a tongue, or that you ain't got much time left 'fore Miss Gwen makes the biggest mistake a her life?"

Not her, too.

"I told you." He raised his hands in the air. "She's made up her mind."

"She done *lost* her mind, if she thinks Mr. Finch is gonna be any kind a husband."

"And you reckon I'd be a better one. Why?"

She removed her coat, and after draping it over the back of a chair, sat beside him. "You got a heart."

She wouldn't have thought that if she'd seen him in August.

"I know what you're thinkin'." She went on before he could speak. "I'm a poor boy from the south with nothin' to offer. An folks from the north hates folks from the south. Right?"

"Yep."

"But Miss Gwen's a northerner, an you love her. An she loves you. Love don't come from a *place*. It comes from the heart."

Sarah had recognized their love before they were willing to admit it and did all she could to encourage it. But all of the love in the world couldn't overcome the obstacles they faced. It was hopeless.

He picked at the sofa cushion. "Love don't put food on the table."

"An every bit of Albert Finch's money won't put a smile on Miss Gwen's face. What's more important?"

"Dyin' happily of starvation?"

She cuffed him upside the head.

"Shame on you, Mr. Carter! We's talkin' 'bout the rest of your lives here. Now you gotta make up your mind whether you're gonna sit on your tail and watch the woman you love go off with another man, or use that voice of yours and speak your peace."

They'd had many conversations over the past month, but he'd never seen her so serious. And though he'd told her he was from Atlanta, he'd never shared the details of his family's deaths. Some things he still couldn't bring himself to talk about. But there was one thing she had to know.

"Sarah." He swallowed hard. "My family owned slaves. Not many. Just enough to help Mama 'round the house. They all left when the war started. 'Cept Isaac. He looked after Mama when Daddy died. I wanted you to know. I reckon it might change your mind 'bout me."

Her face softened, surprising him. A slap in the face seemed more appropriate. And then, when she patted his cheek, a lump rose in his throat.

"Mr. Carter, I expected it all along. The look you gave me when we first met said everythin'. But I have a gift for seein' beneath the surface. An if what you say 'bout Isaac be true, then I reckon your mama was good to your slaves. Some masters was kind. Mine wadn't. But that's all behind us now. An I reckon, even if you could, you'd never own another human. It ain't in your character. You're too good."

Yes, his mama was good to them. And it probably cost Isaac his life. He'd never have left her side.

He sat silently, taking it all in. She was right about slavery. No human should ever own another.

"One more thing, an then I'll leave you be." She took a deep breath and stood. "Mr. Finch sees Miss Gwen as a piece a property. One he'll own the minute she say, *I do.* Ain't that slavery? He may not whip her when she don't do what he want, but there are other ways a bein' cruel. She needs a man with a heart."

He looked into her dark eyes, which glistened with tears reflecting firelight. "Why do her folks want her to marry him if he's not right for her?"

"Cuz they's lookin' at the surface. Not what's underneath. An it ain't my place to set 'em straight." She put on her coat and headed to the door. "But it ain't too late for you."

The room was colder than ever after she left. He put another log on the fire, but still couldn't get warm. Her words haunted him. Did Gwen know what she was getting into? What could he do? Fear kept him glued to his seat.

* * *

The carriage came to a halt. Gwen peered out the window. Why did they stop so far from home? The weather was getting worse and it was too cold to be stopping on the road.

"Do you like the view?" Albert asked.

On any other day, she might. But the flurries kept her from seeing the ocean.

"Albert, why did you have the driver stop? We'll freeze to death out here."

He moved beside her and lifted the blanket he'd covered her with, then tucked it around both of them. "Let me warm you."

So this was his plan. Have her half frozen in the carriage so she'd beg him to be close.

"I want to go home."

"My dear, dear, Gwendolyn." His hand encircled her waist. Though it was warm, she didn't want it there. "How long will you have me wait for your affections?"

She pushed him away. "You'll wait until the preacher pronounces us married."

He grabbed her hands. "We're as good as married now. You're wearing my ring and you accepted my proposal. What's wrong with a small taste of what's to come?" He moved toward her with puckered lips.

Jerking her hand free, it flew to his face as if it had its own will, and hit him hard.

He leaned away from her, and with eyes popping out of his head, rubbed his cheek. "You struck me."

"I—I'm sorry. I don't know what came over me."

He opened the door and beat his hand against the side of the carriage. When he closed the door, the horses moved, and they were on their way again.

Instead of sitting beside her, he sat across from her and the look on his face lacked any trace of affection. Had she crossed the line?

"Gwendolyn." He pursed his lips. "I shan't hold this against you. *This* time. I will assume that the cold made you irritable and unreasonable. But the next time I offer affection, I expect you to accommodate me. I won't tolerate a frigid wife."

"I'm not yet your wife," she muttered under her breath.

"What's that? I didn't quite hear you."

"Nothing. It won't happen again."

He smiled a wry smile. "Good." Leaning forward, he placed his hand on her leg. "I assure you that what I have to offer you will be pleasing. You'll know soon enough." After a squeeze on her thigh, he leaned back and crossed his arms over his chest.

She pulled the blanket tightly around her and tried not to think about what he said. Instead, she thought of how wonderful it would be to get home, have Sarah heat some water for a bath, and soak away today's memories.

* * *

"What was he thinkin' keepin' you out in this cold?" Sarah asked as she poured another bucket full of hot water into the bathing tub.

Gwen sat huddled under a blanket, waiting for the tub to fill. "I don't know."

Sarah set the bucket down. "I know that tone. I reckon you *do* know."

It was always easy to talk to Sarah, but lately Sarah had been pushing her more and more to converse about things she didn't want to. And worse than anything, she kept bringing up John Carter.

"Yes, I know why." It couldn't hurt to tell her. "He thought that if I was cold enough, I'd let him warm me."

Sarah scowled, then mumbled something she couldn't hear. "I'll gets one more bucket a water, then it should be 'nuff."

"Thank you, Sarah."

Gwen couldn't wait to feel the heat surrounding her frozen limbs. There was nothing quite as wonderful as a hot bath.

Cuddled under the blanket, she began to calm. Should she have let Albert kiss her? After all, she kissed John.

What harm could it have done? Aside from the fact that she believed he wanted to do much more.

John ...

How many times had she relived that single moment? Her heart fluttered. If only Albert was John.

Sarah poured the last bucket and then tested the water with her hand. "Just right."

"Thank you again, Sarah."

"I'll leave you to soak." She started to walk away.

"Wait." Gwen didn't want her to leave. "I'd like to talk to you. Can you pull the screen in front of the tub and stay while I bathe?"

"If that's what you want." Sarah complied and positioned the changing screen in front of the bath tub, then took a seat on the far side of the room.

Gwen stood behind the screen and removed her clothes, then stepped into the warm, inviting water. She sighed as she scooted down, letting the heat penetrate her skin. Steam rose into the air and she breathed in deeply. A wonderful way to clear her head.

"Mmm ... This is heavenly, Sarah."

"Glad you like it." Sarah chuckled. "My mama used to fight to get us to bathe."

It was so rare to hear her mention her family. "You didn't like baths?"

"We was bathed in the river. Nothin' like your fancy tub." Sarah's chair scooted in a little closer.

"I know you miss them."

"I does. But I gots you now. 'Til Mr. Finch takes you away."

She'd finally gotten comfortable in the bath, then Sarah spoiled it by bringing up Albert. "Sarah, may I ask you something of a delicate nature?"

"I may not know the answer, but go on an ask."

How would she say it? She wasn't about to ask her mother, so Sarah seemed the logical person to speak to.

"Well ... Do you believe a woman can learn how to enjoy being affectionate with a man?"

Silence.

"Sarah?"

"I's thinkin'."

"You see, Albert wants me to be affectionate, but I don't feel that I want to. Truthfully, I find him offensive."

"Mmm, hmm."

"And, I know that I'll be expected to be affectionate after we're married. What if I still don't want to?"

"You shore you want me to answer?"

Gwen fanned her hand through the warm water and closed her eyes. She could stay here forever, but then she'd die more wrinkled than a prune. Sooner or later she had to get on with her life. She needed an answer. "Yes, I'm sure."

"You don't feels like bein' affectionate cuz you don't love the man. Affection comes natural with love."

"Father says I'll learn to love him."

Sarah grunted. "You're the smartest young woman I knows. But some things ain't meant to be learned. They's meant to be felt. If you don't feels it now, I reckon you may never feels it."

"Never?"

"Uh-uh. 'Specially when you feels it for someone else."

What could she say? Sarah was right. Sarah was always right. But John would be leaving soon. Maybe even before the wedding. Once he was gone, she could let him go. And then, she would have nothing to distract her from Albert.

"You drownin'?"

"Oh—no, Sarah. I was just thinking about what you said."

"Think hard, Missy. It ain't too late to change your mind 'bout marryin' that man."

Yes, it was. The invitations had already been sent. They expected over one hundred guests, and Martha was coming next week to help her with her wedding dress. She adored Martha, and wouldn't hurt her by making a mess of the wedding. And she'd never embarrass her parents over such a scandal.

"I's gonna leave you now, Miss Gwen. I thinks you knows what you needs to do. An I ain't talkin' 'bout bathin'."

Sarah's skirt rustled as she rose from the chair and left the room.

Deciding that she'd best get down to business and scrub her body before the water got cold, Gwen grabbed the bar of lye soap and glided it over her skin. She'd cringed when Albert touched her, but savored John's caress. Skin was skin, but that was not what made contact desirable. It went far deeper. Skin was just a layer over every man's body. What mattered was what drove the touch. Love or lust?

This was something that didn't take much thought. It was easy to know what pushed Albert, and it certainly wasn't love.

Chapter 19

Doctor Young's eyebrows rose. "What's this?

Gwen pushed the book across the desk. "My journal. I've not been writing in it, so I thought I should give it to you now. I doubt my notes will be very helpful."

He pushed it back to her. "Keep it. After all, I'm removing his cast tomorrow. You may want to write your observations regarding how well he copes without it."

She shoved it back. "I don't see him very much anymore. Only at dinner. And we don't ... *talk*."

The doctor arose from his desk, crossed the room, and shut the door. "Sit down, Miss Abbott."

She did as he requested, but knew she wasn't going to like what he had to say. She'd already heard it from Sarah. Nothing would change her mind.

He sat, removed his glasses, and rubbed his eyes. Then, after breathing on the lenses, he polished them with the hem of his jacket and put them back on. "I've been tending Mr. Carter for several months now, and what I've observed is that since you removed yourself from his life, he's become withdrawn again." He looked her in the eye. "And I've also observed that in that same time frame, you have lost what I always admired in you."

"What?" His words pierced her. "What have I lost?"

He frowned and shook his head. "Your spirit. You don't smile like you used to and I can tell that you're deeply troubled. For a woman who's about to be married, you should be ... giddy."

"Did you get your invitation?"

"Yes, I did. Thank you for including me."

The silence that fell between them made her squirm. She finally spoke. "I won't be here next week. And I may not come back. Father hasn't told me whether or not I'll be allowed to continue my schooling after I'm married."

"Miss Abbott, may I give you some advice?"

Why not? Everyone else had. "You may."

"Reconsider your marriage. If you're marrying simply for the comfort of having a husband provide for you, then consider this option. Finish your education. You're close to completing the necessary classes you need to take your nursing exams. I have no doubt you'll pass them. With that, you'll easily find employment. And I will gladly give you a letter of recommendation."

Twisting the ruby ring around her finger, she stared at her hands. If only it was that easy.

"Doctor Young, I appreciate your advice, but I accepted Mr. Finch's proposal. Nothing can change that."

"You've not yet said your vows."

"No, but I made him a promise. I won't break it."

She stood to leave.

"Miss Abbott." Doctor Young came out from behind his desk, holding the journal. "Take this with you. Please?"

With hesitation, she took it from his hands.

He finally smiled. "I don't want it back. I want you to go home tonight and read it, then write what you're feeling regardless of whether or not it has medical implications."

She nodded and left his office, believing it would be her last time there.

* * *

Jeb stared at his leg. It appeared extremely small and lifeless, but at least the cast was gone.

"How does it feel?" Doctor Young asked.

Jeb smiled and nodded at the doctor. The leg felt great, it was the rest of him that needed help.

"I have another gift for you." Dr. Young handed him a wooden cane. "You'll still have some sensitivity and the cane will help you until you get your strength back. But don't over-do." He gave him the look that Jeb would not soon forget. Over the glasses and with the authority of his daddy.

Jeb extended his hand and the doctor shook it firmly.

"You're a good man. I know character. Now, you can get dressed and go on home. I assume Mr. Abbott is waiting for you?"

Yes, Henry was waiting to take him home. Before they'd left work, Jeb had purchased a pair of black wool trousers, knowing he'd need an unaltered pair. Whether from the cast or the cold dry weather, he couldn't stop scratching the leg.

"Go easy on that leg," Dr. Young scolded. "I'll give you some lanolin cream. It will help."

After pulling the trousers up to his knees, he rose from his chair and stood, half afraid that his legs would buckle beneath him.

No pain.

He pulled the pants up to his waist and buttoned them. Whole again. But his heart was empty, knowing it was time to leave Boston.

Doctor Young rested his hand on Jeb's arm. "You look as sad as Miss Abbott. She was here earlier today."

Jeb closed his eyes and shook his head. In three days she'd be married. He couldn't stay around to see that happen.

"Mr. Carter, things aren't always as they seem. You've made a good life for yourself here in Boston. From what Mr. Abbott tells me, you've made great improvements to their business. You don't have to leave."

Spotting paper and pen on the doctor's desk, Jeb wrote:

YES I DO

Again, the eyes-over-the-glasses look. "If you leave, you'll be making a terrible mistake."

I HAVE NO CHOICE

"You always have a choice."

NOT THIS TIME

Doctor Young crossed his arms and shook his head. "Youth ..." he muttered and opened his office door. Henry stood on the other side, waiting.

"Look at you," Henry said. "Ready to do some dancing?" He followed his question with a bit of fancy footwork.

He can't be serious.

"Mr. Carter needs to go easy on his leg, Mr. Abbott," Dr. Young said. "Dancing is out of the question. At least for now."

"That's too bad. Friday night is the bachelor party—the last night of freedom for David and Albert. Of course, the ladies are invited. Without them, we'd not be able to dance."

Doctor Young rested his palm against Jeb's back. "Mr. Carter tells me he's leaving. I doubt he'll be attending your party."

Henry's lip curled. "Leaving? You can't leave before the wedding. And honestly, Father hoped you'd stay. Not in the *guesthouse* forever, but in Boston. He doesn't want to lose a good employee. You're one of us now."

Jeb shook his head.

"Take him home," Dr. Young said. "Perhaps you can convince him otherwise."

They left the office and headed down the hallway. It was strange leaving the crutches behind, and Jeb was grateful for the cane. It helped his confidence in walking.

He'd saved enough money for train fare, as well as food and lodging for a short period of time. Tired of the cold, he'd return to Atlanta. If Mrs. Chambers was right, it would be rebuilt, but needed people there to do the work. Atlanta was in his blood. And now that he had his head in a better place, maybe he could get a job rebuilding the rail lines and eventually another home on the old site.

Large snowflakes descended and a sheer blanket of white covered the ground.

They hustled into the carriage and brushed off the icy flakes.

"There's more room now with your cast and crutches gone." Henry smiled, but then his expression changed. "John, none of us wants you to go."

Jeb let out a long breath and looked apologetically at Henry. He'd grown to like the man and considered him and David both, friends. They'd not mentioned the war even once while they worked together. Maybe Gwen told them not to. He'd learned to like them as co-workers, striving for the same goals. And they'd even made him laugh a time or two, reminding him of his own brothers.

"Have you already bought your ticket?"

He shook his head.

"Good. I don't even know where you plan to go, but wherever it is, can't it wait until next week?"

Jeb stared blankly at him.

"What could it hurt? Besides, Violet's making a feast for the wedding. You could use a little more meat on your bones. Though I must say, you look a lot better than you did when you first arrived."

No, he couldn't bear the wedding.

Unable to respond, he watched the snow fall. Beautiful, but much too cold. The world seemed unusually quiet wrapped in a blanket of white. And when the horses halted and Henry opened the carriage door, silence hung even heavier.

His legs felt strangely light as he stepped out and onto the snow-covered ground. With his luck, he'd probably slip and fall, and end up in a cast again.

"Don't fall," Henry cautioned.

Had he read his thoughts?

A chuckle emerged from Jeb, surprising even himself. It resonated through the air. If Henry read thoughts, he'd have already pummeled him.

"Don't laugh. Even though it would be a way to keep you here, I don't want you to have to go through all that pain again."

Henry took his arm, helping him along the pathway. Now he felt like a toddler, struggling with his first steps.

He walked with Jeb all the way to the guesthouse, then opened the door for him.

"Will you be able to make it by yourself to the main house for dinner?"

Nodding, he walked through the door. The warm, roaring fire beckoned him.

He needed to wash for dinner, but had to hurry. With only ten minutes to spare, he probably should have gone there directly. Maybe Henry saw that he needed a shave. He hadn't bothered this morning and it wouldn't be polite to go to dinner unkempt.

As he glided the razor across his skin, he thought about Sarah. All of her tactics pushing him and Gwen together hadn't worked. Thinking of leaving Gwen—and the entire Abbott family—made his heart ache.

Looking in the mirror, he confirmed what his hands felt. Smooth. No trace of stubble, and surprisingly, no nicks. Time to go.

The snow started to accumulate. The crisp air filled his lungs, stinging, making him feel alive. He never would have experienced all this if he'd pulled that trigger.

What was I thinkin'?

Even with pain, no man should ever consider taking his own life. God had a purpose for him, and by putting one foot in front of the other, someday he'd find out what it was.

He paused and looked over his shoulder. His footprints were there, quickly disappearing with newly fallen flakes. A sense of pride filled him, taking away some of the chill. He'd moved forward with his life and he was grateful.

The main house boasted many fireplaces. One in almost every room, and all were ablaze. The scent of wood smoke drifted into his nose, followed by incredible smells coming from the kitchen. He'd miss Violet's cooking.

It was hard not to limp, even with the cane. Hopefully, in time, he'd walk normally again. But as he limped into the dining room, he froze to the floor when everyone broke into applause.

"Bravo!" David yelled.

"Look at him, Mother!" Katherine cheered.

Every face lit up brighter than the candles, as they expressed their joy.

This was all for him?

Even Gwen smiled, warming him more than all the fireplaces combined. Her smile was so large it pushed up her cheeks, and it made it all worthwhile.

"Come and sit," Mr. Abbott said, putting his arm around his shoulder. "Violet made fried chicken, just for you. We all know how much you like it."

Truly at a loss for words, Jeb took his seat. How would he ever be able to express his gratitude to this family?

As Gwen approached, he stood and pulled out her chair. She was more beautiful than ever in a pink dress. A color as soft as her skin. A whiff of her perfume overtook the scent of food. She smelled nothing like skunk. She was more woman than *any* man deserved.

"Thank you, Mr. Carter." She whispered the words, sending chills down his back.

He returned to his seat, thankful to be beside her. A final time, close to the woman he loved.

"Father, may I say the blessing?" Katherine asked.

"You may, my dear. But remember to keep it limited. We don't want the food getting cold."

Katherine wiggled in her chair, folded her hands, and bowed her head. Jeb couldn't help but grin, then quickly became reverent.

"Lord, please bless this fried chicken that Violet made. Help Mother to understand that I will probably need more than one piece of pie for dessert. And Lord, most important of all, thank you for making Mr. Carter's leg all better and for bringing him to our home. And if you see fit, make him stay. In the name of Jesus, I pray. Amen."

Jeb kept his eyes shut.

Help me find my way, Lord. Amen.

When he opened his eyes, he looked around the table. Everyone was staring at him. The smiles that had been there were gone.

"We truly would like you to stay," Mrs. Abbott said.

"Yes, we would," Mr. Abbott added. "Stay until you can find a place of your own. After all, we have plenty of room. You'll have to share the guesthouse Saturday night with friends coming for the wedding, but you won't need to leave."

"He should move into David's room when he's gone," Katherine said. "Then he won't have to walk so far for dinner."

"Kicking me out already, Katie?" David asked. "I'm hurt." He placed his hand over his heart and feigned pain, then laughed, causing Katherine to giggle.

Jeb's heart raced. He couldn't stay. He didn't belong here. Why couldn't they see that?

"Mr. Carter needs to make up his own mind," Gwen said. "You shouldn't be pushing him so hard. Let the poor man eat."

Poor man. She couldn't have said it better. That was the problem. He had nothing of value to offer her.

The mood lightened again as the food was passed around the table. Though he thought he couldn't eat, after one bite into the chicken leg, his appetite took hold. He needed to eat, because once again, he wasn't sure when he'd get his next meal.

Chapter 20

So little to pack. Jeb couldn't believe Mr. Abbott had given him a travel bag. Another gracious gift from a man he'd come to respect.

Tomorrow, he would have George drive him to the train station so he could get his ticket. Surely, there had to be a train heading south most any day of the week.

The creak of the front door was followed by the howl of the wind. It was late—nearly nine o'clock—who would be coming in? Sarah had to be asleep by now.

"John?"

Gwen?

He hastened from his room with his pounding heart driving him.

She'd already moved across the floor and stood with her back to the fire. As she unwound her scarf, he couldn't take his eyes from her face. The flickering fire-light cast shadows around the room, making her appear larger than life.

He brightened a lantern, allowing him to see her face more clearly. Her nose and cheeks were brilliant red, but she'd never looked lovelier.

"I—I had to come. Since you're leaving soon."

Tell me to stay and I'll stay forever.

He motioned for her to sit and she didn't hesitate complying.

Taking his place beside her, he thought of the kiss. It had happened here, and he wanted more than anything for it to happen again.

"I hoped I might convince you to stay for the party Friday night. I understand why you don't want to come to the wedding. But Henry and David have grown fond of you and they want you there. Father does as well. It's truly a night for the men, but we ladies will have our place in the background."

He stood and went to his room. For once, he was able to get his own paper and pen.

ALBERT WON'T WANT ME THERE

"Albert won't notice one way or another. If you haven't seen it yourself, Albert is only concerned with Albert."

WHAT ABOUT YOU?

"Me? Well, of course, *I* want you there."

NO. NOT WHAT I MEAN. IS ALBERT CONCERNED WITH YOU?

"Oh." She unbuttoned her coat, then immediately began fidgeting with her skirt. "He's concerned about me. But truthfully, I believe he will always put himself first."

NOT RIGHT

"John, I didn't come here tonight to talk about Albert. I came because I have something to say to you."

I'M LISTENING

"I meant it when I told you that I love you. And when you leave, you'll take a part of me with you. But I believe that the kind of love we've felt for each other is a doctor-patient sort of thing. I read about it in my medical books. Patients sometimes become infatuated with their doctors."

YOU'RE NOT A DOCTOR

"No, I'm not. But, I've had a similar role in your life. And since I'm a female, and you're a male, it provided an opportunity for ... infatuation. After all, it would be quite unlikely for you to become infatuated with Doctor Young."

Why was she trying to discount their feelings? Her role as his caregiver gave them time together. Time to realize they shared common interests. Time to see that their hearts were suited for each other—like two puzzle pieces locking together.

I LOVE YOU!

"It will pass, John. Just as I'm certain my feelings for you will go with you. You're the first patient that Doctor Young asked me to journal. He wanted me to be specific with him about your progress and get to know you. I have to believe that is why I feel the way I do."

NO

Maybe another kiss would convince her.

He took her face in his hands and moved toward her, but she grasped his hands, stopping him.

"No, John. Not this time."

He closed his eyes and his shoulders slumped. Her refusal might as well have been a knife in his chest.

"Stay until Friday for my family. Wherever you may be going, most trains have routes on Saturday." She stood and fastened her coat. "I'm sorry if I hurt you."

And as quickly as she came in, she left.

He didn't move from the sofa. After pulling a blanket around his body, he laid his head back.

She was sorry if she hurt him? He didn't believe a word of what she said. All that talk about patient-doctor infatuation was completely ridiculous.

She's just tryin' to convince herself. Make marryin' Albert seem like the right thing to do.

His heart slowed and he made up his mind. He'd go to their party Friday night and watch her with Albert. Prove to himself he was right. And maybe if he was lucky, prove it to her, too.

* * *

Home - November 29th, 1865

Mr. Carter has adjusted well to the use of a cane.

Has gained approximately 20 lbs. since arrival at MGH.

Gwen stopped. Thinking about what Doctor Young had told her, she decided to be a bit bolder in her writing. Since he said to write her feelings and since no one else would ever read this, why not?

His weight gain suits him. His body has filled out, and after the extensive use of crutches, his arms are quite muscular.

Her heart pounded and she had to fan herself with her hand.

I told him tonight of my belief that our feelings for one another will pass. That they are simply a result of our working relationship. So, when he leaves here, I should feel normal again. And that's a very good thing since I'll no longer be …

Single? Is that what she wanted to write? Or that she'd no longer be Gwen Abbott? She would be Mrs. Albert Finch. And just who was that? That person would be the furthest thing from *normal* that she could ever be.

He wanted to kiss me and I didn't let him.

Oh, what she would give for one more kiss from his lips. But the only kiss she had waiting for her was a kiss from Albert that would seal them forever as man and wife.

Her hand trembled, as she continued to write:

Evaluation: John Carter is sane, good, loving, and wonderful. And his leg seems to be healed.

As for his caregiver, she's a complete mess.

* * *

Jeb had never before set foot in the ballroom. Already filling with guests, he blended in. It helped not having the crutches drawing attention.

There were more men than women, but that was the purpose. This was the night that the two *doomed bachelors* kicked up their heels for a final time.

A four piece band made up of a piano player, a guitarist, a man on a bass cello, and a singer, were already entertaining. Some of the lyrics of their songs were a bit off-color, but not so blatant to insult the female guests.

Jeb chuckled, watching the women cover their mouths at the insinuations. Tittering, but not offended.

He was thankful that the Abbott's didn't indulge in alcohol. Adding intoxication to the mix could be disastrous. It appeared everyone in the room came for a good time, honoring the grooms-to-be.

His heart jumped when he spotted Gwen. She stood on the far side of the room next to Martha. David's fiancée was pretty, but paled next to Gwen. Both wore light blue. He shook his head. Soon they'd have to wear darker, more dismal colors, made for mature, married women.

He popped his forehead with the butt of his hand. He'd promised himself not to think about that tonight. It was time to stand back and enjoy the evening. Watch her with Albert and see if she noticed *him.*

Since he'd agreed to attend the party, he'd purchased a black suit. And when Henry insisted that the red tie went with it, he bought it, too.

A bellowed laugh caught his ear and he turned to see who it came from. Of course, it was Albert Finch. Who else would be so happy tonight?

Albert had his head bent close to another man, who was obviously telling a story, one spoken so low that Albert nearly had to put his ear on the man's mouth. The man's hands moved as he spoke, then made a gesture Jeb found more than foul. Again, Albert erupted into laughter.

So this was the man she would marry? Maybe what Jeb needed to do was sneak to her room tonight and steal her away. It was worth a thought.

He inched his way closer to her, only to watch as David whisked her onto the dance floor.

"They love to dance," Martha said, coming up beside him. "Gwen can polka like no one else."

So could he before he'd broken his leg. Polka was a favorite at the barn dances back home. But once the war came, no one felt like dancing anymore.

The air in the room heated as bodies filled the dance floor. With scarce women, some of the men danced together, which only increased the laughter in the room. As men stepped on each other's toes, they cursed in gest and argued over who was supposed to be leading.

"You would think they would mind their language," Martha said. "They forget there are ladies present."

Jeb hadn't forgotten. He couldn't take his eyes off Gwen.

When the song ended, David twirled her a final time, then guided her over to where he and Martha stood.

Gwen was out of breath, but laughing regardless.

So beautiful ...

She finally caught his eye. "Oh, Mr. Carter? I didn't see you come in."

He fanned his arms wide and bowed.

"He's just in time," David said, panting. "Henry's about to sing."

This should be amusin'.

Henry crossed the floor to the stage, then hopped on top of the piano and sat. Laughter filled the room.

"Tonight," Henry proclaimed, and tucked his thumbs into his braces, puffing out his chest. "Is the final night of freedom for my dear brother, David, and future brother-in-law, Albert Finch."

Applause and more laughter. Mr. Abbott clapped louder than anyone, urging his son on.

"As most of you know, David and I spent a bit of time down south not long ago." His final words were said with the worst attempt at a southern accent Jeb had ever heard. But, worse than that, he didn't like where this was leading.

"My brother," he continued, still using the crude accent. "Had a run-in with some good ol' southern boys. But David has an aim like no other and he put them all in an early grave. Thankfully, he managed to leave a few for me."

More laughter. Jeb was ready to run.

"Then, when he got to Atlanta, well let's just say—my brother always knew how to build a good fire!"

Jeb's palms sweat and he tightened his fists. Even though he was aware that David knew Sherman personally, he didn't want to believe he'd ever been in Atlanta.

The applause in the room sickened him and he started backing away.

"So, tonight, I'm gonna sing me a song in tribute to our good neighbors of the south. One that the ladies might just like." He wiggled his brows and nodded to the piano player.

The pianist's hands flew over the keys and his body moved along with the rhythm. Guests began clapping to the beat.

"Well ..." Henry jumped to his feet, still atop the piano. "I come from Alabamy with my banjo on my knee. I'm goin' to Weezeanna, my true love for to see."

Lord, no.

Jeb's chest tightened and he covered his ears.

Please stop.

"Oh, Susanna, oh don't you cry for me! For I come from Alabamy with my banjo on my knee!" As Henry sang the chorus, others in the crowd joined in.

Jeb couldn't take it anymore. Pushing past everyone blocking the doorway, he rushed from the room. With a mixture of a hop and a skip, trying his best to run, he stumbled down the hallway.

How could I think they was any different than any other Yankee?

The man he'd called friend had just hit him harder with words than any fist. It was the one song that reminded him of his mama, and it brought back all the pain. Made him remember where he came from and why he hated the north. For all he knew, David had carried the torch that burned his home. And maybe he and Henry pulled the triggers that killed his brothers.

He wouldn't wait another minute. He'd leave tonight.

* * *

John?

He pushed through the crowd. The torment in his eyes was something Gwen had seen before. It was there the day she'd met him.

Not even considering the cold air, she rushed out the back door without a coat. Snow alighted on her skin, but she didn't care. She had to get to him.

Jerking the door open, she rushed into the guesthouse. "John?"

Lantern light pulsed from his room, so she wasted no time getting there.

Even in the dim light, she could see he was breathing hard. His shoulders moved rapidly up and down as he threw his belongings into the bag.

"John, what's wrong?" She laid her hand on his arm, making him jump.

He turned to face her, flashing more hatred than she'd ever seen before. "What? I don't understand. What happened?"

He glared at her, then turned and began fastening the straps around his bag.

"No. Don't leave. Not like this. You have to tell me what happened."

She grabbed his paper and handed it to him.

He swatted it and it fell to the floor.

Unable to control herself, she started to cry. All of the progress she'd made with him meant nothing if he left this way. "Please, John. Please tell me." She sniffled and tried to stop her tears.

He stood perfectly still, then gradually turned to face her.

His face lost all expression, but at least the hate was gone. He raised his hand and wiped away her tears with his thumb. And then he closed his eyes and shook his head. His body folded in, and she had to hold him.

The warmth from his body permeated her dress. Holding him felt right. He was so much more to her than a medical project, how could she have ever thought otherwise? Her heart ached for him now. Feeling his pain, she wanted more than anything to take it all away.

"Gwendolyn?"

Before she had a chance to say a word, Albert's strong hands grasped her shoulders, jerking her away from John.

"Albert—I-"

"Be quiet, Gwendolyn!" He pushed her to the back of the room and faced John. "What were you doing with my fiancée?" He huffed out the words, then sneered, and shoved John's shoulder.

John took a step back and glared at him.

"Oh, I forgot. You're mute. But it seems you still have a way with the ladies." He drew his fist back, then planted it into John's jaw.

He stumbled backward, hit the wall, then dropped down to the floor.

"What are you doing?" Gwen yelled and grabbed Albert's arm before he could strike him again.

"I'm protecting your honor, my dear. I may have just prevented him from assaulting you."

"That man has more manners than you'll ever dream of having!"

Albert's once-handsome face snarled into something hideous. "You're defending him? Why, Gwendolyn? Has something happened between the two of you?"

Her body quivered, fearful of the man she'd vowed to marry. She looked at the floor, unable to look him in the eye.

"I see." He took her by the arm and dragged her toward the door.

"Albert, you're hurting me." His hand was like a vice on her skin, tightening with each step they took.

"I'm not hurting you, Gwendolyn. I'm going to teach you how to be a proper wife."

"Let 'er go!"

They froze in place. The air fell silent, as if the world itself was astonished by the outcry.

Albert jerked her around so they were both looking at John, whose feet were firmly planted on the floor. His hands were in front of him, formed into fists, ready for a fight.

Albert laughed. "My, my. It seems your mute learned how to speak. And not only can he speak, but was that a trace of southern drawl I heard?"

"I said, let 'er go!" John's chest heaved as he stared Albert down.

"Oh, yes," Albert gloated. "Definitely southern."

"John? I—don't understand." Gwen couldn't believe what she was hearing. Why now?

"Come now, Gwendolyn. Isn't it obvious? He's a rebel." Albert still hadn't loosened his grip. If anything, it was even tighter. "He never intended to be in Boston and pretended he couldn't speak. Otherwise, I doubt they'd have saved him. Doctor Young may be a good doctor, but no man in his right mind would want to help a rebel pig."

John lurched forward and grabbed Albert by his coat. "I told you to let 'er go. I won't have you hurtin' Gwen." Though he'd freed her from Albert's vice, the two men were now wrestling on the floor, grunting and hitting like two bull elk fighting for the rights to a cow.

The front door opened and her brothers rushed in.

"David, Henry," she pleaded. "Make them stop!"

Without questioning what had happened, David grabbed Albert and Henry took hold of John.

"Let me finish him!" Albert yelled. "He's a rebel!"

"What?" Henry held onto John, who was trying to wrench himself free.

"I ain't no rebel! I ain't no different than any y'all. Least *I* didn't burn down *your* house!"

Gwen couldn't believe her ears. Given time to think amidst all the confusion, everything made sense. It was no wonder he didn't talk. He didn't want them to know the truth. And then when Henry sang that song ...

"Everyone needs to calm down," David said, holding fast to Albert. "Albert, take Gwen and go back to the house. Henry and I will take care of this."

"But I-" Gwen tried to speak her mind.

"You heard your brother," Albert said. "They'll take care of Mr. Mute. Come with me."

David released him and he yanked Gwen's arm, hauling her out the door. He forced her down the path.

"I don't want to go anywhere with you." She pushed against his chest, but couldn't get him to loosen his hold.

"Why? Don't tell me you care for that man?"

They stopped on the pathway, paying no attention to the cold wind whipping around their bodies.

"What if I do?"

His body jerked and he slapped her face. "Get over it."

And with those words, he pushed her along the pathway until they reached the main house.

Her cheek stung, but nothing hurt worse than the pain in her heart. She needed more answers from John. But one thing she knew for certain, she'd never marry Albert. How could she get away from him in order to convince her father?

* * *

Jeb plopped down on the sofa.

"You can talk?" Henry asked, sitting beside him.

Jeb nodded. "Yep." Even though he saw these two men through different eyes, somehow he couldn't stop feeling a kinship to them. Maybe his hate went out the door with Albert.

David sat across from them and folded his hands, staring at Jeb. "Why didn't you tell us?"

"Would you a given me the job? Helped me at all?"

David looked at the ground and Henry didn't make a sound.

"Reckon that's a *no*?"

Since they remained silent, Jeb decided to speak his mind. "You shouldn't be sittin' here while that man has his hands on Gwen. 'Fore you got here, he was hurtin' her. Holdin' her so tight she nearly cried. She don't need to be marryin' the likes a him. Are y'all so blind, you don't see it?"

"Albert loves her," David said. "He's a good man. He'd never hurt her."

"So, you're callin' me a liar?"

"Coming from a man who pretended not to have the ability to speak, what can you expect?" David stood and folded his arms across his chest. "It's good that you're leaving. I don't want Gwen hurt any further."

Jeb's blood boiled. "I'd never hurt Gwen. I may a lied 'bout my speakin' an all, but I'll never lie where Gwen's concerned. I love her."

"You love Gwen?" Henry asked, rising to his feet. "No wonder Albert was angry. You have no business loving my sister. You southerners do understand what *engaged* means, don't ya?"

This was the old Henry. The one he didn't like.

"We *southern boys* have more manners than all y'all put together. You could learn a thing or two from us."

The air grew hot and not from the flames. Two brothers against one southern rebel. Jeb didn't stand a chance. Besides, he honestly didn't want to fight them.

"I'll finish packin'. I'll leave tonight."

"The sooner the better," Henry said. "And if I find out that you hurt Gwen ..." He lifted his fist and shook it at Jeb.

"Ask her," Jeb said. "I ain't never hurt her. She knows me better than anyone."

David motioned to Henry. "Let's go back. I don't want Martha worried about me."

They walked toward the door and Jeb stood without moving, watching them go. "I'm tellin' you," he said as they opened the door. "Albert's the one you need to worry 'bout!"

The door slammed shut.

Chapter 21

Jeb glanced at the Bible on the end table. No, it wasn't his, so he'd leave it there. Besides, what good had it done him?

"Why did you make me come here?" He shook his fist toward the ceiling, raging at God.

"He had His reasons."

Startled by the fact that he wasn't alone, he turned toward Sarah. She stood in the doorway of his room with her hands folded casually in front of her.

"Why?"

"You'll understan' one day." She sat in the rocker, but didn't move. "I heard what happened. Folks is all upset. You're lucky they's still in there celebratin', so they don't come lookin' for you. Henry says you're leavin'."

"Course I'm leavin'. I hate it here. I'm goin' home where I belong."

For a long while, she didn't speak. Then she took a deep breath. "What happened to you to fill you full a hate?"

Where should he begin? If he told her everything, it could take all night.

"I'll tell you what happened. That man in there ..." He pointed toward the main house. "Helped kill my family. Maybe both of 'em did. But I know now that David was in Atlanta an helped to see it burned. An my mama—her name was Suzanne. *Oh, Susanna.*" The memory of Henry's song disgusted him and he gritted his teeth. "She an my little sister, Anna, hid in the root cellar. An when the house was set to flames, they died there."

He lifted the porcelain hand from the bed stand and placed it in Sarah's palm. "It's all that's left of my sister. She named her doll Betsy. Carried it with her wherever she went. I found this in the ashes."

Sarah's eyes pooled with tears as she fingered the tiny hand. "You shore they was in there?"

He nodded.

"Yessir," Sarah sighed. "You gots reason to hurt. But hate will only cause you more pain. I seen you with love in your eyes. Love for Miss Gwen. Love don't never die. You gots to hold on to that."

"What's there to hold on to? Albert Finch yanked her outta my life."

"He ain't right for her."

"You don't hafta tell *me* that." He looked deeply into her eyes. "Try to help her. David an Henry don't believe me. But I know he hurt her."

"I'll do what I can. But now, you listen to me. Mr. Abbott told George to takes you to the train station when the sun comes up. So you'd best be ready to go. But tonight, you lock that door. I don't trust Mr. Finch."

Jeb glanced at his packed bag. He'd planned to leave tonight, but it was a ridiculous thought. He'd freeze before he ever made it to the train station. This was going to be a very long night. He'd never be able to sleep.

"Sarah ..." He took her hand in his. "You've been a good friend. Thank you. I'll never forget you."

She patted his hand. "I won't never forget you neither, John."

"Truthfully, my name's Jeb."

"Jeb Carter." She chuckled. "It shouldn't surprise me. It's a good, strong southern name. I likes it."

"It's who I am."

"And who you always need to be. Don't never pretend to be anythin' else. You hear me?"

He nodded. He was done pretending.

Sarah left after giving him a hug and he moved his bag with his few belongings into the living room. After locking the doors, he nestled down on the sofa and watched the fire dance, hoping it would lull him to sleep and quickly bring the morning.

* * *

Albert kept Gwen securely at his side. His fingerprints would be branded into her bruised arm.

When David and Henry returned to the ballroom, they approached them and questioned Albert about the altercation. Of course, he told them he was defending her honor and they believed him. The moment she tried to speak, Albert's grip intensified.

"He'll be leaving in the morning," David said. "Long before the wedding. I'm sorry this happened, Albert. We had no idea."

"You should consider pressing charges," Albert said. "Not only did he assault your sister, his actions were fraudulent. For all you know, he may have been embezzling funds from your father."

Gwen shook her head. "I doubt ..." The pain in her arm was unbearable and she stopped speaking.

Albert smiled at her brothers. "Gwendolyn isn't feeling well. I believe he may have hurt her." He looked directly at her. "Why don't we have some punch, my dear? You look thirsty."

He shuffled her away from the crowd, past the punch bowl, and out into the hallway. Glancing around the room, he moved her further down the hall until they came to the library. He pushed her through the door and shut it tight.

Gwen rubbed her arm. "You can't keep me silent forever, Albert."

"My dear, I'm protecting you. Don't you see that?"

"Protecting me? By nearly breaking my arm in two?"

He motioned for her to take a seat. The calm that came over his face, prompted her to oblige him. At least he'd stopped squeezing her like a boa constrictor.

He positioned himself in a seat across from her, then leaned in and gently took her hands. Raising one hand to his lips, he kissed it. "Now, isn't that better?"

"What's wrong with you?"

"With me? Nothing is wrong with me. All I've done tonight is save you. If something happened between you and that man, it happened without your knowledge of his true identity. He misled you, Gwendolyn. I can't fault you for that. After all, you're a woman. You judge with your heart, not your mind."

Why did he suddenly make sense? Had John purposefully deceived her to manipulate her affections? He kissed her. He made her believe he was someone he wasn't. And honestly, she didn't know *who* he was. Even now. He'd never answer the important questions. How could he love her, but also deceive her?

"All I need to know is ..." Albert rubbed his thumbs over her skin. "Did he *have* you?"

"Heaven's no!" How could he ask such an appalling question?

"Don't be angry, my dear. I needed to know. It's my right, since we're to be wed tomorrow."

She licked her lips and calmed. What did she expect him to believe? He'd walked in and found her in John's arms. "I'm sorry. You're being very understanding. My chastity is not an issue."

Lifting his hand, he brushed her cheek. "Show me that it's me you love." He moved closer, mere inches from her lips.

How could she deny him now?

"I do," she whispered and held her breath.

His lips were nothing like John's. They covered her mouth, engulfing her; wet and warm. He pulled her close to his body and kissed her longer and harder. She couldn't breathe. He was once again the constrictor, squeezing the life from her body.

Finally, it ended, and she gasped for air.

He ran his hand down the side of her face. "My dear, Gwendolyn. Tomorrow I'll give you so much more."

Tomorrow ...

Her mind reeled. Only ten minutes ago she was ready to leave him forever, and now she allowed a kiss. Never had she been more confused.

He lifted her to her feet, and with a gentle hand, led her back to the ballroom. The party was winding down and some of the guests had already departed. Carriages lit by lantern light carried them home along snowy paths. Other guests would be staying in the main house on the third floor. Including Albert. And then tomorrow, his family would arrive for the wedding.

They danced a final waltz, then she told him good-night and headed up the stairs to her room. Albert remained with Henry and David, and as she walked away, she could have sworn she heard the name, John Carter.

Would they harm him?

Please God, no.

Somehow, she knew John meant her no harm. If only he'd spoken sooner.

Chapter 22

The sun had barely peeked into the sky when Jeb awoke to a loud knock at the door. He'd slept little, and the only time he was fully asleep, he'd dreamt about Gwen. Not a pleasant dream, but a horrid nightmare.

How can she marry that man?

If she was his wife, he'd never hurt her. Ever.

The snow had deepened overnight, and as he bundled up in his warmest clothes, as well as the scarf and gloves Sarah was kind enough to give him, he looked behind him one more time. Three months in a city he never meant to be in, two of them in a home he wished was his own.

Would his mind ever be right again?

Even with heavy clothing, he shivered in the carriage. George had said little to him as he opened the door and stepped inside. He'd never gotten to know the man. What was the need?

The further they went down the road, his heart burned in his chest. He closed his eyes and leaned his head against the back of the seat. Soon he hoped to be on a train. If luck was on his side, he wouldn't have to stay long at the station.

"Need help?" George asked, opening the door.

"Thank you, but no." Using his voice was unnatural. But it would be better when he was around other folks that talked the same. They wouldn't look at him as though he was the enemy—which in every sense, he was.

And now, he had to ask for a ticket to Atlanta. How well would that go over?

The agent's lip curled at Jeb's request.

"Leave's at nine. You'll have to change trains in Cincinnati. Think you can manage?"

"Yessir. Thank you." He left the ticket counter, followed by a loud grunt from the agent.

Three hours until the train left the station. Until he was home, he wouldn't speak another word.

* * *

Had she slept at all? Gwen cuddled beneath the blankets, never wanting to leave her bed. She raised her fingers to her lips, thought about Albert's kiss, and shuddered at the memory. The promise of more to come sickened her.

She pressed her palm against her forehead. No fever. So why did she feel so horribly ill? Her stomach churned and her body ached. She had to be coming down with *something*.

"Miss Gwen?"

The gentle rap at her door was Sarah. It was awfully early for her to be coming to her room.

She arose reluctantly, donned a robe, and moved toward the door.

"Sarah, is something wrong?"

Sarah placed one finger against her lips. "Shh. I don't wants to wake the others." She scooted into Gwen's room and shut the door behind her.

"What is it?"

Sarah's brow furrowed and her lips pursed. "Why'd you go an let that man leave?"

"John?"

"Course, John. But his real name's Jeb. Sumthin' else he was 'fraid to tell you. What was you thinkin' lettin' him go? That man loves you more than Mr. Finch ever will. You're marryin' the wrong man."

Not again. They'd been over this too many times already. Gwen didn't want to hear it now. Another lie only solidified her decision. Her wedding was a mere nine hours away, and *Jeb* Carter would be forgotten.

"Sarah," she spoke as calmly as she could. "Mr. Carter lied to me. He pretended to be mute to gain my sympathy. How could you ever believe that was an indication of love?"

Sarah took her by the arm and led her to the bed. "Sit down. We needs to talk."

At least Sarah didn't wrench her arm like Albert had. So, she sat, and gave her full attention. "Go on ..."

"Ain't you figgered out why he done it? That poor man was scared wakin' up at Mass General. Put yourself in his shoes."

Gwen sighed. Maybe he was scared, but it was no reason to lie. Especially to her. She kept her thoughts to herself and let Sarah continue.

"An last night at the party, when your brother sang that song, do you know what it did to him?"

Gwen shook her head.

"I'll have you know that Mr. Carter came from Atlanta, and his mama's name was Suzanne. She an his little sister burned cuz a General Sherman. They was hidin' 'neath the floorboards in the root cellar when their house burned to the ground. He handed me this."

Sarah opened her palm and Gwen gasped looking at the porcelain hand.

Tears filled her eyes, as she tried to focus on the tiny object. It was all coming together. He'd said his sister had burned, but she'd never imagined this.

"David was there," Gwen mumbled. "I have to talk to him." She wiped her eyes with her robe. No wonder Jeb was so angry. He knew that David was in Atlanta and when Henry made light of the way he'd killed all those men and helped burn the city, he might as well have put a bullet in Jeb. *Jeb*. The name was foreign.

"You do that, but I reckon it's too late. They made Mr. Carter leave. He's hurtin' sumthin' awful, Miss Gwen."

"Why didn't you come to me last night? I could have stopped him."

"I tried." Sarah stood and moved slowly toward the door. "Mr. Finch stopped me from comin' to you. He stayed outside your door all night. Din't leave 'til he saw the carriage drive away."

Gwen's fists tightened. If she wasn't a lady, she'd give him a piece of her mind. But she'd do much worse—she'd let her father handle him.

Without bothering to dress, she marched across the room past Sarah.

"What you gonna do, Miss Gwen?"

"What I should have done last night."

Her parent's room was at the far end of the hall on the same floor. As a child, she'd often made her way there on stormy nights, but she hadn't done so in a very long time.

She slowly pushed their door open and paused to listen.

Her father was snoring, so she tiptoed across the floor to her mother's side of the bed.

"Mother," she said in a loud whisper. She gently shook her shoulder.

Her eyes popped wide. "What is it, dear?" She sat up and stared at her.

Her father grumbled and rolled over. "Grace?"

"Gwen is here, William. She doesn't look well."

Wonderful. Her mother just confirmed everything. She grabbed a chair and scooted it close to the bed. "I'm sorry for waking you, but I have something to say."

Both parents were now fully awake and looking at her as though she'd lost her mind.

"Couldn't it have waited?" her father asked. "At least until breakfast?"

"No. There's no time to waste."

Her mother patted his shoulder. "Wedding jitters. I had them, too."

"No, Mother. It's not that. I—I can't marry Albert."

Her father threw his hands in the air. "Can't marry him? Grace, talk some sense into your daughter." He rolled over and yanked the blanket up to his neck.

Before her mother uttered a word, Gwen removed her robe and pulled up the sleeve of her nightgown. "Do you see this?" The bruise on her arm had grown dark overnight and looked horrid against her pale skin.

"What did you do?" her mother asked, peering closely.

"Albert did this. And not only that, he slapped my face. He claimed it was for my own good, but ..." She burst out crying. "In all my life, no one has treated me this way."

Her father flipped over and rose up to look at her arm. "Albert Finch did that?" Air hissed from his nostrils. "And slapped you?" His face turned crimson—his eyes were on fire. "I'll boot him into the snow!"

"Father, please. Don't. Just ask him to leave and break our engagement. I don't love him. Truthfully, I love ..." Could she say his name? Her heart pounded and she sniffled away tears. What would they say?

"You love someone else?" Her mother's eyes blinked slowly.

Gwen gave her a slow, steady nod. "Mr. Carter."

Her father sat fully upright and looked warily at her with his arms folded across his chest. At least he'd stopped fuming. "But we just learned that he's a rebel. Though he may have been the finest employee I ever had, he shouldn't have deceived us."

"He was scared. Would you have allowed him to stay here and work at the store if you'd known? No, you wouldn't. Humans are no different than any other animal. They do what they have to in order to survive."

His arms jiggled against his abdomen as he chuckled under his breath. "You're beginning to sound like a professor. At least I know my money hasn't been wasted on your education."

She didn't want to talk about that now. That would come later. "Father—Mr. Carter came from Atlanta. When Henry said all those things about David at the party, and then sang that song, it hurt him deeply."

Pouring her heart out, she told everything she knew.

"Jeb?" he asked. "No matter how you feel about him, Gwendolyn, it's best he's gone. It would never work between the two of you. You're an Abbott, for heaven's sake. Abbotts cannot align themselves with southern rebels."

"Your father's right." Her mother patted her hand. "But I believe he and I are both in agreement that your marriage to Albert Finch shan't take place. We won't have our daughter bruised and beaten. I have a good mind to speak to his mother about his behavior."

Her father shook his head.

"It may not be a proper thing for me to do, William, but something has to be done. And you know we'll have many devastated guests."

"Our guests will witness a beautiful wedding." Gwen grasped her mother's hand. "David and Martha genuinely love each other. I'll never love Albert. He's—not what you thought he was. I tried, truly I did."

She traced invisible lines around the border of the quilt covering her parents. The relief over their agreement to release her from her marriage obligation was suddenly replaced with fear. Her eyes popped open wide. "How will I tell him?"

"You won't." Her father raised his chin in the air. "I'll deal with Mr. Finch." His words prompted a smile from her mother.

"You don't intend to harm him, do you Father?"

"No more than he hurt you."

Gwen rubbed her hand over her bruised arm, then pulled the ruby ring from her finger and handed it to him. Albert wasn't going to enjoy what was in store for him. After kissing her parents in turn, she left their room. Their grumbles followed her into the hallway.

Returning to her room, she closed and locked the door. Until she was confident that Albert was off their property, she wouldn't risk another encounter with him.

Should she go after Jeb? Her father wouldn't approve, and it was possible he was already out of Boston. Besides, it was David's wedding day. He and Martha deserved happiness. It would be hard enough to deal with their guests' questions. She had to help them as much as she could. If it was meant to be, her time with Jeb would come.

Even so, nothing would stop her from asking David about Atlanta.

Chapter 23

"Gwendolyn!" Albert's loud voice rang out, all the way down the hallway.

Gwen pressed her forehead against her bedroom door as his words become faint, accompanied by the sound of all three Abbott men escorting him from the house. Not one happy sound.

She felt a slight bit sorry for him, but that quickly passed. How could she have ever thought his reasons for hurting her were justified?

Manipulative man.

Thank goodness her parents understood. If it took a bruised arm for them to see him for what he was, then it was worth the pain.

Her white wedding gown caught her eye. It hung on a peg on the side of her wardrobe. What would she do with it now? Not wanting to see it any longer, she moved it inside and placed it behind all of her other dresses.

She let out a deep, weary breath. It would be a very long day.

Selecting a warm, long-sleeved light blue dress, she set about getting ready. This time of year she appreciated all the layers of undergarments. Anything to keep her body warm.

I hope Jeb's warm.

If he was from Atlanta, he wasn't used to this kind of weather—especially snow. Once again, she had an abundant list of questions for him. And now, they could actually converse. She'd heard him say so few words, but the sound of his voice lingered. With an accent she'd once considered an indication of a lack of education; he was one of the smartest men she'd ever known. Even her father agreed with her on that matter.

She fingered the bouquet of paper roses displayed beside her bed.

I have to talk to David.

Knowing it was safe to leave her room, she rushed down the stairs. Voices came from the kitchen and the scent of bacon filled her nose. Breakfast was the last thing on her mind, but she hastened to them.

"We should have listened to John," Henry said, then caught her eye as she entered the room.

"You mean, *Jeb*," her father corrected him.

"Why?" Gwen asked. "What did he tell you?"

David crossed to her and put his arm around her shoulder. "He told us Albert hurt you and we didn't believe him. He said we should ask you. I wish now that we had."

There were a lot of things she wished they'd done differently, but there was nothing she could do about that now.

"David," she looked up into his eyes. "I know you don't like to talk about what happened during the war, but I need to know something." She motioned to the table.

They all sat. An uncomfortable silence hung between them.

She took David's hand and once again retold the story that Sarah had shared.

"Yes," she said, "his mother's name was Suzanne. And both she and his little sister died when their house was burned."

David pulled his hand back and tipped his head, taking in what she said.

"David," she went on. "Why would you burn a house with people inside? I know it was war, but I never thought you'd burn women and children."

He rapidly shook his head. Henry did as well, looking utterly confused.

"We *never* intentionally harmed women or children," David said. "And before we burned Atlanta, General Sherman ordered us to go from house to house looking for them, as well as people who were bedridden—anyone unable to fight—so that we could tell them to leave. People left in droves, fearing what was to come."

The distress in her brother's eyes made her wish she hadn't asked. Even so, she needed to know more.

"So why would he think that they burned with the house? He found this in the ashes." She laid the tiny hand on the table.

David touched it, then drew back and closed his eyes. When they opened again, they were shadowed with un-shed tears. He covered his mouth with his hand and shook his head. "She cried for the doll."

"What?"

"You said his mother's name was *Suzanne?*"

Gwen nodded and swallowed the enormous lump rising in her throat. Her heart pounded.

Every eye followed David as he stood from the table.

"What do you know about this, son?" their father asked.

David crossed to the window and put his hand against the glass. He gazed outside as if he was in another world, far away from the rest of them in the room. Had she pushed too hard?

"The home was grand. Beautiful. Pillared front. Gardens." He ran his finger along the edges of the pane, speaking as though he was caught in a dream. "I sent my men in to make certain it was empty. They found a woman and a child in the cellar. There was also a Negro. He kept saying, *don't hurt Miss Suzanne,* and wouldn't leave her side. She screamed when we threw in the torches and tried to run into the house. My men grabbed her and held her while she kicked and yelled. The little girl clung to the Negro and cried because she'd dropped her doll."

Tears trickled down Gwen's cheeks. "What happened to them?"

David turned to face her, white as a ghost. "The woman was hysterical. Uncontrollable. They took her away. I know some of the women were taken to a hospital in Milledgeville. But there's no way to know for sure if that's where she went."

Gwen's heart beat out of her chest. "We need to tell him! Jeb needs to know that they're still alive." She jumped from the table. "I'm going to the train station. David, will you go with me? Tell him what you just told me?"

David's face showed no emotion. Blank, as if in shock.

"David?" Henry asked, moving to his side. "Why don't I go with her? You'll have guests arriving after lunch. I can tell Jeb what happened."

Shaking his head, David's face regained some of its color. "No, I want to go. I owe it to him. I never thought ..."

"It was war, David." Henry laid his hand on his arm. "You were just following orders."

"We lay to waste an entire city, Henry. Try to put yourself in his place. What if it had been *our* home burned? *Our* mother screaming?"

Their father arose from the table, motioning with his hands for everyone to calm down. "We can't change what happened. But we can do our best to help the man and make amends. After all, he did a great deal for us. The least we can do is let him know about his mother."

Gwen kissed him on the cheek. "Thank you, Father. We'll hurry and be back before any of the wedding guests arrive. And hopefully, Mr. Carter will be with us."

He gave her a wary look, but said nothing. How could he not be concerned knowing how she felt about Jeb? But getting to him quickly was all that mattered. For the first time in weeks, she had hope.

* * *

This was the first time Jeb had ever been in a passenger seat on a train. Though he'd gone with his daddy to see them at the station, he'd never had the privilege to actually ride. Train hopping was a thrill when he was a boy, and even when his mama came into her inheritance, the excitement kept him hopping rather than paying a fare. It was odd showing his ticket to the conductor.

"Changing in Cincinnati, I see," the conductor said. "And then on to Atlanta?"

Jeb nodded.

Why did he hafta say it so loud?

"Not much there these days. You working on the rails?"

Again, Jeb nodded. When the conductor's brows drew in, Jeb rubbed his throat, then touched his finger to his lips and shook his head.

"Oh. You a mute?"

Another nod. So much easier than speaking and being shunned.

"Well then ..." The conductor's voice grew even louder. Why was it that when folks thought he was mute, they thought he was also hard of hearing? "Hope you have a nice ride. If you need help in Cincinnati, let me know." He tipped his hat, then headed down the aisle to the next seat.

Jeb leaned his cane against the wall of the car and looked out the window. More snow. At least it wasn't so deep that the train couldn't run.

He glanced around taking in his surroundings. Nice upholstered seats, brass wall lanterns, shutters with gold tassels on the windows. Expensive-looking. Then his eyes shifted upward.

The man approaching him was finely dressed, fitting in perfectly with the extravagant fixtures. Business suit, top hat, and looks that caused every woman he passed to turn her head. It was obvious he liked the attention. He smiled at each one in turn, regardless of whether or not they had a man accompanying them. But oddly enough, he appeared to be heading to the seat beside Jeb.

"May I?" the man asked, pointing to the empty seat.

Why not? Jeb wouldn't be carrying on a conversation with him, and he seemed harmless enough. So, he nodded, and the man sat.

"Thank you." He leaned in and Jeb got a whiff of cologne. He smiled inwardly, thinking of Katherine's *skunk*. But it was nothing to smile about. Gwen would be marrying the skunk in less than six hours.

"I heard the conductor," the man said. "I know you can't speak, but it's to my benefit. I tend to find myself sitting beside a woman who can't keep her mouth shut. For the most part, I listen, and often times I'm rewarded for my attentions." He wiggled his brows. "I'm certain you understand my meaning. But today, I need to watch myself. Not get carried away." A sly grin curled the man's lips. He removed his hat and placed it in his lap, then primped his hair. Never before had Jeb seen a man so concerned over his appearance.

He should have told him *no*.

Are all men from the north arrogant and rude in regard to women?

"My name's Martin. John Martin. I'm an attorney." He puffed out his chest and sat more upright.

An attorney. That explained the expensive suit. Jeb sighed. It wasn't long ago that *he* answered to the name *John*.

"My practice is in Bridgeport. So, if you're ever there, or in need of legal help, look me up."

The man's arrogance oozed from every part of his body. One of the ladies who had watched him pass by, turned to look at him. He acknowledged her with a slight lift of his head and one raised eyebrow. She covered her mouth, tittered, then faced forward.

"That one shows promise," he said through the side of his mouth. "But I dare not. I'm meeting a woman in Buffalo." He cupped his hand over the side of his mouth. "For a tryst."

Was this man always so bold? Talking to a complete stranger about his personal life? Maybe he thought he would be impressed, or did he simply find Jeb to be non-threatening?

"You're a handsome young man." Mr. Martin rubbed his chin. "Even with your impairment. May I give you some advice?"

This could be interestin'.

"Circus women."

What?

Jeb's face must have shown his confusion, because Mr. Martin laughed aloud. An arrogant, sophisticated sort of laugh.

"I'm personal friends with Mr. P.T. Barnum. *Phineas Taylor Barnum.* I'm certain you've heard of him. Well, he knows all sorts of interesting people and women with unique talents. Of course that mermaid was a hoax, but she brought him incredible wealth."

Jeb nodded, intrigued by the man's story. Not to mention that it took his mind off Gwen and helped the time to pass.

Mr. Martin leaned in again. "He introduced me to a contortionist. I highly recommend every man should give one a try. At least once. They can move their bodies in ways that you can't even begin to imagine."

Intriguing or not, Jeb couldn't take another minute. He grabbed his cane and rose to his feet.

"Oh." Mr. Martin looked up at him. "Do you need to use the facilities?"

Jeb scowled at the man and stepped by him, into the aisle. Glancing toward the rear of the car, he spotted an empty seat and made his way toward it. He pitied the woman in Buffalo and hoped she knew what kind of a man he was.

Why did men treat women like *things?* Objects to be used for their own selfish purposes and then tossed aside at will?

He settled into his new seat and closed his eyes. He should have followed his first instinct and took Gwen away with him. Now she was destined to marry a man who wasn't much better than this attorney from Bridge-port.

God, help the women of this world.

* * *

"Sorry, Ma'am, the train already left the station."

Not the words Gwen wanted to hear.

Her head dropped, her shoulders slumped. With David on one side of her and Henry on the other, she was escorted back to their waiting carriage. They'd missed him by only fifteen minutes.

As cold as it was, she was surprised her tears didn't freeze on her cheeks. Though tired of crying, she couldn't help herself. Jeb was on a train headed far from her, and all she could think about was the brief moment, holding him in her arms before Albert yanked her away.

"Don't cry, Winnie." David offered a handkerchief. "The agent said there will be another train on Monday. We'll go after him then."

She dabbed at her tears and stared at her brother. "We? But you can't. You have very little time with Martha before you have to leave for Washington. I could never ask you to go with me."

The carriage moved slowly through the snow. She could see every word spoken in puffs of icy air. Though covered by blankets, she still couldn't stop shivering.

Henry scooted closer to her and placed his arm around her. "I'll go with you."

"No," David said firmly. "Father needs you at the store. He's already replaced *me*. Besides, I need to do this.

Perhaps I'm being selfish, but somehow I hope it will ease at least some of my guilt."

"David." Gwen took hold of his hands. "As much as I want you with me, what about Washington? If you go with me, you'll arrive late. It's not wise to be late when meeting the president."

He patted her hands. "Perhaps not, but family is more important. I'll send a telegram and explain that I'll be delayed."

Henry shook his head and grinned. "The president knows all about delays. Look what he did to Thanksgiving this year. Why on earth do you suppose he had it fall in December? Especially after Lincoln declared it would always be in November?"

"To prove he's the president," David said.

Gwen smiled at her brother, then laid her head back against the seat. If only she hadn't waited. If only ...

Fifteen minutes late. Had she been a man, she would have hopped on a horse and gone after him. Such silly thoughts. But soon, she would follow him, and if all went as she hoped, she'd reunite him with his mother and Anna. It could be a very happy Christmas.

Chapter 24

When the wedding guests learned only one couple would be saying their vows, the room sighed with astonishment. Gwen had made up her mind to tell them Albert had had a change of heart, though her mother already revealed the horrible truth to several of her close friends.

Gwen passed by one of them, who looked at her sympathetically, then whispered to someone else, "Grace said her arm is bruised." Gasps followed her everywhere she went.

Gwen didn't intend to tarnish Albert's reputation, but then again, he'd brought it on himself.

"She's twenty."

Gwen froze, listening to what was being said. With her back to them, the two women hadn't recognized her.

"What man will have her now?"

"William Abbott will find *someone* to take her. Even if he has to pay them."

Pay them? Gwen's good intentions of helping ease the guests were rapidly fading. If these two pompous women were a sample of the attendance, then she wanted nothing to do with them. She didn't even know half of them. Most were her father's best customers and vendors. Some were acquaintances of David's from the war, and men he'd be working with in Washington. The elite of Boston and other parts of Massachusetts.

She inched past the women and up the stairs to her room.

Initially, they'd intended to have a church wedding, but due to the elaborate reception, her parents had decided to hold the entire ordeal at their estate. Considering the snowfall, it had been a wise decision. But since Gwen wasn't getting married—aside from the gossip—no one seemed to care about her. Honestly, she'd rather not be there at all. She'd wait until right before the wedding march, then take her place beside Martha. Henry had graciously stepped in to stand with David.

"Hidin'?" Sarah peered around Gwen's doorframe.

"Yes. I don't belong down there."

Sarah entered her room. "You was too late for the train, wadn't ya?"

She nodded. "Fifteen minutes. He's somewhere between here and Cincinnati by now. And he left thinking I'm marrying Albert." Flopping back onto her bed, she sighed.

"But you's goin' after him, ain't ya?" It wasn't a question; it was a statement of fact.

"Yes. Monday. But how will I ever find him? Atlanta is a big city."

"I wouldn't worry none 'bout that. Your brother will know where to look. An I hear you're gonna look for his family, too. I knew the good Lord had sumthin' in mind when he brought you two together."

Gwen sank deeper into the mattress. "So why didn't He keep Jeb from leaving before we could tell him about them?"

"They's a reason, but we don't knows it yet. Seems you needs to go on a longer journey."

"I'd rather it was simple."

Sarah shook her head. "If life was simple, we wouldn't appreciate the good. Sometimes things hasta be hard for us to knows how good they is." She crossed the room and ran her hand over the top of Gwen's head. "Rest for a spell. I'll come getcha when it's time."

"Thank you, Sarah."

After closing the door behind her, Sarah was gone, leaving Gwen to her thoughts.

Hard times make us appreciate the good.

They'd had their share. And coming from Sarah, it meant a great deal. But no one had harder times than Jeb.

He must feel more lost than ever right now.

A light rap at her door made her think Sarah must have forgotten something. It couldn't be time for the ceremony.

"Come in." Gwen remained flat on her back, enjoying the comfort of her bed, but looked toward the door.

Katherine?

Her little sister stood timidly in the doorway, dressed in pink frills. But the frown on her face didn't complement the dress.

"Katherine, what's wrong?" Gwen sat up and patted the spot beside her. As her sister stepped nearer, evidence of shed tears lingered on her face. Puffy eyes and a signature red nose that all the Abbott women wore when they cried.

"I don't understand," Katherine cried. "Why did Mr. Carter leave? And what happened with Albert?"

Gwen hadn't considered that Katherine knew nothing about last night's events or anything that transpired this morning. One of the downfalls of an early bedtime.

In as gentle a manner as she could, Gwen told her what had happened. And being that Katherine specifically asked to see her arm, she knew rumors were spreading like wildfire on the lower floor.

"I'll have to find me another beau," Katherine whimpered.

"Another beau?"

"I told Mr. Carter I'd marry him one day. But I knew all along that he loves you. Besides, I don't think he wanted to wait for me to grow up."

Gwen pulled her into her arms, resting her sister's head against her shoulder. She kissed the top of her head, then smoothed her long hair with her hand. "I knew he cared for you when he gave you the paper rose."

"But he gave you a bouquet of them. I didn't stand a chance."

"One day, when you're grown up, I know you'll get many more flowers."

Katherine sniffled. "Well I know for sure I don't want to marry Mr. Finch. I don't want to marry any man who would hurt me like that." She pointed to Gwen's arm. "It wasn't very nice."

"No, it wasn't. And you have the good fortune that Father learned a lesson from what I went through. I doubt he'll push you into marrying someone you don't love."

Sitting upright, Katherine looked into Gwen's face. "Are you going to marry Mr. Carter? You love him, don't you?"

If only it was that simple. They had many obstacles to overcome. Marriage or not, she wasn't done helping him. Hopefully, reuniting him with his family would begin to heal his heart.

"Yes, I love him. But sometimes that's not enough."

Katherine jumped to her feet and threw up her hands. "Now I really don't understand. I'll never figure out grown-ups."

"I hate to tell you this, but it doesn't get any easier when you become one." She stood and walked with her sister to the door. "I'll be down soon. Go and wash away your tears. I noticed a few young men downstairs closer to your age. They might appreciate seeing your pretty face."

Katherine shook her head. "Uh-uh. I'll wash my face, but only to keep Mother happy. I'm done with men." Throwing her shoulders back and tossing her head in a gesture far beyond her years, she strode out the door.

It would be much easier for Gwen if she felt the same. Of course, Katherine would grow out of it one day and would marry well. Probably have half a dozen children.

Before Gwen met Jeb, she'd never thought about spending her life with any particular man. She was at peace studying medicine and medical procedures. Her heart was content until her *study* captured it. But she would likely have to overcome her feelings. Understanding what it meant to be an Abbott, she knew she wasn't free to marry whomever she chose. Being released from her obligation to Albert didn't in any way open the door for Jeb.

* * *

Gwen ignored the hushed tones as she walked by the seated guests in the ballroom. Dressed in pink, similar to Katherine, but without the frills, she floated by them and took her place beside Martha.

Gossip never bothered her. She just hoped things wouldn't be blown completely out of proportion.

She glanced at David. *So handsome.* He'd be a fine husband to Martha. Their faces beamed with love for one another.

That's what I want.

Admitting it to herself was the first step. Thinking she could go through life married to books was behind her now. The way she felt in Jeb's arms had changed all that.

Casting those thoughts aside, she focused on the bride and groom.

"And do you, Martha Candace Marie Clayton, take David William Alexander Abbott to be your lawfully wedded husband?" The preacher's face was stoic. How many times had he performed a wedding ceremony?

"I do."

Gwen looked sideways at Martha and smiled. Now they were sisters. She couldn't have asked for a finer one.

And soon, there would be food and dancing. This time she had no worries about being hounded by Albert Finch.

* * *

The conductor passed by Jeb, brightening the lanterns to offset the setting of the sun. Another full day of travel before they reached Cincinnati. Amazing how far he'd traveled before without knowing it. How long had he been unconscious before they'd found him? He'd probably never know.

At least being unconscious cleared his mind. He no longer had that luxury. And as darkness was the only thing to see out the window, he knew that night had also come to Boston. Gwen's wedding night. His head pounded at the thought. She was in the arms of a man who didn't have a clue what a rare gem was in his grasp.

They'd stopped in Buffalo briefly and Jeb watched Mr. Martin exit. Jeb even peered out the window, hoping to catch a glimpse of the contortionist. And he did. But she wore a heavy coat and her head was covered by a large hat. Though she wasted no time rushing into the attorney's arms, she looked no different than any other woman waiting at the station.

Mr. Martin sauntered away with her; tall and proud. They too must be enjoying a wedding night, even without a ring. Not the way Jeb wanted his future. There was nothing lasting about that kind of relationship. He'd seen similar behavior during the war. Men finding comfort with women who sold themselves. He'd had the opportunity, but knew it was wrong. This was one thing in life worth waiting for and should never be taken lightly.

Oh, how he ached for Gwen ...

He didn't want to accept that she'd never be his, and if he thought much more about Albert and what they might be doing now, he'd go mad. So he concentrated on the click-clack of the rails and huddled beneath his blanket. He could have afforded a sleeping car, but wanted to save his money. If he was going to rebuild his home, he'd need all he had and more.

Chapter 25

Two days to Cincinnati and then two more to Atlanta. Gwen and David followed the same route they were told Jeb took. But once they reached Atlanta, they would take a secondary line to Milledgeville. She wanted to find his mother before looking for him. If she'd died, she didn't want to give him false hope. It would be horrible to make him go through her death all over again.

Her father insisted they stay in a sleeping car and gave them more than enough money to pay the train fare as well as purchase accommodations in Atlanta and Milledgeville. Unsure how long it would take them to find Mrs. Carter, he didn't want them to run out.

Her mother didn't understand why they couldn't simply send a telegram to Jeb. But neither Gwen nor David believed it was the right thing to do. This was a task that had to be handled in person.

Gwen placed her bag under the seat in their small chamber. The seat pulled down into a bed. It was nothing like her bed at home, but at least it gave her a place to rest. She glanced at the small package setting on the chair. Hopefully it would help. Purchasing a doll for Anna seemed like the right thing to do. The doll's porcelain hands were similar to the one Jeb had.

What made him give it to Sarah?

After he'd wrenched it away from her so long ago, she knew how much it meant to him. Perhaps he'd left it accidentally. She patted the small cloth bag hanging from her wrist. Maybe it was odd to bring the hand, but it was almost like having a part of him with her.

David had already pulled down his bunk and appeared to be sleeping. No wonder. He and Martha had honeymooned for two nights in a row. Gwen thought they would never say goodbye at the train station. Martha clung to him. Something had changed between them and Gwen was certain what it was. The two were not merely in love, they'd become lovers.

She tilted her head. Her brother's chest rose and fell. He was content. At least for now. But what would he do when he had to face Atlanta again? And what would she see there?

Since she wasn't in the least bit tired, she picked up a book given to her by Doctor Young as an early wedding gift. Though she should return it, she knew what he would say, looking at her over his glasses. *Keep it. The book was for you, not him. Besides, I'm glad you came to your senses.*

So, she opened it to page one. Hopefully *Alice's Adventures in Wonderland* would keep her mind busy and help the time to pass.

* * *

Changing trains in Cincinnati was no problem for Jeb. He'd always been comfortable around trains and train stations, thanks to his daddy. And the conductor pointed him in the right direction. Having *impairments* had its advantages.

Was it wrong to mislead him? Maybe so. But it was so much easier than being judged for his accent. And—he didn't intend to have an ongoing relationship with the conductor, so what harm could it do?

Now that the train neared Atlanta, his heart fell into his boots. Signs of the war became evident and painful. Could he face the burned remains of his home again?

It was surprisingly cold. Maybe he'd brought the weather with him. He recalled only a handful of snow-falls in his lifetime, none of which had stuck to the ground for more than a few hours.

When he stepped off the train, icy crystals alighted on his face. It was good that he'd not shaved in four days. Though he must look a sight, he didn't care. The whiskers kept his face warm.

Told that there was a reconstructed boarding house several blocks from the train station, Jeb made his way there. It was going to take time before he had anything livable on his old home site.

Passing by shanties with folks huddled together around small fires, his stomach churned. Could he do this? He thought of the smiling faces at Abbott's as folks prepared for the holidays and the beautiful buildings and houses lining the streets of Boston. A different world. But At-lanta was home and they needed him here.

With his room key in his fist, he went down the hall to number three and turned the key in the lock. It couldn't have been simpler; Bed, wardrobe, night stand, lantern. It needed a fireplace, but the larger rooms that had them were already taken. The stack of blankets at the end of the bed would help.

Since he had little to unpack, it didn't take long to get settled, but he was interrupted by a knock at the door.

"Did I forget sumthin?" Jeb asked Mr. Thomas, the owner, who stood in the doorway scratching his head.

"No, but my wife wanted me to remind you that t'morra is Thanksgivin'. We'll be eatin' 'bout one. We got plenty a rations for a nice, big meal. Don't you worry none, it won't cost you extry. It's part of your board. My wife likes to cook a big meal for the holiday, even though food's kinda hard to come by these days."

"Thanksgivin'?"

"Yep. Not sure where you been, but the president decided to have it in December this year. Can't figger why, but he's the president."

Jeb thanked him and accepted the invitation. With everything going on in Boston, he'd not thought about Thanksgiving. So much attention was on Christmas, especially where Katherine was concerned.

His heart ached thinking of her, and her suggestion they might marry one day. Such a sweet child. After piling blankets over his body, he nestled into bed and dreamed about her sister.

* * *

Gwen's eyes popped wide. She yawned and stretched, then picked up the book she'd dropped on the floor of the train car. She was more tired than she'd thought. Strangely, she'd dreamed of white rabbits.

Curiouser and curiouser.

She giggled. Doctor Young had an interesting sense of humor giving her the book. It was entertaining, and one of the most unusual stories she'd ever read. Far different from her medical books.

Having always loved adventure stories, now she could write her own. But would her story have a happy ending?

"Good morning," David said, grinning. "Still chasing rabbits?"

"I—How did you know?"

"You mumbled something in your sleep." He stood and pushed up his bunk, securing it to the wall. "Everyone in the family knows you talk to animals. But don't worry, I won't tell anyone your secrets. *Any* of them." He followed his words with a little wink.

Had she revealed more than rabbit chasing in her sleep?

"Don't look so nervous," David said. "I'm teasing you. You've been a mess lately and I'm trying to help. Let's find something to eat and talk over breakfast."

She loved the idea and gladly followed him out of their room and down to the dining car.

"How do they keep their balance?" she asked David, nodding to the waiters bustling around serving guests.

"They're used to the movement. But if I were you, I wouldn't ask for hot tea."

She laughed and felt good doing so. Her nerves had kept a sour expression glued to her face. David always knew how to break through.

When the waiter poured her steaming tea from the silver teapot, she held her breath.

After he left the table, David chuckled. "I was teasing about the tea."

"I know you were. Otherwise, I wouldn't have ordered it."

"So why did you hold your breath?"

He read her like a book. "Well ..." Knowing that spilling hot tea wasn't what was actually on David's mind, she decided to change the course of the conversation. "You miss Martha, don't you?"

He cocked his head and gave her a look she knew well. Yes, she'd changed the subject. "Of course I do. You know that I'm smitten. There's no one in the world quite like her."

She smiled her agreement. "You were fortunate she came from a respectable family. I wouldn't advise anyone to fall in love with someone of lower stature."

Saying the words made her smile vanish. She poked at her pastry with her fork. The silence between them caused the sounds around her to intensify; clanking of silverware, soft-spoken words of other passengers, the clacking of the wheels, and even the beat of her own heart.

"Winnie ..." He took hold of her hand. "That's what I want to speak to you about."

Raising her eyes from her plate, she met his. "Jeb?"

"Yes. Though he's from the south, I doubt he's lower in stature. His home was—*grand* to say the least. Unlike some of the other estates, his was not a plantation. Their money had to have been made elsewhere."

"Why does money have to matter? Sometimes I hate it." She looked down at the table. Fine china, linens, crystal, and a silver fork perched in her hand. Was it fair when others had so little?

"Don't say that." He lifted her chin, making her look at him. "Hate doesn't become you. You're too good. And as for money, Father worked hard to get where he is today. That's what's wonderful about this country. Any man can work hard and better his life."

"Until it's burned down around him."

His face fell. She shouldn't have said it. She reached out to him. "I'm sorry, David."

"No. You're right. We burned it all. And now the government is sending money to help rebuild it. Though it seems to make little sense, I do know this. Sherman's plan worked. The things we did put an end to the war and now we can come together and make the Union strong again. And that's why I agreed to go to Washington. To help piece it all back together."

He was right. If it hadn't been done, the war may have gone on forever. More men would have died. More lives destroyed. She somehow managed to smile. "The president couldn't have a better man for the job. I *am* proud of you, David." Her words seemed to ease him and he sat a little taller. "And I'm grateful you're with me. But how can knowing all of this help my situation?"

He breathed deeply and leaned back in his chair. "I intend to go to Father and encourage him to have a change of heart regarding Jeb Carter. After all, he likes him, respects him, and until we discovered his deceptions, he trusted him. All I have to do is convince him to trust again."

"What if he doesn't?" She was afraid to even hope.

"I'll explain that no other man will ever have you, considering your age."

She dropped her fork. "David Abbott!" When several guests stared at her, she calmed. "I'm not that old." She leaned in to him, lowering her voice. "At least I have more sense than the silly little girls some men court."

He chuckled aloud. "Winnie, I will never tire of teasing you."

She should have seen it. But everything else he said was of such a serious nature that his jest snuck up on her. Or maybe she was just sensitive regarding her age. "Teasing only about my being twenty? Or teasing about going to Father about Jeb?"

"Oh, I intend to go to Father. You deserve happiness, Gwen. And even though I didn't see it right away, looking back now, I remember how he used to look at you. Unlike Albert, who broke into a sweat when he saw a scarce amount of your bare flesh, Jeb saw you with eyes of devotion. Real love. And you saw him exactly the same way. Father put you in a horrible predicament pushing you and Albert together."

"He hoped we'd be like you and Martha." She glanced out the window, becoming almost dizzy watching the scenery fly by. "Speaking to Father may not be necessary."

"Why?"

"There's no guaranty Jeb will want to be with me."

David folded his arms across his chest and shook his head. "I'm a man. I have no doubt I'll be speaking to Father."

Time would tell. Two different worlds could never easily come together.

* * *

Yesterday's Thanksgiving meal on the train suddenly felt like a rock in Gwen's stomach. She stood aghast, staring at the rubble that was once Union Station.

"C'mon, Gwen." David took her arm. "I was told there's a small eatery close by where we can wait for the train to Milledgeville."

She heard his words and felt the tug of his hand, but it was almost impossible to move. The desolation pained her heart. After trying to visualize what it must have looked like, nothing could have prepared her for this. A once great thriving city reduced to ash.

Yes, there were signs of reconstruction, but how long would it take?

People gawked at her as she and David entered the restaurant. When he ordered their food, the scowl from the waitress was unexpected.

"Now I understand how Jeb felt," Gwen whispered to David. "Maybe I should pretend to be mute." Staying silent wouldn't change her attire. Her coat alone screamed wealth.

Fortunately, they only had to wait two hours.

With no appetite, she picked at her food.

"What's wrong?" A man hissed the words from another table. "Food ain't good enough for ya?"

"Ignore him," David whispered.

"Hey, Sal." The man waved down the waitress. "What we doin' caterin' to Yanks?"

The waitress hurried to the man's side, motioning with her hand for him to be quiet. "Hush, Fred. We need the business."

After taking a couple more bites, Gwen pushed her plate away. "David, let's go somewhere else to wait. I don't feel comfortable here."

He nodded and went to settle the bill. She tried not to look at anyone, but she felt their eyes on her like she was something wretched. Their muttering caused her skin to crawl.

"Go back where you came from!" the man yelled as they walked out. "Ain't you done enough damage already?"

David wrapped his arm around her and led her quickly away. The air had warmed enough they opted to sit on a bench at the make-shift station and wait for the train. With their backs to a wall, they were as safe here as any-where. At least they could see what was coming.

"Just keep reminding yourself that we're doing this for Jeb," David said.

"It's his face in my mind that keeps me going." She grabbed David's hand and squeezed it tight. "But I'm scared. I can't deny that."

"I'm here for you. I'm doing my best *not* to be scared. But honestly, it's much different being here out of uniform and without my men to back me. That being said, I doubt anyone will harm us."

She wasn't comforted. She trembled, and not from the cold.

"Gwen?" His body deflated beside her. "I need to tell you about Milledgeville."

This didn't sound good. She shifted to face him.

"The hospital I mentioned, where I believe Mrs. Carter was taken ..." He paused and rubbed his temples.

"What about it?"

"It's a—lunatic asylum. I didn't know how to tell you."

"Oh, David." Now she felt even worse. "I've heard horrible things about-"

"I know." He stopped her from finishing her sentence, but it didn't stop her thoughts. Some of those facilities were known for using restraints on their patients. Chaining them to their beds.

Barbaric.

Gwen grabbed his hand and squeezed. "If we find her there, we have to take her away. I don't care how, but we'll have to find a way." Her trembling had stopped, replaced with something much worse. Dread of what was to come. Jeb may not want to see his mother this way. "What about Anna? They wouldn't keep *her* there."

David slowly shook his head. "I don't know."

They knew so little. Going on a hunch and a prayer, they boarded the train.

Chapter 26

After being directed to a local livery stable, David managed to hire a carriage and driver to take them to the asylum.

The man was leery at first, but David told him that Gwen was a nurse, sent by the president himself to inspect the facility. A few choice tidbits from David about President Johnson convinced the man they were who they claimed. And it cast aside his concern over their obvious northern accents and attire.

Although their silver-haired driver was at ease, Gwen was anything but.

She peered out the tiny carriage window as they drove the long, winding path leading to the facility. Rows of barren pecan trees eerily lined the way. Their naked branches stretched high into the sky. Far off, cotton fields lay at rest, waiting for spring.

They'd seen Sherman's work in Milledgeville and David told her about an incident where honey was poured into the pipes of a church organ. He said it was done without the consent of officers and tried to explain that sometimes soldiers got out of hand. Did things on their own. Again, war seemed to excuse almost any form of intolerable behavior.

When the carriage came to a stop, the driver didn't open the door, so David arose and opened it himself, then helped Gwen. She stepped to the ground and glanced upward at the driver, who was huddled under blankets, blowing on his hands.

"Will you wait?" David asked him.

The man extended his hand and rubbed his fingers together, wanting money.

After handing him more than enough, the man grinned and nodded.

David swung open a tall wooden gate and they walked toward the front entrance. The three-story building was made from white brick and had a wooden roof. Windows with iron bars lined the walls of every floor. Nothing was ornate, looking more like a large box with windows. It resembled a prison rather than a hospital. This building was not created for beauty, rather a place to hide the tormented souls no one else cared to cope with.

She gripped David's arm almost as fiercely as Albert had held hers. "I don't like this place."

He shook his head. "Neither do I, but we have to start here."

They were met almost immediately by a middle-aged nurse dressed in a uniform reminiscent of her own. Gwen plastered a smile on her face. "Good afternoon."

The raised eyebrows of the nurse were no surprise.

Yes, I'm from the north.

"How can I help you?" The nurse folded her arms defensively in front of herself. There was no trace of a southern accent in her speech. Wherever she was from, she seemed hard and cold.

A loud shriek from a distant room caused Gwen to jump. Her reaction prompted a smirk on the nurse's face.

David stepped forward. "President Johnson sent us to evaluate this facility. My name is David Abbott, and this is my sister, Gwendolyn. She studied at Boston Women's Medical College."

The woman's upper lip twitched. "Do you have written orders?"

Gwen's heart jumped. What now?

Without a moment's hesitation, David reached into his jacket pocket, pulled out a letter, and handed it to her. "As you can see, President Johnson is expecting me in three weeks. With a full report."

The nurse lost her smirk and replaced it with wide-eyed horror, staring at the document. "Yessir, Mr. Abbott, sir. Where would you like to start?"

Gwen should have known David would have thought this through. Having his work orders readily available was brilliant. The reply to his telegram to President Johnson gave him until after Christmas to relocate to Washington.

As they wandered down the corridor, Nurse Jamison waved her hands, telling the history of the asylum.

"This floor houses our male patients. Each floor has twenty rooms and we're currently filled to capacity. The war brought many troubled soldiers to our doors."

The more the nurse spoke, her tone became less defensive and more compassionate.

"The upper floor is for our female patients. We have a matron who oversees their care. Women oftentimes need delicate handling."

Another shriek followed by a series of low moans, sent chills down her spine. "Why do they cry out?"

"There are many disturbed minds here. It's their only means of communication."

"Are they ever violent?" David asked.

"Nothing we can't control."

Gwen couldn't hide the frown on her face, thinking about the means they must use to control the patients.

Nurse Jamison placed her hand on Gwen's arm. "Nothing to fret over. Our asylum has come a long way since its founding. The current superintendent, Doctor Green, saw to it. They used to use restraints on the patients, but he doesn't allow them. We do our best to treat our residents with respect."

Maybe this wouldn't be as bad as she'd feared. "May we speak with Doctor Green?"

"I can facilitate that. He likes to have meals with the patients. Why don't you join us for dinner?"

Gwen looked sideways at David before agreeing to the invitation.

"Thank you," David said. "Speaking with Doctor Green is important for our report. I'd like to put in a kind word for him to the president."

Nurse Jamison folded her hands in front of her body and tilted her head. "Why is the president interested in our asylum? Doesn't he have more important things to do?"

"President Johnson is trying to put our country back together. He finds that learning about every aspect of reconstruction in the south is beneficial. Especially when it concerns rebuilding the lives of soldiers who are citizens of the Union."

She touched her hand to her chest and smiled. "My, oh my. I may have developed a new respect for the man."

They returned to the main entrance and David excused himself to give instructions to their driver. Gwen hoped he would return for them later in the evening, but after paying him so much to stay, he may not return at all.

"Are you a nurse?" Nurse Jamison asked.

"I'm studying to be a doctor," Gwen replied, and it felt liberating saying the words.

She was repaid with a very large, respectful smile. Gwen was beginning to like Nurse Jamison.

"I apologize for being cold to you when you arrived," the nurse said. "We've experienced many unpleasant things over the years. Mostly strangers who come to spy on us, looking to tell terrible tales of the *horrors* here. I've been here for five years. Saw it through the war. *That* was the horror. I enjoy my work and care a great deal for my patients. I don't care for ill reports."

If all the staff felt this way, there was hope for Mrs. Carter. But how would they go about finding her? Just come out and ask? Maybe David had already worked that out. Gwen would wait for him to take the lead.

With David once again by her side, they were led to a small dining room where they were introduced to Doctor Green. He wasn't as old as Doctor Young, but Gwen guessed him to be older than her father. He had a salt and pepper beard and a kind smile.

The room they were in was large enough for forty patients to eat at one time. The doctor explained that some were so ill they stayed in their rooms, but he encouraged as much of a family atmosphere as possible, which included eating together.

After being seated at a round table, Gwen scanned every face in the room. None of the women looked like Jeb. But that didn't mean she wasn't here.

There were a handful of people who seemed completely *normal,* then many more who were acting odd, to say the least. Twitching, drooling, outbursts, and flailing arms went unnoticed by the staff, but Gwen found it disturbing. The look on David's face showed that he must feel the same.

"I'm glad you came," Dr. Green said with a smile. "We rarely have such honored guests. And it may be selfish of me, but I hope you can speak with the *powers that be* and help us with some necessary funding. We've suffered horribly since the war. Money is scarce, as is food."

Gwen frowned at her plate.

"Miss Abbott, please don't feel poorly. We're happy to offer what we have."

"I can almost guaranty that my father will make a contribution to your facility," Gwen said. "Though it wouldn't be polite of me to make that commitment before speaking to him. We'll see to it when we return to Boston."

The room became uncomfortably chilly. She hadn't seen a single fireplace. "Doctor Green, how do you heat this building? Or ... do you?"

He chuckled. "I'm certain you understand that we can't risk open flames around our patients. We have a large iron stove in our basement that heats the building. I can show it to you, if you'd like."

"Yes, please," David said. "It must be enormous to heat the entire facility."

"That's the problem," Dr. Green said. "It doesn't do a very good job. Your sister will attest to that."

Gwen smiled, more at ease than ever. Even the occasional outcry wasn't quite so bothersome.

They finished their scarce meal, then the doctor led the way to the basement. A large Negro tended the fire.

"Isaac," the doctor said. "We have guests."

The man faced them and dipped his head. He was covered from head to toe in soot. Nervously wiping his face with the back of his hand, he smudged it, making it even worse.

"Ma'am," he nodded at Gwen. "Sir." A similar nod to David.

"Isaac's been with us for a year now," Dr. Green said. "He's a very hard worker."

After scanning the large oven, David thanked him and they headed back up the stairs to the main floor.

"Doctor," David said. There was hesitation in his voice. "Was Isaac a slave?"

The doctor paused on the stairwell and turned to face them. "I'm pleased that you said *was*. At least you have some faith in me."

David smiled nervously.

"Yes, he was a slave, but as you know, was freed. However, he refuses to leave the asylum." He took another step upward. "He's devoted to one of our patients."

Gwen's mind whirled.

No, it couldn't be ...

"One of your *male* patients?" Her heart fluttered as she posed the question.

"Oh, no. The patient is female, but it's not what you're thinking. His devotion is not of the amorous kind."

They continued on to the main floor. David tugged on her hand. Had he realized the same thing?

"Well, then," the doctor said. "You'll want to be on your way before dark. Do you have a carriage coming?"

"Yes—that is, I believe so," David replied. "Doctor Green, may we sit for a moment? There's something else I need to discuss with you."

"Certainly." The doctor motioned to a long bench on the far side of the hallway.

Gwen's heart pounded, waiting to hear what David would say. She sat comfortably, but her insides tumbled.

"There's more to our visit than we first indicated," David began. The doctor said nothing and simply nodded, seeming not to be the least bit surprised. "This matter is of a personal nature."

Gwen needed water for her dry throat. She cleared it, then motioned for David to go on.

"You see, the president has a close friend who had family from Atlanta. I say *had* because most of them perished in the war."

"Oh. I'm very sorry," the doctor said.

"It seems their home was burned, and this friend's cousin—a woman—may have been brought here. She didn't take the losses well. She was accompanied by a Negro slave, and her daughter, who would be approximately six years old by now. Her name is Mrs. Carter. *Suzanne* Carter."

Gwen rubbed her hands together anxiously and took several deep breaths as she waited for the doctor's response.

Doctor Green stroked his chin, then looked upward as if contemplating his answer. "And if she's here, does the president's *friend* wish to take her home?"

"Yes." Gwen spit out the word without thought. Her eagerness made the doctor chuckle.

"Yes." David gave Gwen the eye. "She's terribly missed and one of her sons, whom she believed died, is alive. Her cousin would very much like to see them reunited."

Rising from the bench, Doctor Green folded his arms and leered down at both of them. "Suzanne Carter is here, but she's in no condition to leave. I can't allow it."

No! She couldn't have heard him correctly. Gwen jumped to her feet. "Why? What's wrong with her?"

"She doesn't speak, she rarely eats, and she isn't healthy enough for travel. I'm very sorry, but you'll need to tell this *friend* that if he or she wishes to see her, it will need to be done here."

During all the time they were with the doctor, he'd been gracious, cordial, and willing to tell them anything and show them everything. But he was suddenly guarded. Protective of his patient.

Gwen persisted. "Doctor Green, I have medical training. Will you at least let me see her? Perhaps if I give her the news about her son-"

"I doubt she'll understand, but I'll allow you to try. And I apologize, Mr. Abbott, but I can only allow Miss Abbott to go into her room. You may wait here."

David nodded and pulled Gwen close. "Prepare yourself for the worst. And don't push her too hard."

"I'll be fine, David." She leaned down and kissed his cheek, then filled with hope, smiled.

She followed the doctor to the far end of the hallway and up another stairway to the upper floor. Though they appeared to keep the facility clean, there was still an odor hovering in the air. The scent of unwashed bodies filled her nose. She dabbed at it with a handkerchief.

"We're short of staff here," Dr. Green said. "Most of our patients can't bathe themselves. We do our best."

Ignoring the odor, Gwen pressed on. As they walked, she tried to decide what to say to the woman. The fact that she didn't speak, reminded her of her son. But Mrs. Carter's silence was not for the same reason. Gwen suspected it was a combination of extreme depression and shock.

The doctor motioned to the next room. "She likes to sit by the window. I don't feel comfortable allowing you to be alone with her, but I'll stand close to the door so you can speak freely with her. I won't interrupt you unless I see fit."

"Thank you." Gwen let out a long breath and walked through the door.

Mrs. Carter was faced away from her, staring out the window. Her long hair hung loose and fell to her waist. White as the snow in Boston. She had a tiny frame, which was evident even through the blanket wrapped over her shoulders. Her body rocked to and fro as though she were keeping time with the world passing by outside the glass.

"Mrs. Carter?" Gwen's voice shook.

Silly. Don't be afraid of the woman.

"Mrs. Carter, my name is Gwen Abbott. I've come a very long way to see you." She inched over to the woman and perched herself on the edge of the small bed. Her room was cold. Not just from the lack of heat, but there were no wall hangings, no color of any sort to brighten it. Her bedspread was white, and the iron bedframe was also painted plain white. It seemed starker than any hospital room she'd ever entered.

Suzanne stopped rocking. Her head turned just enough so that Gwen caught her eye and profile. Pale skin, with a few freckles, and though her lids drooped half closed, there was a trace of blue just like Jeb's. There was no doubt in Gwen's mind. She'd found his mother.

Wanting to reach out to her and whisk her away to find him, Gwen had to push her desires aside. There had to be a way to reach this woman and have her released from the asylum.

Suzanne shivered, so Gwen readjusted her blanket, then got another from the base of the bed, which she placed across her lap. "Is that better?"

She nodded and Gwen's heart leapt.

So like Jeb ...

Gwen glanced over her shoulder. The doctor was watching every move she made. Time to be bold.

She reached out and took her hand. "Your hands are cold. Let me help warm them." Gwen rubbed her hands over Suzanne's, then looked in her eyes. Suzanne grunted, trying desperately to force her lids fully open.

"It's helping, isn't it?" Watching her struggle was painful.

Another nod. Progress.

"Mrs. Carter, I know you've been through a terrible ordeal."

Doctor Green cleared his throat, but Gwen didn't care, she would press on. After all, there wasn't much time. David couldn't stay in Milledgeville indefinitely. He had other obligations.

"I know about your family and your losses."

Suzanne's hand tightened around hers.

"But I have some wonderful news. Your son—Jeb—is alive. He's in Atlanta. He thought you'd died in the fire. Otherwise he would have come for you earlier. He's devastated over losing you and I want more than anything to take you to him."

A low moan emerged from somewhere deep within her. Her hands trembled and she started rocking again, faster than ever. Her face contorted, then her eyes scrunched tight. "Jeb ..."

Gwen flashed a look at Doctor Green, who was scratching his head. He stepped closer and motioned for her to continue.

"Yes, Jeb." Gwen stroked the woman's hair, trying to calm her, and she slowed her rhythm. "He loves you so much. And you see—I'm a nurse. I can take care of you. I want very much to help you so that you don't have to stay here."

Blinking slowly, Suzanne shifted her body toward Gwen. "Jeb?"

"Yes. Do you want to go to him?"

A slow, deliberate nod was all Gwen needed to see. But then, once again, Suzanne's face twisted. "Anna ..."

"Your daughter? Yes, she can come, too. Where is she?" Suzanne's shoulders slumped and tears fell.

"Miss Abbott?" Doctor Green motioned her out of the room.

Gwen stood and before walking away, patted Suzanne's back and leaned toward her. "I'll return soon."

In an unexpected flash, she grabbed Gwen. "Soon." One simple word from the woman's lips and her tear-filled eyes broke Gwen's heart.

Ignoring the persistent grunts coming from the doctor, Gwen knelt beside her. "Yes, soon." She leaned in and whispered in Suzanne's ear. "I won't leave you here."

A hint of a smile crossed her face, warming Gwen to the core. She cupped her cold cheek and left Jeb's mother with a smile and a promise to return.

Chapter 27

Doctor Green said nothing to Gwen as he walked briskly down the steps to the first floor. Was he angry that she'd gotten Mrs. Carter to speak? Certainly not.

They returned to the hall bench where David sat cross-legged, swinging his upper leg. Gwen knew that look. He'd been up to something, but what?

Doctor Green pointed to the bench and glared at Gwen. "Sit."

"What did I do wrong?" Gwen complied and sat beside David who immediately uncrossed his legs and put his arm around her.

"I don't appreciate you giving orders to my sister, Doctor," David said.

"And I don't appreciate charades. There is no *cousin*, is there?" The doctor crossed his arms and looked sternly at both of them.

With a sideways glance at Gwen, David raised his eyes with a *what did you do* look.

She gazed downward, ashamed of their deceptions. "No, there's not."

"And your interest in Mrs. Carter? I shall assume that the president didn't order you here."

"Our interest is genuine," Gwen said with earnest. "We know her son, Jeb. He truly is alive and we want to take her to him."

"Why not bring him here?" The doctor's face had not softened.

"Because he was devastated losing her the first time. If we'd brought him here and found her buried in your graveyard, it would have destroyed him. It would have burdened him with guilt for not coming sooner. But now, reuniting them will help both of them to heal."

Doctor Green shifted his attention to David. "Do you even know the president?"

"Oh." David sat up straight. "That part of our story is true. I have to be in Washington after Christmas. I'm an advisor to President Johnson."

The doctor lowered his arms and hissed breath out his nose. "Forgive my disappointment. Believing that you were here for a noble purpose gave me hope for aid. Our financial situation is dismal and because I refuse to turn away anyone seeking help, it makes our burden even greater."

"Perhaps we misled you," Gwen said, to which she received raised brows from the doctor. "But our purpose is honorable. You promote a family atmosphere. All we want to do is bring a family together."

"And," David added. "I won't let you down in regard to the president. I'll do what I can to help you with funding. I would never mislead you about something so important."

The tension in the air eased. Gwen's heart finally calmed and it seemed the doctor might forgive them. Since she had nothing to lose, she decided to ask the question that had been haunting her.

"Doctor Green, do you know where Mrs. Carter's daughter is?"

He nodded, then fidgeted with the lapel of his white frock coat. "A family on the other side of town by the name of Olson. We had to find a home for her. A lunatic asylum is no place for a child."

Gwen agreed wholeheartedly and was about to say more, but David pressed his fingers against her arm. A sign to hush. He then lifted her to her feet. It seemed that he was eager to leave.

"Come back tomorrow," Dr. Green said. "And we'll see what we can do for you."

He escorted them to the entrance and stood in the doorway as they headed down the pathway to the front gate. Gwen stopped before exiting and looked over her shoulder. He hadn't moved and was watching them. The eerie feeling she'd had when they'd arrived, returned. Something was amiss.

Thankfully, the carriage was waiting. The little old man rubbed his fingers together at the sight of them. *More money*? Hadn't they given him enough already?

"We should have dressed like paupers," Gwen whispered to David.

Once again, the man remained seated while they helped themselves inside. And as soon as they sat, David beamed.

"Tell me," Gwen urged. "I know you're up to something."

Sitting tall and puffing out his chest, David looked a bit like Albert. But this was his way of being playful. Pulling her along until she was ready to burst with curiosity.

"David! Tell me!"

"I know about Anna." He wiggled his brows.

And so did she. Doctor Green just told them where she was. "She's with a family named Olson. I heard."

"But I know where they live. *Exactly* where they live."

"How?"

"When you went to Mrs. Carter's room with Doctor Green, I returned to the basement and had a nice chat with Isaac."

Her eyes widened. This was better than she thought.

"When I told Isaac our reason for being here, he was elated. And even though our time was brief, he told me about his devotion to Mrs. Carter. She's been like a mother to him."

"But she's not that old. Though her hair is white, she has very few wrinkles. She can't be more than forty-five. Isaac looks to be in his thirties."

"He was born at their estate. His mother died when he was a toddler. Suzanne was a young girl at the time and took it upon herself to care for him."

Gwen leaned back in her seat, taking it all in. Piecing together the puzzle of Jeb's family. "So, the estate belonged to Jeb's *mother's* family. That's where the money came from. Not from his father."

"Yes. Isaac said that when Suzanne married, she moved away, but when her parents died, she and Mr. Carter returned to the estate. He said he felt like his *mama* had come home to him." David grinned broadly. "The man likes to talk."

Gwen wished she had her journal so she could write everything down. Such an amazing story and one that wasn't nearly finished. More than anything, she wanted to discuss it all with Jeb.

"Isaac visits Anna every Sunday afternoon." David's voice became somber. "And from what he tells me, the Olson's aren't a fit family. He begged me to take her from them."

"Oh, David. Have they hurt her?"

"I don't know. But we'll find out tomorrow."

Tomorrow. If only they could go tonight. But she knew it was impossible. It would be dark soon and they needed to find lodging. She'd had no idea what to expect when they'd left Boston and it hadn't gotten any easier. As Sarah said, *they needed to go on a longer journey.* Was this why God brought Jeb into her life?

It seemed that now she would not only help him, but was being given the opportunity to save an entire family. It felt good—healing the whole bird, not just a broken wing.

* * *

Their money-hungry carriage driver had a room for rent, so they took him up on his offer. As many times as the man rubbed his fingers together, he must have acquired callouses.

The man's wife cooked a pot of stew, which Gwen reluctantly ate. It had very little seasoning and the meat was questionable. It wasn't beef, it wasn't pork, and it certainly didn't taste like chicken. She wasn't about to ask. Food didn't seem to matter and hopefully they would only be here for one night.

When morning came, Gwen and David both rose quickly, dressed, and after giving directions to *Charlie*— as he asked to be called—they were on their way to the Olson home.

Gwen cradled the doll in her arms. She would leave it in the carriage until she knew it was wise to give it to the child. Once again, she had no idea what to expect.

Charlie claimed he'd heard of the Olson's; knew where they lived, but didn't know them personally. The way he said it made her more nervous than ever.

The sun shone brightly, warming the air enough that Gwen didn't see her breath. But she still cuddled beneath her wool coat and kept her hat tied firmly on her head.

As the carriage slowed, she peeked out the window. "Oh, dear ..."

In response to her, David also looked. They then sat back in their seats, shaking their heads.

"Worse than I thought," he muttered.

They waited a moment after the carriage stopped, before venturing out.

"We're taking her with us." Gwen opened the door.

"My thought exactly," David replied and followed her out.

The tiny, one-room shack looked as though a slight wind could easily blow it over. Chickens ran about freely, and a couple of pigs were penned in a make-shift structure beside the house. Smoke billowed from a chimney and firewood was strewn about, accompanied by assorted tools and overturned buckets. There was no order here.

Even if they're poor, they could tidy up the place.

"Want me to wait?" Charlie asked, chuckling.

Gwen was prepared for the finger rub.

"Please," David said. "We shan't be long."

Threadbare curtains hung over the one window beside the front door. Stepping over what appeared to be feathers from a recently plucked chicken, Gwen approached the door, ready to knock.

"Let me." David rapped hard.

The door creaked open and a young woman with messed hair and a baby on her hip stared back at them. She couldn't have been much older than Gwen. "Can I help ya?" She was missing her front teeth and Gwen doubted she'd bathed in a very long time.

Gwen tried to see into the house for any sign of a six-year-old girl.

"Yes," David said. "We've come from Atlanta. We were told that you've been caring for a young girl whose mother is ill and whose father is deceased. Her name is Anna Carter. Is she here?"

Thank goodness he didn't waste any time. Her brother was good at getting down to business.

The woman scratched her cheek. Gwen had to close her eyes so she didn't have to look at the woman's filthy fingernails. "Reckon she is. You come to take 'er?"

"May we see her?" Gwen asked, craning her neck.

"House is a mess. I got five little uns to tend. We was told we'd get some money for takin' care a her, but all we ever get is what that darkie brings. It ain't much." She stepped to the side. "Come in if ya like. Tommy here just got over the pox. Doc says he ain't contagious no more." She patted the child's head, while Gwen scanned his face for indication of the illness.

Oh, Lordy ...

What were they getting into?

David gave her a slight nod and they walked in.

At least the house was warm. A crackling fire did the job well and the wood smoke helped to cover the scent of unwashed flesh.

The cry of a newborn turned Gwen's head.

"That's little Gertie," Mrs. Olson said. "She's three weeks."

Before Gwen could object, Mrs. Olson handed her Tommy, while she went to pick up the infant.

While jostling the child on her own hip and hoping she wouldn't get some sort of disease, Gwen's eyes moved to the children sitting on the floor by the fire. They were playing a game with sticks, unfamiliar to her.

No toys?

"Gwen," David whispered. "Look at the girl." He nodded toward the child, then took the baby from her arms. "Go talk to her."

Gwen didn't waste a moment and knelt down beside her.

Though she had a smudged, dirty face, and long brown hair full of knots, she was by no mistake a Carter. "Anna?"

The girl blinked slowly and shyly lifted her blue eyes. "Yes'm?" Reaching up, she gingerly touched Gwen's hat.

"You like my hat?"

"Yes'm."

"Yep," Mrs. Olson said. "That there is Anna. She's a quiet child. Not like little Markie there. He an Frankie go at each other sometimes. An when their daddy's out huntin' I have a hard time makin' 'em mind."

The two boys laughed aloud, then punched each other in the arm. Point well made.

"Is he hunting now?" David asked.

Mrs. Olson scratched her neck, then her head, making Gwen squirm. She'd check Anna for lice as soon as they got her out of here.

"He's been gone a couple a days. Figger he's huntin'. Hope so anyways. Kids are gettin' hungry. Them chickens ain't gonna last forever. 'Sides I hate killin' 'em. We like the eggs."

Gwen stood and took hold of Anna's hand. The little girl stood beside her without question.

"Mrs. Olson ..." Gwen inched toward the door. "We have papers stating that we can take Anna with us."

"Can't read," Mrs. Olson said, wrinkling her nose. "Got any money?"

David reached into his pocket and gave her so much that she stumbled backward, nearly dropping Gertie.

"That'll do." Mrs. Olson swallowed hard. "I 'preciate it. One less mouth to feed may keep us all alive a tad bit longer."

Gwen bent down, coming to Anna's level. "I want to take you home with me. Is that all right with you?"

Anna's timid face transformed into a bright smile, followed by a vigorous nod.

"Does she have a coat?" Gwen asked.

"Nope. Just what's on her back."

What was on her back could scarcely be called a dress. Torn at the hem and much too short. David handed Tommy over to his mother, then removed his jacket and placed it around Anna.

They left the woman with a baby on each hip and two boys wrestling on the floor. A sight Gwen wouldn't soon forget.

"Are you my new mama?" Anna asked as Gwen helped her into the carriage.

"No," Gwen replied with tears in her eyes. "Think of me as your new sister. We're going to see your mother soon."

Anna hugged her with as much strength as her tiny body could muster. "I prayed that God would send me an angel. Are you an angel?"

"Some people think she is," David said. "She's my sister as well."

Anna tipped her head, studying David. "So, are you my brother?"

Gwen never intended to confuse her. "He can be. But I have another surprise for you. Your *real* brother is waiting for you in another city. We're going to surprise *him* very soon. Do you like surprises?"

She seemed so small and frail cuddled under David's coat, but when Gwen mentioned a surprise, her face lit up brighter than ever, making her larger than anything around them. Gwen knew it was time.

"I have a present for you." Gwen reached down beside the seat and lifted the doll. The only thing she had to go by when choosing the doll was the porcelain hand. This doll had long, flowing auburn hair and painted brown eyes. She wore a pink cotton dress with tiny pearl buttons. She prayed it would be similar to the doll Anna had lost.

Anna's chin quivered as Gwen placed the doll in her arms. "Mine?"

"Yes." Gwen had to fight back her own tears.

Anna closed her eyes and held the doll close to her heart, cuddling it, and rocking side to side. "Betsy," she whispered. "I won't lose you again."

Hearing David cough, Gwen looked at him and caught a tear rolling down his cheek as he turned his head.

Chapter 28

It was a very good thing that their father had given them plenty of money for the trip. It seemed that every time they turned around, David was reaching for his wallet. He assured Gwen he had enough to get them home again, but if they continued dealing with people like Charlie and Mrs. Olson, they'd be in trouble.

Anna's bath alone had cost two bits, but it was money well spent. And Charlie's wife was kind enough to give her—for another two bits—a small dress she said had belonged to a niece. At least it was better than the rag Anna had been wearing.

Gwen held a lantern close to Anna's head, looking for lice as she combed through her long brown locks. A few of the knots in her hair were so bad they required cutting, but Gwen assured her it would grow back quickly. Besides, her hair was so thick that the few cut lengths weren't even noticeable.

Betsy didn't leave Anna's arms, but Gwen had to insist that Betsy not take a bath with her. Anna was satisfied as long as the doll was within view.

And now that all of them were thoroughly bathed, they were on their way back to the asylum.

"I checked your scalp, David," Gwen said with a grin. "You're fine."

He rubbed his knuckles over the top of his head. "I scratched all night long. Just the thought of it ..."

Anna covered her mouth and giggled.

David cocked his head. "It's not funny." But then, he, too, laughed. "She'll get along well with Katie."

Gwen thought about what he'd said, and it struck something deep within her. "What if Jeb refuses to go home with us?"

"Then you'll explain to him how it will benefit his family. We have room for them and it was the plan all along. Now that we've found Suzanne and Anna, we'll reunite them and have everyone home in time for Christmas."

He made it sound simple enough. But how could she persuade Jeb to return to a city and people he hated?

"Who's Katie?" Anna asked. Her meek voice grew bolder the further they went.

"Our sister," Gwen said. "She's just a few years older than you."

"Another sister?" Anna asked. "Will we all sleep in the same room?"

Gwen had only caught a brief glance of the bed in the Olson home, but she'd never forget it; a pallet on the floor for all of them together.

"You'll have your own room." Gwen stroked her smooth hair, then kissed the top of her head. In such a short period of time, this child had worked her way into her heart.

* * *

The asylum wasn't as ominous as it was the previous day. Knowing there weren't monsters lurking inside, helped. But Gwen was still cautious. After the strange look she'd received from Doctor Green, she wasn't sure what to expect.

Even though children were more than likely not allowed around the patients, they weren't about to leave Anna in the carriage. With their luck, Charlie would drive away and hold her for ransom.

Anna held tightly to Gwen's hand while clutching Betsy with her other arm. David protectively draped his arm around Gwen's shoulder, huddling them all together.

Their intention today was to leave with Suzanne. David had added money to his wallet in the event bribery was necessary.

Nurse Jamison rapidly approached them, shaking her finger. "No! No children are allowed."

"Nurse," Gwen said sweetly. "This is Anna. Mrs. Carter's daughter."

Anna hid behind Gwen.

"I see." She peered around Gwen's body, causing Anna to retreat further. "A shy child? You don't expect to take her to Mrs. Carter's room, do you?"

"No." Gwen didn't care for the tone of Nurse Jamison's voice. "We expect to take Mrs. Carter home with us."

"Out of the question. Doctor Green had to sedate her last night."

This wasn't going well. Gwen's stomach turned flips as she determined where to go from here.

"Why?" David asked in a tone not to be challenged.

Nurse Jamison took a step back. "She was—*talking*. She wouldn't stop."

"But that's wonderful," Gwen said. "Why sedate her for talking?"

The nurse looked completely befuddled, trying to form words, but with nothing coming from her lips. "It —it was *unlike* her."

"Where is Doctor Green now?" David demanded.

"On the women's floor. I imagine he's with *her*. The matron is ill and Doctor Green has taken it upon himself to tend to all of the women."

With a jerk of his head, David motioned for Gwen to follow him. They crossed the hall to the now-familiar bench.

"I'll stay here with Anna. Go to Mrs. Carter's room and do what you can."

"That's not much of a plan, David. What if he won't let her go? Or, what if she's still asleep? I can't carry her out."

"I can."

Their heads whipped around, facing Isaac. In the bright hallway, Gwen saw him much clearer than she had yesterday in the basement. He was a handsome man with rigid features and eyes as black as coal. He was well over six feet tall, with muscles larger than any she'd seen on a man. Years of hard work showed.

"What are you doing up here?" Nurse Jamison scolded him, shaking her finger in his face.

"I's heppin' take Miss Suzanne home."

The nurse frantically waved her hands. "No, you can't. Go back downstairs this minute!"

"Uh-uh." He shook his head. "C'mon now, Miss Abbott. I's gonna hep ya."

How could she refuse his help? At least it was a plan.

With Nurse Jamison running about looking a bit like Mrs. Olson's chickens, Gwen hurried down the hallway with Isaac right beside her.

"Negro's ain't allowed up here," he said. "They makes 'em sleep outside in tents. I has a bed in the basement, but I ain't never been up here neither."

"How would you like a real room to sleep in?"

"Where?"

"Help me get Mrs. Carter out of here and I'll take you with us." What was she saying? What would her father say? The plan was never meant to include a Negro. But then again, he was part of the family.

The door to Suzanne's room was shut. Gwen tried to open it, but it was locked. "Doctor Green, are you in there?"

Pressing her ear to the door, she heard shuffling of feet.

She beat on the door. "Doctor Green, I know you're in there!"

More shuffling. "No, I don't want it!" It was Suzanne.

"Doctor Green! Open this door!"

"I'll open it." Isaac gently pushed her to the side. Leaning back, he lifted his leg, then slammed his foot into the door. Wood splintered and the door broke into pieces.

Effective.

"How dare you?" Dr. Green yelled. He was seated on the edge of Suzanne's bed and in his hand was a syringe, positioned to administer medication.

"Don't do it," Gwen said. "She doesn't need it."

"I'm her doctor. Don't tell me what she needs."

Suzanne's tear-filled eyes pleaded with Gwen. "Take me ..."

Isaac stomped past Gwen and grabbed Doctor Green by the shoulders, stopping him from placing the needle. "You don't hurt Miss Suzanne."

"I wasn't hurting her!" The doctor's eyes were on fire, his breathing heavy. "I'd never hurt her. I love her. You can't take her from me."

Isaac held him fast.

Gwen gaped at the doctor. Now it made sense. What other reason would he have for keeping her from her family? "No. You don't. If you loved her, you'd want what's best for her. And pumping her full of sedatives to keep her quiet isn't what's best. We're removing her from your care."

"No. Please ... no." His head dropped to his chest. "She's special. You don't understand."

Gwen's sympathetic side took hold and she approached the doctor with caution, motioning for Isaac to step aside. He hovered close by. "Yes, I do. I know what it's like to care for a patient. But she wants to leave. Don't you see?"

Doctor Green took Suzanne's hand. Her eyes were fully open, with no indication of sedation. She pulled her hand away, then placed it against his face. "Please, let me go."

Staring at her as moments ticked by, finally, his head nodded against her hand.

The men stepped out of the room while Gwen helped Suzanne dress. Then she folded her remaining clothes together and bundled them into her arms.

"Jeb?" Suzanne asked, looking toward the door.

"Soon," Gwen replied. "But Anna is waiting downstairs."

Suzanne's trembling hand covered her mouth and her face wrinkled, ready to cry. "Anna?"

"Yes."

It appeared that Suzanne was about to buckle at the knees, so Gwen called out for Isaac. He rushed in and placed his large arm around her waist, keeping her on her feet. "I hep ya, Miss Suzanne."

"Thank you, Isaac."

Isaac's cheeks rose to his eyes with a smile broader than a river. "We's goin' home."

They passed by a defeated Doctor Green, who sat on a chair outside the broken door.

"Don't worry, Doctor," Gwen said. "My brother will leave enough money for repairs. I know you've done your best here, but you've lost sight of reason. You may have implemented a plan to remove chains as restraints, but sedation is just as binding."

He stretched out his hand, stopping her. "Take care of her. Please?"

"It was my intention all along." She managed to smile at the distraught man. In her heart, she believed his intentions for the asylum were good. Removing Mrs. Carter from his care would eventually get his mind back in the right place. In many ways, he was no different than most of his patients.

* * *

Gwen would never forget this moment. Her heart tightened in her chest and she was unable to control her tears. Tears of utter joy as mother and daughter embraced, holding one another as if their very next breath was dependent on each other. They gazed into each other's eyes, touching faces, reminding themselves of their existence.

Isaac stood back, allowing them time, with glistening tears of his own.

"Mama," Anna muttered over and over.

Suzanne clung to the little girl, sobbing all the while.

Why had Doctor Green kept them apart all this time? Was he so selfish that he didn't want to share her with her own daughter? Whether or not children were allowed in the facility shouldn't have mattered. He could have arranged regular meetings.

While still holding tightly to Anna, Mrs. Carter turned toward Gwen. "Thank you."

Gwen linked her arm in David's. "You'll need to hold on to me when we have their reunion with Jeb. My heart may not be able to take it." She sniffled and wiped away her tears.

He patted her arm. "We did the right thing, Winnie. And don't worry. We'll hold each other up." He cleared his throat and coughed. Yes, her brother had a very big heart.

David settled financial matters with Nurse Jamison, who willingly took the money, but muttered all the while. They'd upset the order of the asylum, but as far as Gwen was concerned, it needed it.

Charlie's head drew back as they approached the carriage. "I didn't expect so many." Finger rub.

David sighed. "We'll settle up with you after you take us to the train station."

Rubbing his chin, Charlie shook his head. "Not that I don't trust ya, but a man's gotta make a livin'."

So, once again, David dug into his wallet.

"You ain't plannin' on takin' that Negra on the train, are ya?"

"Yes, we're all going to Atlanta."

Charlie chuckled. "You northern folk don't know nothin' 'bout how things work 'round here. They ain't gonna let him on the train."

That hadn't crossed Gwen's mind. Of course, she never thought they'd be taking him along to begin with. She looked at David. "What will we do?"

"I'll take care of it." David patted his pocket.

The carriage was almost too small for the five of them, but at least they were warm. David's assurance of taking care of things helped, but her mind could not rest. The next step was finding Jeb. Isaac would be able to help, and if Mrs. Carter was in a better state of mind, she'd also know where to go. But it wouldn't be wise to have her see the remains of the house. Gwen wasn't sure she wanted to see it either, but if it meant seeing Jeb, she'd go anywhere.

Chapter 29

Lacking motivation, Jeb needed something to lift his spirits.

The church bells rang loud and clear as he approached the old building. If Mrs. Chambers was here, would she recognize him? Maybe this time he'd have the courage to introduce himself and deal with her condolences.

The white brick church looked just the same as it had in August, but something about it felt different. Maybe it was because he was coming to worship, not looking for handouts.

He trudged up the concrete steps—still relying on his cane for support—and pulled his black coat tighter around his body. Though it wasn't very cold, a chill swept over him as he walked through the tall doorway.

Feeling the need to be nearer to God, he moved to the front pew. Odd for him, since he used to sit in the back. He understood that God was just as close to the people in the back pew, being that God was everywhere. Still, something pushed him forward.

The piano made him jump. Why was he so uneasy?

Folks were filtering in around him and part of him prayed that no one would speak to him. He'd gone to his old home site and grew more discouraged, realizing just how much work had to be done. Work that he could in no way accomplish by himself. And now, here he was at the church he'd grown up in, feeling like a complete stranger. Maybe it had something to do with the fact that he was all alone.

The words on the page of the hymnal stung. He couldn't sing them. So he read them silently.

Now thank we all our God with heart and hands and voices,

Who wondrous things has done, in whom his world rejoices;

Who from our mothers' arms has blessed us on our way

With countless gifts of love, and still is ours today.

He couldn't breathe. The song was one of thanks, but what did he have to be thankful for? Everything he cared about was gone.

Hanging his head, he limped back down the aisle, doing what he could to shut out the words and even the music. There was no joy in his heart. A few more steps and he'd be out the door.

"Jeb?"

He stopped and closed his eyes. No, it couldn't be her, but she'd said his name. His heart pounded, scared to raise his head.

She touched his arm. "Jeb, I'm so glad I found you."

Yes, it was her.

Swallowing hard, he forced himself to look at her. "Gwen?"

She nodded with a timid smile, then sniffled and covered her mouth.

"But ... how ..." It didn't matter, she'd come for him. He pulled her into his arms and held her tight, ignoring the gasps from members of the congregation. Her body vibrated against his as it shook with sobs.

"Jeb," she whispered his name again and nothing had ever sounded so perfect.

"I don't understand," he said in her ear. "I can't believe you're here."

She pulled away and nodded. "Let's go outside."

A very good idea, since they were getting frowns from every direction. She took his hand and he stared at hers. *No ring?*

How was it possible?

Before he could ask another question, David was there with a grin on his face larger than any he'd seen before.

"Jeb." David chuckled. "You look confused."

"Don't tease him," Gwen scolded. "Of course he's confused."

With his cane to steady him, Jeb eased himself down onto the church steps and held his head in his hands. "Tell me what's goin' on."

After tucking her skirt, Gwen sat beside him. This had to be a dream. There was no way she could really be here.

David remained standing with his confusing grin.

She took his hands. Skin just as soft as ever. "We had to come." Her grip tightened, and when he looked in her eyes they were intense. Something was wrong.

"You're scarin' me, Gwen."

"Oh ... no. No, I don't want you to be scared. But this is very hard. There's so much to say."

You're telling *me* that? His mind spun with every possibility. But none made sense. Why did their daddy ever let them come?

But no matter what she had to tell him, she was beside him and lit a glimmer of hope in his heart. "I'm listenin'."

The trepidation in her eyes turned to joy. "Like old times. But I must say, I like hearing you talk."

And I've always liked hearin' you talk.

She inhaled deeply, then blew out a long breath. Why was she nervous?

"Sarah told me about your family and what happened."

He shook his head and pulled his hands from hers. He didn't want sympathy.

"No, Jeb—please hear me out." She placed her hand on his arm.

"Fine."

"It was good that she did, because I went to David and told him. I was so upset about what the soldiers did and couldn't understand how they could harm a woman and child."

Jeb looked up at David. The grin was gone, replaced by a soft smile. He nodded toward Gwen as if to say, *give her a chance to explain.*

"I don't wanna hear 'bout what happened to my mama. Don't you understand how hard it is? How many nightmares I've had?"

When he stopped feeling sorry for himself, Jeb realized she was gently rubbing his arm. A gesture that reminded him of the way his mama used to soothe him.

"That's why we came. Jeb ..." She swallowed hard, then took his face in her hands, forcing him to look at her. "They didn't die that day."

His heart stopped beating—his body froze. She had to be mistaken. If they weren't dead, then where were they?

She stroked the side of his face. "We found them. They're here. And they're waiting to see you."

His entire body shook. Not knowing whether to scream or cry, he remained silent. It was always easier.

She stood and extended her hand. "Come with us."

His legs wouldn't work. He tried several times to rise, but with no success.

"Let me help you." David hoisted him up.

Even with more questions than Jeb could ever ask mulling around his brain, they walked silently down the road. He couldn't stop trembling and had to tell himself to put one foot in front of the other. Much to his surprise, they went straight toward the boarding house.

"There?" He pointed.

"Yes," Gwen replied. "There were very few accommodations here. We took what we could get. And we had to sneak Isaac in after dark. We weren't about to leave him out in the cold."

"Isaac?" He stumbled and David steadied him.

She grinned and bit her bottom lip. "Yes. He's a very nice man."

They approached door number seven and Jeb made them stop. "I want to know everythin'. None of this seems real."

"We'll have plenty of time for that. But for now, your mother needs you." Gwen pushed the door open.

The last time he'd seen her was when he'd left for the war. She'd held him and cried, dressed in black as if already mourning him. And now, it was his turn to cry. Vowing never to shed another tear when he cried for Anna, all that changed. These were tears of joy.

He dropped his cane and rushed to her, pulling her to him and kissing her cheek, then he buried his face in her shoulder and sobbed. "Mama ..." Wanting to know how, where, why—all of those things disappeared. She was alive. Nothing else mattered.

"Jeb," she whispered through her tears. "My Jeb."

* * *

Gwen stepped back and braced herself against her brother. This was even more powerful than watching her with Anna. Gwen's love for Jeb intensified every emotion. This moment made all of the hard times getting here worth it.

Anna crossed to Gwen and tugged on her skirt. "That's my real brother?"

"Yes, sweetheart. That's Jeb."

"I don't remember him." She wrinkled her nose. "But he looks nice. And Mama loves him."

Gwen knelt down beside her. "He's *very* nice. And I know he loves you. You don't remember him because you were a very little girl when he left home."

"Do you think he'd like a hug from me?"

"More than anything."

Anna moved beside Jeb and pulled at his pant leg. "Mister? Miss Gwen said that you're my brother."

Jeb released his mother and turned to face Anna. His swollen eyes blinked away tears that trickled through his beard. "Anna?" With one swoop, he lifted her into his arms and swung her around, kissing her all over her face. "You've gotten so big!"

She giggled until he came to a stop. Then she wrapped her arms around his neck and hugged him. "I'm six."

"Yes, you are." He broke into a laugh, completely out of breath.

Isaac stood at the far side of the room and Jeb crossed to him, still holding Anna. "Isaac, it's good to see you again." He extended his hand and Isaac shook it hard.

"I did what I could to look after 'em," Isaac said.

"You did a good job."

Gwen looked at David and nodded toward the hallway.

"Jeb," she said. "I know there's a lot you need to discuss with your family. David and I are going out for a while to give you time."

"You're comin' back, ain't ya?" Jeb asked.

She nodded. "Of course we are. You and I also have a lot to discuss."

"I'll be waitin'." His blue eyes sparkled with hope and she prayed she wouldn't have to let him down again.

* * *

Isaac sat. "I'd leave too, but them folks don't know I's in here. I's tryin' not to cause trouble."

"I don't want you to leave, Isaac," Jeb said. "I owe you so much, lookin' after Mama." He held her hand, never wanting to let go.

Her hands were smaller than he remembered, and her body frail. And now it would be his job to look after her, make sure she was strong and healthy again.

It took time for her to tell him all she'd been through, and knowing she'd been in an asylum was almost unbearable. Isaac said that he rarely got to see her. But even so, he hadn't left the place.

"I din't do much," Isaac mumbled. "Wish I coulda done more. Least I was able to see little Anna. She was in a bad place. They was nice 'nuff to her, but they was poor."

Jeb glanced at his little sister who was content, sitting on the floor, playing with ... "Where'd she get that doll?"

"Miss Abbott gave it to her," Isaac said.

"Gwen?" He should have known. Thinking hard, he couldn't recall what he'd done with the porcelain hand from Anna's old doll. He'd shown it to Sarah. *Thank God I told her.*

His mama squeezed his hand, warming his heart. "She's a sweet girl, Jeb. She gave me this dress I'm wearin', then apologized for not havin' crinolines for me."

"That sounds like Gwen. She and her family helped me. I can't believe she came so far. She lives in Boston."

"Tell me how you met her."

How would he tell her without hurting her? There was no way to explain how he'd ended up in Boston without telling the reason why he'd left in the first place. He stared at the floor, shaking his head.

"Jeb?" She touched her hand to his face. "I'll be fine. I wasn't crazy. The only reason they took me there was I was hurtin' and didn't handle things well. Then Doctor Green didn't want me to leave. But I already told ya 'bout that. What I'm gettin' at is that I reckon you're afraid to tell me what happened to you. But I'm strong enough to hear anythin' you have to say. We're together again and we're gonna help each other through."

It was no wonder Gwen reminded him so much of his mama. Both were strong, determined women, and both held his heart.

He decided to start at the beginning, and by the end of his story, not only did he have the attention of his mama, but Isaac and Anna as well.

"Are you gonna marry her, Jeb?" Anna asked, wide-eyed. She sat on the floor with her knees drawn to her chest, looking at him like he'd just told the best bedtime story ever.

His mama leaned in. "Are you, son?"

"I—I don't know. She an I have things to talk 'bout. I reckon she an David will be goin' back to Boston soon." They had to. If he remembered things correctly, David was supposed to be in Washington by now.

"But ..." Isaac's brows drew in. "I thought we was *all* goin' to Boston."

"What?" Jeb couldn't have heard him right.

"Miss Abbott said I'd have my own room if'n I hepped get Miss Suzanne outta that asylum."

"Me, too," Anna chimed in. "They said that Katie would be my friend."

Jeb ran his hand back through his hair. That was their intention? To take everyone back to Boston? Why? It wasn't right for Gwen to make these plans and promises without talking to him first.

"We can't go to Boston," Jeb said as calmly as he could. "We belong here."

"But where will we stay?" his mama asked. "I know you didn't plan for this, but we can't live in this boardin' house. Unless you've come into some kinda money, we can't afford another room or two. And what 'bout Isaac? Sneakin' 'round ain't gonna be good for him."

"So, you're all willin' to up and move to a city you've never been to before, just to have a roof over your heads?"

All three nodded simultaneously.

"Mr. Abbott said you did a fine job workin' for his daddy." His mama rubbed his arm. "I know you wanna make things work here, but our home is gone. Long as we're together, does it matter where?"

Jeb stood and paced the floor. This wasn't what he'd planned, but then again, nothing was as he thought it was.

Nothing.

Deep in thought, he startled when Anna tugged on his pant leg. "How you gonna marry Miss Gwen if she's in Boston an you're here?"

His mama let out a laugh as light as air. A sound he'd missed. How would he answer?

The door creaked open. Isaac jumped to his feet and moved to the corner of the room.

"It's just me." Gwen stepped inside. "David is trying to find somewhere we can eat."

"You didn't answer my question, Jeb." Anna stood with her hands on her hips.

"Did I interrupt?" Gwen asked, shutting the door.

"Yep," Anna said, boldly. "I asked Jeb how he was gonna-" Jeb secured his hand over his sister's mouth.

"Why don't I go help David?" Jeb said. "You can come with me, Gwen." He glanced back at his mama, whose eyes sparkled with laughter. "Will you be all right without me?"

She nodded and motioned for Anna to sit beside her. With a promise to return quickly, Jeb took Gwen by the hand and went out the door.

Chapter 30

Her hand felt natural in his. Like it had always been there. As if she'd always been a part of him.

"I didn't think I'd ever see you again," Jeb said, as they walked down the road. She'd told him that David had gone to the train station to ask about a place to eat, so they were headed that way.

She tightened her grip on his hand. "That night was horrible. I know you were trying to protect me from Albert. I just didn't know what to think when you started talking. I was happy, but ... *hurt*."

He stopped, halting her with him. "I'm sorry, Gwen." He looked down. Saying the words didn't seem like enough.

"I know why you did it. I may have done something similar if I'd found myself in your situation. Heaven knows I got a taste of it when David and I arrived in Atlanta."

"No southern hospitality?" He grinned at her, trying to remove the frown from her face.

She shook her head. "Oh, there were a few people who seemed to like us. As long as David opened his wallet." His comment worked. She laughed aloud, making her more beautiful than ever. But it also drew his eyes to her mouth. Thinking about their kiss was probably not the best thing to do right now.

Even though seeing her happy was what he wanted more than anything, there were important things to discuss. "Gwen? Why did you tell my family you'd take 'em to Boston?"

Her face fell and she shifted her eyes to the ground. "I —I hoped you'd go with me. Father would love to have you back at Abbott's and we have plenty of room for all of you in our guesthouse. I hadn't planned on Isaac, but David believes there's work at the estate for him. George always needs help with the horses. And ..."

"And?"

Her chest rose and fell and she appeared as if she was about to lose her breath. She looked deeply into his eyes and he felt that he might crumble right there on the road.

"And ..." She licked her lips. "I want you—back at the estate."

"What about Albert?"

She wiggled her naked hand in front of his face. "When Father saw my bruises, he and the boys threw him out of the house. Albert's no longer a concern."

Jeb's fists tightened. "Bruises? I wish I'd been there to help 'em."

"I don't want to talk about Albert."

Neither did he. If he'd stayed in Boston, he'd have known she didn't get married, but then they may have never found his family.

"So, you want me back at the estate. Why?"

"Because—because ..."

He didn't want to wait for the answer.

Placing his hands on the sides of her face, he became lost in her eyes. This time, she didn't say no.

Their lips met like familiar friends, but lingered like lovers. And when they parted, he pressed his forehead against hers, staying locked in the embrace. "Because you love me?"

Her head bobbed up and down, moving his along with it. "Yes, I love you."

"And if I agree to go to Boston, will you agree to be my wife?"

She pulled away and his hopeful heart dropped. "It's not that easy."

"Why?"

"Father-"

"So, I'm good enough to work for 'im, but not to marry his daughter?"

Her face twisted as though she was going to cry. This was not what he wanted. Everything was supposed to be fine now. He had his mama, his sister, and the woman he loved back in his life. So why this?

"Out looking for me?"

David's timing may have saved her from an explanation, but they still needed to settle this. At least David didn't spoil their kiss. How could she kiss him like that and *not* marry him?

"Yes, David." Gwen smiled. It seemed forced, but at least she wasn't crying.

"Good news. We can eat at the church tonight. I was told they're serving stew and anyone can come and eat."

"How does that sound to you, Jeb?" Gwen asked. "Or would you rather eat at the boarding house?"

He weighed the ideas in his mind. Right now he didn't feel like eating anything. He and Gwen had too much to settle. "Let's ask Mama what she wants to do. I reckon the church won't turn Isaac away. It might be best to go there, but I want her to decide. She might not feel like goin' there."

"She would have gone to services this morning," Gwen said. "But we didn't think it would be a good idea for you to see her for the first time in such a public place."

"How'd you know I'd be there?"

Gwen shrugged. "It was a hunch ... and a hope."

This time, returning to the boarding house, she didn't hold his hand. Was it because of David, or was she pulling away? Jeb refused to lose her again.

Stew at the church. It was decided with no objections. His mama's face lit up at the suggestion and she commented about looking forward to seeing some old friends again.

Jeb was confused over her enthusiasm. He believed that she wasn't even bothered by the city's desolation. Instead, she walked beside Gwen, pointing out what *used* to be there.

He lagged behind, lost in his thoughts, watching his family enjoy the company of the Abbott's, feeling suddenly left out.

"Have you decided to go with us?" David asked, snapping Jeb out of his self-pity.

"I don't know."

"The decision isn't hard. Look at it this way. On one hand, you have no home, no job, and no Gwen. On the other hand, you have a home, a good job, and the woman you love. Not to mention a very nice place for your family to become reacquainted." He held up his hands like a balance scale and shifted them up and down. "How can you not know?"

"There's a small problem with your examples."

"What?"

"Even if we go with you, I won't have your sister."

David raised his brows and grinned. "What makes you so certain?"

Regardless of the fact that David had something to do with the destruction here, he couldn't help but like him. There'd been too many families torn apart by the war and he couldn't fault David for still having his. A family that he'd grown to love.

"Your daddy-"

"My *daddy* ..." David chuckled. "Likes you. I intend to have a talk with him when we get home. But, it won't do any good if you're still here. Think about that." He increased his pace and joined the others, leaving Jeb to do just that.

With David on his side, maybe there was hope.

* * *

Jeb's kiss had Gwen tingling all the way to the tips of her toes. It might have had something to do with the beard that tickled her skin. She shouldn't have spoiled it with a dose of reality. But she could never have him.

"Miss Abbott," Suzanne took her by the hand. "I'd like you to meet my dear friend, Mrs. Chambers."

Mrs. Chambers held Suzanne's arm, and a warm smile covered her face. "She told me how you helped her get out of that horrid place. I was so angry when they took her there. It never shoulda happened."

Gwen nodded politely to the woman, then caught Jeb's eye.

What's wrong with him? His face had turned as white as a sheet.

"Excuse me for a moment," Gwen said. "I don't mean to be rude and it was a pleasure to meet you, but my friend needs me." She did a half curtsy and rushed to Jeb's side.

He leaned against his cane, breathing rapidly. And when she took his arm to help steady him, he didn't resist. "I need to sit down."

"Let me help you." Holding him by the arm, she led him to a chair. "I'll get you some water."

As she walked away, she glanced back and he was bent over with his head in his hands. Suzanne must have noticed him, too, because she was crossing to him, leaving Mrs. Chambers.

When Gwen returned with the water, Suzanne was holding his hand.

"Drink this." Gwen handed him the glass.

He took it and drank it down, then wiped his mouth with the back of his hand. "I'm sorry."

"What happened? You looked as though you'd seen a ghost." Gwen took her place on his other side and received a smile of gratitude from his mother.

"I learned a horrible lesson 'bout keepin' my mouth shut."

She already knew that.

"It's not what you think," he went on. "I never would a gone to Boston if I'd a just told Mrs. Chambers who I was. She knew Mama was alive and even where they took her. I came here after the war, needin' help. She gave me clothes and food, but didn't know me. And I was too embarrassed to tell her who I was. And—I didn't want her feelin' sorry for me cuz a Mama."

Suzanne looked sympathetically at her son, then turned her attention to Gwen. "He never would a met you, my dear." She patted Jeb's leg. "Don't you see, son? Things happened the way they was supposed to happen. God wanted you to meet Gwen, so He sent you on a journey."

A journey?

It was the same thing Sarah had said. Everything happened as it was supposed to happen.

"And broke my leg to make a point?" Jeb asked with a grunt.

"It worked, didn't it?" Gwen smiled at him, then reached out and took his hand. "Please, finish the journey with me and come home."

He peered around the room and sighed. "And if I wanna come back here one day?"

"Why don't we wait and see. Maybe your journey will bring you back."

"Is David buyin' the tickets?"

She couldn't help but laugh. "He's paid for everything else. That is—Father has. I'm certain he'll find a way for you to repay him."

And then he said, "Yes." Gwen wanted to hug him, but not only would it be inappropriate in the church fellowship hall, but she didn't want to give him false hope. At least things would be somewhat like they were. She could keep attending school and he'd be working for her father. They'd see each other at dinner, and ...

The rest remained to be seen.

Chapter 31

The train ride was more enjoyable this time, but Jeb couldn't believe he was going back. Deep down inside, he knew it was the right thing to do. He liked working at Abbott's and with only ten days until Christmas, it was sure to be hectic. They'd need him there.

"Don't look so worried," his mama said. "From what you've told me, we'll be blessed livin' in such a fine home."

"But it's not *our* home. Do we really belong there?"

She sat beside him. After just five days, she already had more color in her cheeks. The navy blue dress Gwen had given her looked beautiful with her snowy white hair. She'd told him that Gwen had helped her twist it up on her head, then covered it with a matching hat. Every day she became more and more like the mama he'd left behind so many years ago.

"Jeb, maybe this is their way of sayin' they're sorry. I don't reckon many folks from the north wanted to do the things they done. And if I was to ask you 'bout what you did in the war, I reckon there'd be things you wasn't proud of. If you had the chance, don't you think you'd wanna fix it?"

She was right. He hated the killing. Destroying lives and property. He'd take it all back if he could. "Yes, Mama, I would."

"Then give 'em a chance to do what they think's right. And one day, maybe you can do the same for someone else."

He hugged her, breathing in every memory in her arms. Always knowing how to ease him—just like Gwen.

He'd offered to take them all by the old home site before they left Atlanta, but his mama refused. That was one memory she didn't want to hold onto or relive. She said she'd much rather remember it the way it once was.

"Snow!" Anna yelled, jumping up and down.

Everyone laughed and gathered their belongings to exit the train. Anna was in for more snow than she'd ever imagined.

George tipped his hat and smiled at Jeb, then looked curiously at Isaac. Jeb would never be able to thank David enough for bringing Isaac with them. It hadn't been easy. They'd gone through more money than Jeb could have imagined it would take to bribe his way onto the train. Luckily, the further north they'd gone, the more sympathetic the rail workers were.

When David introduced Isaac to George and told him that he'd be helping him in the stable, George shook Isaac's hand so hard that Jeb feared he'd wrench it from his body.

"Best Christmas present the Abbott's ever gave me!" George exclaimed.

Jeb hadn't realized that George was overworked. Maybe now he'd be a bit more talkative.

They piled into the carriage and when they got settled, Jeb noticed Isaac's hopeful expression was gone.

"Isaac, are you all right?"

He frowned. "Is I still free?"

"Course you are. Freer than ever. I reckon they worked you hard at that asylum."

"What's wrong, Isaac?" Gwen asked.

"Well—I ain't never been no one's present before."

It took both Jeb and David to explain George's meaning—by the time they were done, Isaac was himself again. And when David went on to tell him that he'd be living in the caretaker's house by the stable, and would also receive pay, Isaac was beside himself.

Anna hopped off their mama's lap and climbed into Isaac's. "You was *my* present every Sunday." She laid her head against his chest and closed her eyes, while Isaac blinked away tears.

Everything felt right, and with Gwen beside him, Jeb was home. But then he tried to take her hand and she pulled away. A dull, familiar ache tugged on his heart, as the carriage came to a halt.

"Is this really our home?" Anna asked, as Isaac lifted her down to the ground. Her wide eyes blinked away a flake of snow.

Jeb remembered his first impression of the estate and knew how she felt. "Over there," he said, pointing to the guest house.

He shifted his eyes to the main house. Mrs. Abbott and Katherine were hurrying along the pathway toward them, followed by Sarah and Martha. The hugs that followed made him forget his troubles with Gwen.

Watching as Martha covered David with kisses, Jeb envied what they had. She led him away quickly. He doubted he would see David again for some time.

Gwen introduced their mamas to each other. As for Anna and Katherine, no introduction was needed. Within moments, they were on their backs in the snow making snow angels, until Mrs. Abbott fussed at Katherine and told her to go inside and get Anna a proper coat before playing in the snow.

Jeb took it all in, knowing he'd made the right choice. And when he heard Sarah's unmistakable laugh, he smiled. She and Isaac were talking and laughing like old friends.

Isaac may be someone else's present this year.

He shook his head, chuckling to himself. Wouldn't it be something if this was the reason for it all? To bring someone into *Sarah's* life?

Gwen looked at Jeb and nodded toward the couple. She'd noticed, too. The grin on her face was something he'd hold in his heart until a time when he was allowed to hold her again.

* * *

And just like he'd never left, Jeb fell into a routine; rising with the sun, taking the carriage to work with Henry and Mr. Abbott, then coming home before the sun set to have dinner at the main house.

The difference was, he shared it all with his mama and sister. While he worked, they kept busy at home. His mama and Mrs. Abbott became friends and Anna was included when Katherine's tutor came to their home for lessons.

The Abbott's were kind enough to put up a Christmas tree in the corner of the guesthouse living room, which elated Anna. In the evening, he'd sit with her on his lap in front of the fire, sometimes reading to her, and other times having her try to read to him. She got better as each day passed.

His mama was content. Mrs. Abbott gave her some needlework to keep her busy and he loved watching her dainty hands move the needle in and out of the fabric. Bundled under a lap blanket, she looked beautiful with the firelight reflecting off her hair.

This should be enough, but he was unsettled. Would he have a happy Christmas?

"Christmas is in two days, Jeb. I hope you got them things finished for the Abbott's. They've been awful good to us." His mama set aside her sewing.

"I did."

"You don't seem happy 'bout it."

Anna hopped off his lap and lay down on her belly in front of the fire. He could tell she was tired and he should tuck her into bed.

"Mama, what if Gwen don't say *yes*?"

"I thought she already did."

He shook his head. "Every time I try to get close, she pulls away. Worried 'bout what her daddy will say."

Worse than that, he was afraid it was something more. Maybe now that he could talk, she didn't like what she heard.

"Hasn't that been taken care of?"

"We'll see ..." He scooped Anna into his arms. Luckily, he no longer needed the cane. "I'm gonna turn in after I put her to bed." He jostled her little body against his, then bent down to kiss his mama's cheek. "G'night, Mama."

She patted his face. "Night, Jeb. Don't you fret. Things will be just fine."

He started walking away.

"Jeb? You might wanna think 'bout shavin' before Christmas. Gwen might appreciate a smooth face. I know I liked your daddy smooth."

She hadn't mentioned his daddy before now. "Thank you, Mama. I'll think 'bout it."

A shaved face wouldn't matter if Gwen turned him down. But maybe it would help. As he tucked Anna into bed, he thought about Gwen's reaction the first time he'd shaved. Sarah's manipulation. Women were smart about those things. Taking his mama's advice might be a good idea.

* * *

Christmas break had always made Gwen happy in the past, but now she wished that school was still in session so she'd have things other than Jeb to occupy her mind. It was all supposed to be better now that he was here, but somehow it made it harder.

"You sleepin', Miss Gwen?" Sarah peered into her room.

"No. Come in, Sarah."

Sarah had been scarce over the past week and Gwen hoped she wasn't ill. She knew she should have checked in on her before now, but was too caught up in her own troubles.

"Miss Gwen, I has sumthin' to say." She crossed the room and motioned to the bed. "Can I sit by you?"

Gwen scooted up in the bed and made room for her. "Please do." *Has she been crying?*

"Member when I told you that your journey wadn't done yet?"

Gwen nodded, urging her to continue.

"I never figgered that God had me in mind when he sent you away." Tears pooled in her eyes. "But you brought me Isaac. An from the first time he spoke to me, I felt sumthin' inside. He felt it, too."

Yes, Gwen had noticed it that first day. "Sarah, I'm so happy for you." She rubbed Sarah's back. "Please don't cry."

"Happy tears, Miss Gwen. They's happy tears."

Though overjoyed for Sarah, Gwen wished she could have some happy tears of her own.

Stop feeling sorry for yourself. You have so much ...

"Anyways," Sarah said, rising. "I just wanted to thank you. I ain't been this happy in a long time."

Gwen extended her arms to her dear friend and pulled her into an embrace. "He's a good man, Sarah. I'm happy for you both."

As Sarah backed away, she shook her finger at Gwen. "Don't give up hope, Miss Gwen. It's all gonna be just fine."

Gwen laid back and pulled her blanket up to her chin, then closed her eyes and prayed Sarah was right.

Chapter 32

"Gwen, get up!" Katherine yanked on her arm. "Mother says we have to have everyone there before we can open presents. You're holding up everything!"

Christmas morning and she'd overslept. How was it possible? Every year past, excitement woke her before the sun came up.

"I'll be right down. I need to get dressed."

"Why?" Katherine's hand went to her hips, accentuating her flannel nightgown. "You never have before."

"We have guests this year. It's not just family."

Katherine rolled her eyes and scurried out the door, yelling behind her to hurry.

Gwen wasn't about to go downstairs in her nightgown and robe. What would Jeb think? Surely he and his family wouldn't have come over from the guesthouse in their bedclothes. Would they?

Heavens, no.

It took her several minutes to decide on the perfect dress to wear. It shouldn't have been so difficult. The mint green, with the tiny red roses, was perfect for the holiday. As a final touch, she tied a green ribbon in her hair. A quick glance in the mirror and she decided it would have to do. Why was her heart racing?

As she descended the stairs, the incredible scent of cinnamon and apples drifted into her nose. Her stomach grumbled and her mouth watered. *Hot cider.* She quickened her steps.

"Hurry!" Katherine peered at her from the end of the hallway, then popped back into the living room.

The house looked spectacular, decorated with fresh green boughs and large red silk bows. And as she rounded the corner into the living room, her breath hitched. This was more beautiful than any decoration. They were all waiting—her entire family—even Isaac and Sarah. Their smiles burned brighter than the fire crackling in the fireplace.

Jeb stood and took her by the arm, then led her to a sofa with room for both of them. She couldn't remove her eyes from his smooth, clean face. Why did it increase the rhythm of her heart seeing him this way?

"What's wrong?" he asked, but she believed he knew the answer.

She touched his cheek. "You shaved." She gulped and watched his eyes sparkle with amusement.

To make matters worse, she glanced around the room, realizing that every eye was on them. Her face became hot and her throat dry.

"Your cheeks match the roses on your dress," Jeb whispered through the side of his mouth. "And—you look beautiful."

"Thank you. So do you." She turned just enough to look into his blue eyes. The air around them was heavy and warm, or perhaps it was simply being near him. Whatever it was, she wanted it forever.

"Miss Gwen," Anna said, breaking the spell. "Would you like some cider?" She teetered a cup in her little hands.

Gwen took it quickly to prevent a hot spill. "Thank you, Anna."

"You're welcome." She beamed. A miniature female version of her handsome brother. "Merry Christmas."

"Merry Christmas." Gwen patted her on the head and she returned to her spot beside Katherine at the base of the Christmas tree, waiting with anticipation for gifts to be passed.

"She likes you," Jeb said. "We all do."

Henry looked across the room and winked. Why was Jeb speaking so loudly? Had he become so comfortable with her family that he no longer found the need to hide his feelings for her? What would they think?

Her father took his place beside the tree and loudly cleared his throat. "With so many of us this year, this may take some time. I don't believe I've ever seen so many gifts under the tree." He leaned in toward the two girls. "Santa must have heard you were very good this year."

They both bobbed their heads, looking as though they would burst at any moment. Gwen missed those days of being young and excited about Christmas presents. But now, it was just as enjoyable watching them.

Jeb's body shifted, causing her heart to skip a beat. What would he think of her gift?

They sat, silently watching boxes opened and shrieks of joy from the girls. Santa must have known that Betsy needed a friend. This doll wasn't quite so fancy, but a hand-sewn rag doll.

"Mama made her," Jeb whispered in her ear.

"She's adorable." How was it that his warm breath on her neck gave her shivers?

Gwen's parents gave both Anna and Suzanne new clothes; coats, dresses, socks, boots, hats, and even crinolines. Everything they would need to dress like proper ladies. Their gratitude shined through gasps and words of thanks over and over again. Jeb was also given new clothes and seemed almost ashamed to receive them.

"They've done too much," he said, for only Gwen to hear.

"They wanted to do it, Jeb. Don't feel bad."

"But I gave 'em so little."

"You're wrong. The things you made are beautiful. I never knew you had a gift for woodworking as well as paper roses."

"There's a lot you don't know 'bout me. But in time, we'll know each other much better."

She let out a long sigh. It was what she wanted, but how?

Every gift was given except the gift she had for Jeb. That and ...

"Jeb? I have something for you that I'd like to give you privately. And not that I expect a gift from you, but ..."

He chuckled. "Yes, you do."

"Well—yes. I hoped."

He stood from the sofa and extended his hand. "C'mon."

She took it and let him lead her from the room. Whispers followed them into the hallway, as well as giggles from the girls.

"Wait." She let go of his hand, and hurried back into the living room. Reaching far behind the tree, she retrieved his gift. As she lifted her head to leave, she caught a wink from David, followed by an enormous smile. Her heart thumped. What did he know?

Jeb waited with his hands folded comfortably in front of him. She took him in from head to toe; well groomed, black trousers, crisp white cotton shirt, and black braces over his shoulders.

As if he knew she was looking him over, he tucked his thumbs under the braces and slid them up and down. The movement drew her eyes to his chest. Strong and firm, with arms that could hold her and keep her safe.

Taking her hand, he guided her to the library where he led her to a leather sofa, then crossed to the fireplace, stoked it, and added another log. Finally, he took his place beside her.

"You first," he said, nodding toward the package in her hand.

She stared at it. Long ago, he may have thrown it at her, but that was far behind them. "It's not much, but I thought you might like to have it." She placed it in his hands and he loosened the string binding the paper to it.

"I know it's a book." He grinned as he removed the paper. And when he saw it, he froze, then slowly ran his hand across the pages. "Your journal?"

"*Our* journal. I couldn't have written it without you. I thought you might find it—humorous."

"My recovery was humorous?"

"Sometimes." Would it reveal too much to him? "If you don't want it, I'll understand."

He clutched the book against his chest and shook his head. "I want it."

She smiled timidly, still uncertain what to do with him.

"My turn," he said, and closed his eyes. His demeanor changed as he produced a small box and placed it in her palm.

No, it can't be.

Her hand trembled as she stared at the box.

"Jeb. I-"

"Open it, Gwen."

A single red ribbon held the lid on the box. One pull and it dropped in her lap. She lifted the lid.

"How?"

"I love you, Gwen. I want you to be my wife. We've been runnin' 'round tryin' to avoid each other for too long now. Tell me you love me. Please say yes."

"But—Father ..." The lump in her throat, hurt. Her heart ached. She wanted to say yes, but was too afraid.

"Where do you think I got that ring? Your daddy, Henry, and David helped me pick it out. Oh, and Martha was the biggest help of all."

"They all know?"

He took her hand and pulled it to his lips with a kiss so gentle it took her breath. "Yes, they know. Everyone in that other room knows how we feel 'bout each other. David went to your daddy an talked to him 'bout me, but what he found out was that your daddy had already made up his mind. He wants you to be happy, Gwen. Can you be happy with me?"

She gaped at him. He'd never talked so much. And it seemed he wasn't done.

"If you love me, say yes. But you gotta love me for what you see sittin' here right now. I ain't gonna change. I ain't never gonna talk like men 'round here. I reckon maybe I embarrass you by the way I talk, an act, but this is-"

She'd heard enough and covered his lips with her hand. "Yes, Jeb."

"Yes?" His mouth dropped wide open.

And to prove her commitment, she closed his mouth with a kiss. They melded together and his arms encircled her waist, drawing her close. Their journey was now truly beginning.

* * *

Jeb took the box from her hand, lifted out the ring, and placed it on her finger. She'd said yes, and now all his fears were gone.

The setting suited her. Martha was the one who'd seen it first, and he was grateful for her help. He wanted it to be completely different from the ring Albert had given her, and this one was. A green emerald set between two small diamonds.

"It's perfect, Jeb." She stared for a moment at the ring, then gave him another kiss he would not soon forget.

Jumping to his feet, he lifted her up and into the air. He wanted to dance, to sing, to scream his joy to the world.

She laughed aloud as he brought her down again and her feet touched the floor. Then her face became somber and her brows drew in.

Please don't change your mind.

"What do you want from me, Jeb?"

"What do you mean? I want you to be my wife."

"But what about my education? Will you want me to stay home all the time?"

How could she even think that?

"No. You're the smartest woman I've ever met. I asked you to accept me as I am. It would be wrong a me to want to change you. I love you for who you are, an one day, you may be the best doctor this country has ever seen. I ain't gonna stop that." He ran his hand down the side of her face. "I fell in love with every part of you, Gwen. Don't ever change." She burst into tears and he held her close. "Please don't cry."

"These are happy tears," she mumbled against his chest.

"Then let's go share 'em."

She nodded into his shoulder, and for a moment gripped him so tight he could hardly breathe. Then after she took a deep breath, she took a small step back. Linking her arm in his, they returned to the celebration and were greeted with hugs and congratulations.

The most joyous day of the year became the best day of his life.

Chapter 33

"And do you, Gwendolyn Marie Antoinette Abbott take Jeb Carter to be your lawfully wedded husband?"

The minister stared at her. So stoic. *Why doesn't he smile?*

Gwen shifted her eyes to Jeb, which was where they should have been. After already committing himself to her, he was smiling from ear to ear. But something about the minister's dour expression bothered her.

Jeb squeezed her hand and nodded toward the preacher. She turned her head and looked at him again. His brows rose. "Well, do you?"

She licked her lips and smiled. "I reckon so."

With one eyebrow raised, the man showed a glimmer of a smile, then chuckled and shook his head.

Jeb touched his hand to her cheek and mouthed the words, *I love you.* Gwen expected admonishment from her parents. But this was her special day and she wanted to be certain everyone in attendance had a smile on their face. Including the minister.

After a few more words and a prayer to send them on their way, they were legally man and wife. Now they could seal their love in the church with a kiss no one could frown at.

The sanctuary was filled with friends and family. They'd invited everyone they could think of—even Nurse Phillips. She may have just come for the free food, but it didn't matter to Gwen, who smiled and remained glued to Jeb's side. She'd never let him go again.

She made a point to thank Doctor Young. He didn't mind in the least that she'd given the journal to Jeb.

"I knew the two of you would come to your senses sooner or later," Doctor Young said, eyeing them both over the top of his glasses. "I'm rarely wrong with my diagnosis."

"Except when you thought I was mute," Jeb said. "Reckon I fooled you on that one."

Gwen rubbed his arm. "You fooled everyone. But that's in the past now."

"I ain't proud a what I done, but I'm curious, Doctor Young. Would you a operated on me if you knew I was southern born?"

The doctor rubbed his chin and peered upward. Why was he taking so long to answer?

"I was none-the-wiser when they brought you in," he finally said. "Even so, my doctor's oath requires I give care to anyone in need regardless of where they're from." He patted Jeb on the back. "You're a good man, Jeb Carter. Now stop worrying about all this and see to your wife. That's what truly matters."

Gwen released Jeb's arm and gave Doctor Young a kiss on the cheek. "I'll never be able to thank you enough."

"Be happy and continue your studies. That's all the thanks I need."

Happiness consumed her.

With cheers following them, they headed for the carriage. She paused and gave the mare a loving pat, whispering soothing words.

"Katie told me 'bout this," Jeb said with a chuckle. "You talk to the horses."

"Yes, I do, Mr. Carter." She playfully tossed her head. "Be grateful. They taught me how to put up with silence."

He circled her waist and drew her to him. "I *am* grateful. Thankful I had the most patient woman in the world as my nurse." He kissed her. Longer than their wedding kiss. Igniting more desire within her than she knew she possessed.

They hopped into the carriage.

Jeb held her against him. "I hope you told that horse to go fast."

"You heard me, didn't you?" She grinned at him and cuddled close.

The Boston Hotel boasted of fine rooms, but they would have been happy anywhere as long as they were together. They stood side-by-side, looking out the window as the snow drifted to the ground. Beautiful and cold, but Gwen had never felt warmer. Jeb's presence was all she needed—he was the never-ending flame that would keep her heart lit for eternity.

Something wonderful had come from the ashes of Atlanta. The devastation had brought him to her and he'd never be taken away. She placed the tiny porcelain hand on the bed stand, then slipped beneath the blankets and nestled her body against his.

He pulled her even closer. "I can't believe you're really my wife."

"I *am,* and will be forever." She nuzzled into his neck and allowed her fingers to roam mindlessly across his chest. All of this felt right. Unlike every moment she'd spent with Albert. Never had she been more content—at ease—or so blissfully happy.

"I thank God I didn't end it all before it even began," he muttered, while caressing her arm with his fingertips.

"What do you mean?"

"I thought 'bout endin' my life. Thought I had nothin' to live for."

She rose up and peered deeply into his eyes. "Oh, Jeb." She kissed him, wanting to wash away any trace of pain that might remain somewhere deep inside of him. "Please, never think that again. We have everything to live for."

And soon she would tell him that he'd saved *her* life, just as he credited her for saving his. But not tonight. Tonight they were done talking.

Sarah had told her that affection would come naturally with love, and she was right. In no time at all, their bodies joined. Perfectly. Beautifully. Entwined as one, never to be parted again.

Not another word was uttered, but much was said.

'Tis my happiness that renders me silent.

THE END

Acknowledgments

What a blessing it is for me to be able to share *From the Ashes of Atlanta* with you. God continues to surround me with incredible people who support my efforts and give me the boost of confidence I need whenever I get ready to start a new book.

I'm grateful that I married a southerner who has shown me the rich history here, and the amazing stories that lie beneath the ashes of many fallen soldiers. Though it was a difficult time in our nation's history, I believe it's something we should never forget. By remembering, my hope is that it will never happen again.

A special thank you goes out to Mary Ann Brooks who offered to Beta read for me. She'd not read anything written by me prior to this, and her fresh set of eyes was extremely helpful. She gave me some insightful suggestions.

Thank you also to Lyla Red. Lyla and I have followed each other down many different paths through the course of our lives, and now she is encouraging my writing. She, too, did a thorough read-through and gave me some great feedback as well as some astute, fine-tuned corrections.

In preparation for publication, I was happy to have the same great team that I had with *Marked*. Cindy Brannam did a *fantastic* job editing. She's always able to see the little things that I miss. Her extraordinary abilities made the book better than ever. And once again, Rae Monet came through with a beautiful cover. This one was a bit more complex than the last, but she certainly didn't let me down. Jesse Gordon handled all of my formatting, and Karen Duvall laid out the back cover and spine for the print version. You all make my life so much easier, and I can't thank you enough!

I also have a regular group of readers who love to give my stories a test run. Once again I'd like to thank: Birgit Barnes, Bobbie Bauer, Diane Gardner, James McCormick, Joy Dent, Kim Gray, Marie Nichols, and Stacy O'Brien. And of course, my mom, Janet Launhardt. It's nice to know you're always looking forward to my next book!

If you enjoyed *From the Ashes of Atlanta*,
you'll want to read:

Marked
River Romance, Book 1

A Novel by Jeanne Hardt

Cora Craighead wants more than anything to leave Plum Point, Arkansas, aboard one of the fantastic steamboats that pass by her run-down home on the Mississippi River. She's certain there's more to life out there...*somewhere.* Besides, anything has to be better than living with her pa who spends his days and nights drinking and gambling.

Douglas Denton grew up on one of the wealthiest estates in Memphis, Tennessee. Life filled with parties, expensive clothing, and proper English never suited him. He longs for simplicity and a woman with a pure heart—not one who craves his money. Cora is that and more, but she belongs to someone else.

Cora finally gets her wish, only to be taken down a road of strife, uncertainty, and mysterious prophecies. When she's finally discovered again by Douglas, she's a widow, fearing for her life and that of her newborn child and blind companion.

Full of emotions, family secrets, and the search for true love, you'll find it's not just the cards that are marked.

Coming Soon!

Tainted
River Romance, Book 2

A Novel by Jeanne Hardt

Despite her new position as manager of the *Bonny Lass,* Francine DuBois doubts her abilities. After all, the only skill she's ever been recognized for is entertaining men and giving them pleasure. But she'll never let her insecurities show in the presence of the new captain. In her opinion, he's not old enough to be a pilot and will never measure up to his predecessor.

Luke Waters may be young, but he's determined to prove that he's more than capable. He'll show everyone that he's the best pilot the Mississippi River has to offer. His only problem is the new crew manager. His religious upbringing taught him to frown on women of her profession, so how can he bring himself to overlook her way of life and work beside her?

Which is worse? A tainted past, or a tainted opinion?

* * *

For information on upcoming releases, be sure to follow Jeanne Hardt:

facebook.com/JEANNEHARDTAUTHOR
jeannehardt.com
amazon.com/author/jeannehardt
goodreads.com/jeannehardt